ACCLAIM FOR COLLEEN COBLE

"A law enforcement ranger investigates a cold case and searches for her kidnapped sister in this exciting series launch from Coble (*A Stranger's Game*) . . . Coble expertly balances mounting tension from the murder investigation with the romantic tension between Annie and Jon. This fresh, addictive mystery delivers thrills, compassion, and hope."

—*Publishers Weekly* on *Edge of Dusk*

"This Christian romantic suspense novel packs a lot of plot into its pages, wrapping up only two of its biggest plot lines while leaving plenty of material for a sequel. Some of the plot twists were excellently paced surprises . . . Fans of Colleen Coble's works will welcome this brand new series set in the same world as her previous thrillers. Her love for the UP is palpable, and I really liked learning about the Finnish influences on the area. Ms. Coble is a great ambassador for the UP's natural beauty and cuisine, and speaks knowledgeably and at length on celiac disease, including recommendations at the end of the book that are super helpful for anyone wanting a list of gluten-free brands."

—*Criminal Element* on *Edge of Dusk*

"Coble's clear-cut prose makes it easy for the reader to follow the numerous scenarios and characters. This is just the ticket for readers of romantic suspense."

—*Publishers Weekly* on *Three Missing Days*

"Colleen Coble is my go-to author for the best romantic suspense today. *Three Missing Days* is now my favorite in the series, and I adored the other two. A stay-up-all-night page-turning story!"

—Carrie Stuart Parks, bestselling and award-
winning author of *Relative Silence*

"You can't go wrong with a Colleen Coble novel. She always brings readers great characters and edgy, intense story lines."

—BestInSuspense.com on *Two Reasons to Run*

"Colleen Coble's latest has it all: characters to root for, a sinister villain, and a story that just won't stop."

—Siri Mitchell, author of *State of Lies*, on *Two Reasons to Run*

"Colleen Coble's superpower is transporting her readers into beautiful settings in vivid detail. *Two Reasons to Run* is no exception. Add to that the suspense that keeps you wanting to know more, and characters that pull at your heart. These are the ingredients of a fun read!"

—Terri Blackstock, bestselling author of *If I Run*, *If I'm Found*, and *If I Live*

"This is a romantic suspense novel that will be a surprise when the last page reveals all of the secrets."

—*The Parkersburg News and Sentinel* on *One Little Lie*

"There are just enough threads left dangling at the end of this well-crafted romantic suspense to leave fans hungrily awaiting the next installment."

—*Publishers Weekly* on *One Little Lie*

"Colleen Coble once again proves she is at the pinnacle of Christian romantic suspense. Filled with characters you'll come to love, faith lost and found, and scenes that will have you holding your breath, Jane Hardy's story deftly follows the complex and tangled web that can be woven by one little lie."

—Lisa Wingate, #1 *New York Times* bestselling author of *Before We Were Yours*, on *One Little Lie*

"Colleen Coble always raises the notch on romantic suspense, and *One Little Lie* is my favorite yet! The story took me on a wild and wonderful ride."

—DiAnn Mills, bestselling author

"Coble's latest, *One Little Lie*, is a powerful read . . . one of her absolute best. I stayed up way too late finishing this book because I literally couldn't go to sleep without knowing what happened. This is a must read! Highly recommend!"

—Robin Caroll, bestselling author of the Darkwater Inn series

"I always look forward to Colleen Coble's new releases. *One Little Lie* is One Phenomenal Read. I don't know how she does it, but she just keeps getting better. Be sure to have plenty of time to flip the pages in this one because you won't want to put it down. I devoured it! Thank you, Colleen, for more hours of edge-of-the-seat entertainment. I'm already looking forward to the next one!"

—Lynette Eason, award-winning and bestselling
    author of the Blue Justice series

"In *One Little Lie* the repercussions of one lie skid through the town of Pelican Harbor, creating ripples of chaos and suspense. Who will survive the questions? *One Little Lie* is the latest page-turner from Colleen Coble. Set on the Gulf Coast of Alabama, Jane Hardy is the new police chief who is fighting to clear her father. Reid Dixon has secrets of his own as he follows Jane around town for a documentary. Together they must face their secrets and decide when a secret becomes a lie. And when does it become too much to forgive?"

—Cara Putman, bestselling and award-winning author

"Coble wows with this suspense-filled inspirational . . . With startling twists and endearing characters, Coble's engrossing story explores the tragedy, betrayal, and redemption of faithful people all searching to reclaim their sense of identity."

—*Publishers Weekly* on *Strands of Truth*

"Just when I think Colleen Coble's stories can't get any better, she proves me wrong. In *Strands of Truth*, I couldn't turn the pages fast enough. The characterization of Ridge and Harper and their relationship pulled me immediately into the story. Fast-paced, with so many unexpected twists and turns, I read this book in one sitting. Coble has pushed the bar higher than I'd imagined. This book is one not to be missed. Highly recommend!"

—Robin Caroll, bestselling author of the Darkwater Inn series

"Free-dive into a romantic suspense that will leave you breathless and craving for more."

—DiAnn Mills, bestselling author, on *Strands of Truth*

"Colleen Coble's latest book, *Strands of Truth*, grips you on page one with a heart-pounding opening and doesn't let go until the last satisfying word. I love her skill in pulling the reader in with believable, likable characters, interesting locations, and a mystery just waiting to be untangled. Highly recommended."

—Carrie Stuart Parks, author of *Fragments of Fear*

"It's in her blood! Colleen Coble once again shows her suspense prowess with a thriller as intricate and beautiful as a strand of DNA. *Strands of Truth* dives into an unusual profession involving mollusks and shell beds that weaves a unique, silky thread throughout the story. So fascinating I couldn't stop reading!"

—Ronie Kendig, bestselling author of the Tox Files series

"Once again, Colleen Coble delivers an intriguing, suspenseful tale in *Strands of Truth*. The mystery and tension mount toward an explosive and satisfying finish. Well done."

—Creston Mapes, bestselling author

"*Secrets at Cedar Cabin* is filled with twists and turns that will keep readers turning the pages as they plunge into the horrific world of sex trafficking where they come face-to-face with evil. Colleen Coble delivers a fast-paced story with a strong, lovable ensemble cast and a sweet, heaping helping of romance."

—Kelly Irvin, author of *Tell Her No Lies*

"Coble . . . weaves a suspense-filled romance set during the Revolutionary War. Coble's fine historical novel introduces a strong heroine—both in faith and character—that will appeal deeply to readers."

—*Publishers Weekly* on *Freedom's Light*

"This follow-up to *The View from Rainshadow Bay* features delightful characters and an evocative, atmospheric setting. Ideal for fans of romantic suspense and authors Dani Pettrey, Dee Henderson, and Brandilyn Collins."

—*Library Journal* on *The House at Saltwater Point*

"Set on Washington State's Olympic Peninsula, this first volume of Coble's new suspense series is a tensely plotted and harrowing tale of murder, corporate greed, and family secrets. Devotees of Dani Pettrey, Brenda Novak, and Allison Brennan will find a new favorite here."

—*Library Journal* on *The View from Rainshadow Bay*

"Coble (*Twilight at Blueberry Barrens*) keeps the tension tight and the action moving in this gripping tale, the first in her Lavender Tides series set in the Pacific Northwest."

—*Publishers Weekly* on *The View from Rainshadow Bay*

"Filled with the suspense for which Coble is known, the novel is rich in detail with a healthy dose of romance, allowing readers to bask in the beauty of Washington State's lavender fields, lush forests, and jagged coastline."

—*BookPage* on *The View from Rainshadow Bay*

"Prepare to stay up all night with Colleen Coble. Coble's beautiful, emotional prose coupled with her keen sense of pacing, escalating danger, and very real characters place her firmly at the top of the suspense genre. I could not put this book down."

—Allison Brennan, *New York Times* bestselling author of *Shattered*, on *The View from Rainshadow Bay*

"Colleen is a master storyteller."

—Karen Kingsbury, bestselling author

BREAK
OF
DAY

ALSO BY COLLEEN COBLE

ANNIE PEDERSON NOVELS
Edge of Dusk
Dark of Night
Break of Day

PELICAN HARBOR NOVELS
One Little Lie
Two Reasons to Run
Three Missing Days

LAVENDER TIDES NOVELS
The View from Rainshadow Bay
Leaving Lavender Tides (novella)
The House at Saltwater Point
Secrets at Cedar Cabin

ROCK HARBOR NOVELS
Without a Trace
Beyond a Doubt
Into the Deep
Cry in the Night
Haven of Swans (formerly titled *Abomination*)
Silent Night: A Rock Harbor Christmas Novella (e-book only)
Beneath Copper Falls

YA/MIDDLE GRADE ROCK HARBOR BOOKS
Rock Harbor Search and Rescue
Rock Harbor Lost and Found

CHILDREN'S ROCK HARBOR BOOK
The Blessings Jar

SUNSET COVE NOVELS
The Inn at Ocean's Edge
Mermaid Moon
Twilight at Blueberry Barrens

HOPE BEACH NOVELS
Tidewater Inn

Rosemary Cottage
Seagrass Pier
All Is Bright: A Hope Beach Christmas Novella (e-book only)

UNDER TEXAS STARS NOVELS
Blue Moon Promise
Safe in His Arms
Bluebonnet Bride (novella, e-book only)

THE ALOHA REEF NOVELS
Distant Echoes
Black Sands
Dangerous Depths
Midnight Sea
Holy Night: An Aloha Reef Christmas Novella (e-book only)

THE MERCY FALLS SERIES
The Lightkeeper's Daughter
The Lightkeeper's Bride
The Lightkeeper's Ball

JOURNEY OF THE HEART SERIES
A Heart's Disguise
A Heart's Obsession
A Heart's Danger
A Heart's Betrayal
A Heart's Promise
A Heart's Home

LONESTAR NOVELS
Lonestar Sanctuary
Lonestar Secrets
Lonestar Homecoming
Lonestar Angel
All Is Calm: A Lonestar Christmas Novella (e-book only)

STAND-ALONE NOVELS
Fragile Designs (available January 2024)
A Stranger's Game
Strands of Truth
Freedom's Light

BREAK
OF
DAY

AN ANNIE PEDERSON NOVEL

COLLEEN COBLE

THOMAS NELSON

Since 1798

Break of Day

Published in Nashville, Tennessee, by Thomas Nelson. Thomas Nelson is a registered trademark of HarperCollins Christian Publishing, Inc.

Thomas Nelson titles may be purchased in bulk for educational, business, fund-raising, or sales promotional use. For information, please email SpecialMarkets@ ThomasNelson.com.

Scripture quotation is taken from the Holy Bible, New International Version®, NIV®. Copyright © 1973, 1978, 1984, 2011 by Biblica, Inc.® Used by permission of Zondervan. All rights reserved worldwide. www.zondervan.com. The "NIV" and "New International Version" are trademarks registered in the United States Patent and Trademark Office by Biblica, Inc.®

Publisher's Note: This novel is a work of fiction. Names, characters, places, and incidents are either products of the author's imagination or used fictitiously. All characters are fictional, and any similarity to people living or dead is purely coincidental.

Library of Congress Cataloging-in-Publication Data

Names: Coble, Colleen, author.
Title: Break of day / Colleen Coble.
Description: Nashville, Tennessee: Thomas Nelson, [2023] | Series: An Annie
  Pederson Novel ; 3 | Summary: "Annie Pederson's happily ever after is finally
  within sight . . . if she can stay alive long enough to grasp it. Return to the beloved
  town of Rock Harbor in the final installment of the Annie Pederson trilogy by
  bestselling suspense author Colleen Coble"—Provided by publisher.
Identifiers: LCCN 2023000514 (print) | LCCN 2023000515 (ebook) | ISBN
  9780785253785 (paperback) | ISBN 9780785253815 (library binding) | ISBN
  9780785253792 (epub)
Subjects: LCGFT: Christian fiction. | Thrillers (Fiction) | Romance fiction. | Novels.
Classification: LCC PS3553.O2285 B74 2023 (print) | LCC PS3553.O2285 (ebook) |
  DDC 813/.54--dc23/eng/20230106
LC record available at https://lccn.loc.gov/2023000514
LC ebook record available at https://lccn.loc.gov/2023000515

Printed in the United States of America

23 24 25 26 27 LBC 5 4 3 2 1

For my mother, Peggy Rhoads,
who went to join my brother Randy
in heaven on July 29, 2022.
Miss you so much, Mother.
Hug Randy, Grandma and Grandpa, and Tiff for us.
We'll see you soon.

ONE

STUPID KAYAK. **ELLA ANDERSON LAY SPREAD-EAGLED ON**
her back on a tiny spit of land in Lake Superior. She was cold, wet,
and tired, but snuggling against Scout, her golden retriever, would
warm her. The dog licked her arm and went back to sleep.

Right now she wondered why she'd even decided to tangle
with the big lake when she could have been warm and comfy in
a tent underneath the big trees. But her kayaking trip had cleared
her head. She'd chafed under her parents' constant orders—clean
your room, be home at a decent hour, help with laundry and
housecleaning. She was eighteen years old and should be able to
make her own decisions, but her dad had always rattled off that
"as long as you're under my roof" spiel.

She would be under their roof until she went off to college
next month. Once she was in the dorm, she could manage her
own time. She loved them, but a little distance would be a good
thing. Getting through the anniversary party was the first priority, and it was a small price to pay for all they'd done for her.
Then she could move on to her own life.

Most of the trouble had started when she'd met Alex. Just
because he was married didn't make him a bad person. He was

separated and getting a divorce, but her dad thought he was the devil. And yeah, he was ten years older than her, but that was nothing now that she was an adult herself.

Things would change soon.

She sat up and brushed the sand off her arms and tried to reach her upper back. A fingernail snagged on her necklace, and it broke. She tried to catch it as it flipped off her neck, but the necklace went flying off into the weeds. She scrambled up to search for it but gave up after fifteen minutes. Her parents would get her another one.

The July sun warmed her skin, and the breeze from the water lifted her blonde hair from the back of her neck. She should shove off in the kayak before she fell asleep or she wouldn't make it back to the Kitchigami boat launch before sundown. She had her tent with her so she could sleep anywhere, but she was done with this big lake. She wasn't the best at directing the kayak, and those vigorous waves were looking bigger and harder to navigate.

She rose and called Scout, who jumped into the front of the kayak with no prompting. Ella shoved her yellow kayak into the water, then grabbed the paddle and settled herself. The waves bobbed around her, and before she knew it, she was yards away from the island's shoreline. No matter what she tried, the paddle wouldn't take her in the direction she thought she was heading. The waves bounced her in the opposite direction, and another island loomed in the distance.

Her arms were tired, and her head hurt. Maybe she should just let the kayak go that direction. It was a larger island, and there were probably people on it. Maybe even cell service, and she could ask her mom to hire a boat to come get her. Fighting this big lake was too exhausting. She'd underestimated how fatigued she'd be after a few hours on the water.

The waves lifted her kayak and it slid down the trough in a surge that took her closer to the other island. If it wasn't taking all her strength, she'd pull out her map and figure out where she was, but there would be time for that once she was safely ashore. She'd assemble her tent and sleep for a week.

She paddled for a few minutes and realized she was getting farther from the island, not closer. What was going on? She could have cried with frustration and fatigue until she heard the sound of a motor and spotted a boat heading her way.

She didn't dare stand up, but she waved her arms to help them see her. "Help!" Scout barked and added more noise to her call.

The craft switched direction and skimmed over the waves toward her. Two guys were aboard, and her gut clenched when she recognized one of them. Wasn't he the man who'd gotten a little too friendly when she was setting off on her adventure? There had been a sinister edge of danger to him, and she didn't like the big knife or the gun he carried on his belt.

She lowered her hands, then waved off the boat. "I'm okay. Go ahead!" she shouted.

But the boat engine cut off, and the craft slowed and came to bob near her. The man she feared smiled and beckoned to her. "Hello again. We can take you wherever you want to go."

She began to tremble and shook her head. "I'm not going with you."

"We won't hurt you."

The soothing words contrasted with the fierce stare he focused on her, and she clenched the paddle in her hands. "No thanks. I don't want to leave my kayak."

"We can take it with us. Climb aboard." His smile turned wolfish.

"No."

His smile vanished, and a gun appeared in his hand. "Get up here or I'll shoot you where you sit."

The other guy put his hand on the armed guy's shoulder. "Easy. Don't scare her. I won't let him hurt you, Ella."

They knew her name? She swallowed down the fear clogging her throat and shook her head. "Just leave me alone."

"We can't do that," the second man said.

His eyes were kinder than the first guy, and Ella hoped he would protect her. She maneuvered her kayak close enough for her to lift her dog up for them to get onto the boat.

She didn't have a choice.

/ / /

Lake Superior was in a pensive mood this morning, with swells from an incoming storm slapping at the boat's hull.

Annie Pederson tensed as the Tremolo Island dock loomed nearer, and she spotted an asylum of loons patrolling a small cove. Their short hoots of communication didn't bother her, but she wanted to be out of here before the loons' crazy laugh would begin to sound around dusk. She had too much to do to deal with the nightmares the birds' tremolo always brought.

Max Reardon lifted a hand in greeting and came to tie up her boat. "Anu is resting on the porch while my cook whips up our lunch. I hope you're hungry." His smile widened when his gaze landed on Kylie. "And you brought my favorite little girl with you. I'm sorry Jon couldn't make it."

A handsome man in his sixties, Max's bearing and clothing oozed money, from his styled salt-and-pepper hair to his Italian leather shoes. He'd leased this island from Annie when she needed the income most, so she harbored a soft spot for him.

She threw him the line. "His dad had a doctor visit in Houghton. He was sorry to miss lunch." She paused to help her eight-year-old daughter to the freshly stained boards.

Kylie was a carbon copy of Annie with big blue eyes and shoulder-length blonde hair. Kylie promptly went to hug Max before moving to the edge of the water to watch the loons.

"Anu is recovering nicely from her surgery."

"I'm eager to hear how it went." While Bree had filled her in that the ovarian cancer surgery had gone well, Annie was eager to hear the results—and to see her friend Anu Nicholls with her own two eyes.

She spotted Anu on the expansive porch along the front of the massive log home Max had built. Anu saw her and waved. Though the older woman was in her sixties, she looked forty-five. Her silvery-blonde hair just brushed her chin, and her clothing was always impeccable. She rose as Annie reached the porch, and she seemed as strong and steady as usual.

Annie went up the steps ahead of Max and Kylie to embrace her. Careful not to hug her tight enough to press against her incision, Annie inhaled Anu's perfume, a light scent with a citrus note.

Annie guided her back to the chair. "How are you feeling?" She pulled another Adirondack chair closer to Anu and settled in it. Kylie perched on her knee.

Anu smoothed the crease in her tan slacks. "Quite well. I am still sore, but I am healing every day." She smiled and reached over to take Annie's hand. "I can see the question on your face, *kulta*. I do not have the biopsies back yet, but I am most optimistic. The doctor told Max, Bree, and Hilary that it appeared the cancer was confined to the ovary. If the biopsy confirms that prediction, I will not need to have chemo or radiation. I am praying that is the case."

"Jon and I are praying for that too."

"So am I!" Kylie chimed in.

Anu's smile widened. "I appreciate that very much, my Kylie. And it is thanks to dear Jon that we had such good news."

"And Milo!" Kylie said.

Anu nodded. "It was most astounding to discover such a young puppy has the ability to sniff out cancer. And that Jon's intuition led him to the right reason for Milo's behavior. I am very blessed."

"Annie!" Max came hurrying toward her holding a satellite phone. "It's Jon."

Jon Dunstan, the love of her life and Kylie's father, had suddenly reappeared after nine years. "Hey, Jon, what's up?" He wouldn't bother Max on the satellite phone unless it was important.

"Hussert escaped."

Annie's stomach bottomed out. Glenn Hussert had imprisoned a woman to try to hide his embezzlement from a women's shelter. Sheriff Mason Kaleva suspected he might know more than he was telling about other crimes in the area. Glenn had kept Sarah locked up, too, and for all Annie knew, he might have killed her if her sister hadn't managed to escape.

"Does Mason think Sarah is in danger? Or Michelle?" Michelle Fraser had been kept in an abandoned cabin for over a week while Glenn demanded evidence she'd hidden.

"He thinks it's possible. Without the kidnapping victims' testimonies, Hussert would only be charged with fraud, which is a much lesser crime. I heard about it when I went to pay Sarah's bail. Bree and Kade are taking the kids to Wisconsin Dells for a week, so Mason's concerned Bree's guest cottage might not be as safe as we'd like with no one in the lighthouse. What should I do about Sarah?"

While Annie had been willing to bail her sister out even though she'd kidnapped Kylie, Annie hadn't wanted to see her, but did she have a choice? "I don't know."

"I could let her stay in Dad's cottage. No one would know she was there."

"She's not trustworthy, Jon. She's likely to talk about it in town."

"Maybe not if she's scared of Hussert. And I could drop off food and supplies to her. She wouldn't have to go to Rock Harbor at all."

"I'm not sure she has the good sense to be afraid." Annie winced at how bitter her words sounded. "I'm sorry, that didn't come out well."

"She's hurt you a lot, love." His voice went soft. "We could revoke the bail."

Annie was reluctant to toss her sister back in jail, but the thought of having her near Kylie gave her pause too. Was there anywhere safe Annie could send her? She didn't want to be responsible for Hussert getting hold of Sarah again. Her baby sister had been missing and presumed dead for twenty-four years, but her recent return had not been the joyful event Annie had hoped for.

"How did he escape?" she asked to delay a decision. "He

7

barely woke up." Hussert had been in a coma after a mountain lion's stranglehold nearly killed him.

"The deputy guarding him was drugged, and there was some kind of incident at the nurses' station that caused a distraction. A security camera showed three men in a back stairwell taking him out in a wheelchair in the wee hours this morning."

More evidence Hussert's crimes involved more than embezzlement and kidnapping. And clearly others were involved as well. Her gaze went to Kylie skipping rocks across the placid pond.

Nothing mattered to her more than her daughter. Kylie was her priority. "Take Sarah to your dad's cottage. I think it's the only option."

"It's the right decision," Jon said. "I'll see you at dinner. I have a killer recipe for gluten-free orange chicken Kylie will like."

"See you then." She ended the call and handed the phone back to Max.

Sarah would be closer than Annie would like but still far enough away that she might be able to forget her betrayal for a while.

TWO

THE GEESE UNDERFOOT ALONG THE PATH SCATTERED as Jon neared the steps to the back deck. The scent of charcoal and grilling steaks wafted to him from the campground, and his stomach rumbled. With the injuries he'd suffered from falling off a cliff ten days ago, it was difficult to balance the two sacks of groceries in his good arm while digging in his pocket for the key to Annie's cottage. He'd had to go to Houghton to find all the ingredients he needed for orange chicken, but it would be worth it when he saw Kylie taste it.

The pain in his head was better, at least for now, which left him looking forward to the evening. He found the key and got the door open, then set the bags on the counter. His phone vibrated before he could unpack everything and get to work.

His finger paused midswipe when he saw the name and picture on his screen. His former boss, Olivia Thompson, was calling. Did he even want to talk to her, or should he let it go to voice mail? The horrific accusation against her of euthanasia had left him reeling.

Shaking his head, he accepted the call. Who was he to pronounce judgment without giving her a hearing? "Jon Dunstan."

"Jon." Her voice rose with a note of relief. "I wasn't sure you'd answer my call. No one seems to be taking them these days. How are you?"

He began to unload the groceries while Milo, a German shepherd–chow puppy sired by Samson, squirreled around his feet yipping with excitement. "Doing okay. Concussions and dislocated shoulders are no joke. You'd have thought I would have figured that out without having to experience them myself." Might as well cut to the chase. "I heard about your trouble, Olivia. Is it true? Did you actually euthanize some patients?"

The silence on the phone continued so long that he pulled back the phone to check the screen. Still connected. "Hello?"

"You believe that of me?"

His gut clenched at her tormented tone. "They have it on camera, Olivia."

"He was *dying*, Jon. He asked for my help."

"That doesn't make it right. We doctors aren't God. We took an oath to do no harm. You did the ultimate harm."

"He was a Christian. I knew he was going to a better place."

Had she done this with any other patients? Since this news broke, he'd checked his patient files, and one other patient had died when he'd thought she would pull through. The official cause of death was a heart attack, but they wouldn't have checked for potassium chloride.

Was it too late to find out? His patient had died a year ago, but if he brought it up now, would the police think he was in on it? It would be far easier to say nothing, but Jon cared about his patients, and he didn't think he could ignore that.

Olivia's voice took on desperation. "My daughter is going off to college in August, and I can't go to jail, Jon. I just can't.

Would you testify for me and tell the court you believe in me? That would help."

He put the milk in the fridge and shut the door before he sank onto a chair at the table. "Olivia, I can't lie. You just admitted you did it. And what about Tessa Abston?"

"What about her?"

Was it his imagination or did she sound guarded? "Did you kill her? She'd just found out she had stage-four pancreatic cancer before she broke her ankle. I told you about it."

"Look, I'm not some kind of serial killer!"

But was she? Jon didn't know anymore.

Her voice hardened. "I gave you a start, Jon. Took you on when you were brand-new and taught you the ropes. You owe me this."

What she said was true enough. He'd been delighted and honored to be offered a position with her and her colleagues. People came from all over the world to see Olivia or one of her practice's doctors. But that didn't mean he was willing to lie for her. And what would this do to his reputation?

"I can't lie for you," he repeated.

The line went silent, and he glanced at his phone to see the call had ended. A text came through on the heels of the conversation. He stared at the phone for a long moment. It was his duty to report his uneasiness about Tessa Abston. Sometimes duty was painful.

What would it mean for his career if Olivia had killed one of his patients? Nothing good, that much was sure. He'd been proud of how far he'd traveled up the ladder at his age of thirty-four, but it might all explode in an instant. He clenched his fists and rose to finish putting away the groceries.

/ / /

Annie was nearly to the dock at Tremolo Marina and Cabin Resort when her phone sounded. The phone screen showed Unknown, but in her line of work as a law enforcement ranger, that happened a lot. "LEO Annie Pederson."

The caller was a man, but that was all she could tell from the garbled, "Annie."

"Hello? This is Annie."

"Help me." The words were a harsh whisper. "He's going to kill me."

She cut the engine and let the boat idle in the Superior waves. A gull landed almost immediately on the bow of her boat and stared at her with hungry eyes. "Who's going to kill you? Who is this?"

"Took me, eh. Hospital."

Something in the man's Yooper accent tickled her memory. She knew that voice. "Glenn? Glenn Hussert?" Annie glanced at Kylie, who thankfully didn't seem to be paying attention as she tossed bread crumbs to a gull.

"Glenn. Yaass." His voice vibrated with relief as he drew out the word.

"Where are you, Glenn? I'll come right now." She turned on the speaker so she could hear while she called up her message app and shot off a swift text to Mason. *Track my number. Glenn is on the other end.*

If she could only keep him on the line long enough, Mason might be able to track him. But it was a long shot. That kind of thing wasn't instantaneous even if Mason happened to be in the office at the moment.

"Need help. Kill me," Glenn muttered again.

He hadn't spoken much since he'd come out of the coma.

Just mumbling and nonsense. The doctor had said he might have some memory loss, and there was no guarantee they'd get much information out of him. Should she press for more information about who had him or try to find out where he was?

Maybe something more personal would keep him on the line. "Have you seen Lissa? Was she trying to get you help?"

"Lissa?" His voice held bewilderment. "No Lissa."

Before Annie could ask anything more, she heard an angry shout on the other end. It sounded like a man's voice, but she didn't recognize the speaker. The sound ended a few moments later.

"Hello? Glenn?" She pulled the phone away from her ear and checked the screen. The call had ended, and she was sure it hadn't been long enough to track, but she called Mason to check anyway.

"You didn't get the location, did you?"

"Not enough time," Mason said. "You sure it was Hussert?"

"Positive." She told him about the man's garbled words. "I think he's in trouble."

"He certainly wasn't well enough to walk out under his own power. Makes sense with what we gathered from the hospital cameras. Keep your phone on you in case he calls back, and I'll have your calls monitored until we find him."

"Okay." She throttled up the engine and motored for her dock.

The gull flapped its wings and took off to skim across the white caps on Lake Superior. The wind tugged at Annie's blonde strands and blew them around her head and into her eyes. The humid air cooled with the breeze as night began to fall, and it felt good against her skin, baked by the sun on this hot day.

Kylie turned off her tablet. "Who was that, Mommy?"

"The sheriff," Annie said.

"The call before that. It sounded like he was in trouble. Are you going to help him?"

"He didn't tell me where he was. The sheriff is in charge, and he will take care of things."

Annie's work usually involved much lower-profile cases than she'd investigated recently, and she didn't like Kylie knowing about the more dangerous circumstances. Her little girl worried enough about her when she was checking out a car break-in. It was time for life to settle down here for them, but so far, there'd been no sign of normalcy.

By the time she tied up at the dock, the sun had sent its dying rays into the fading light of the evening sky. The scent of ginger and garlic wafted her way, and her stomach rumbled.

Kylie sniffed the air. "That smells good."

"Jon is fixing us orange chicken."

"You wouldn't let me have it at the restaurant the other day." Kylie's voice vibrated with outrage. "It has gluten."

"Not this one. Jon said he found a good recipe."

Kylie followed Annie across the soft grass toward the back deck of their cottage. "Does he have to come over every night? I miss being with you by myself."

Annie stopped at the bottom of the deck steps and pulled her daughter in for a hug. "I thought you liked Jon after he saved your life. That should count for something, honey."

Kylie stiffened in Annie's embrace. "I like him fine, but he's never really going to feel like my dad."

Would Kylie ever adjust to the truth that Jon was her biological father? She clung to Nate's memory with everything in her, and Annie couldn't fault that. Until a few weeks ago, she'd thought he was Kylie's father too. It was a sea change of tsunami proportions for them both.

Headlamps swept over the grass, and they both turned toward the parking lot as a big SUV parked. Two people got out, and Annie straightened when a familiar voice called her name.

Kylie squinted in the dark. "Grandma?" She ran toward the figures.

Annie's chest compressed as the realization sank in that Nate's parents were here. Without warning and without her being prepared to tell them what had happened. This wasn't the way the truth was supposed to come out with them. She'd wanted to wait until Jon's DNA test came back for absolute confirmation in case they wanted to see it, and it was due anytime now. Yet here they were.

She shot a glance through the window toward Jon moving around in the kitchen. Running wouldn't work, though everything in her wanted to bolt for the safety of her truck.

THREE

KYLIE'S BEAMING FACE AS SHE HUNG ON HER GRAND-
parents after dinner shattered Annie's heart. This was Nate's
parents' usual behavior—an unexpected visit laden with gifts
followed by a quick departure and long silences.

Jon's surprise orange chicken had fallen flat with Kylie, who
barely touched her food because she was so eager to dive in to
the gift bags her grandpa Lars had hauled into the living room.
Maryanne claimed they'd eaten already so they hadn't touched
the meal either, but she'd peppered Jon with questions about what
he'd been up to for the past nine years. Jon and Nate's friendship
had existed since their teen years, and Maryanne hadn't given
any indication she suspected Jon's presence was more than a
casual visit.

Annie tried to encourage Jon with sounds of delight about
the food, though she barely tasted the bite of ginger in the meal
over the taste of fear on her tongue.

Kylie put down her fork. "May I be excused?"

Annie started to order her to eat more, but it would be a waste
of breath. "Go ahead. I'll be right there."

Jon's wink as he rose and gathered dishes from the table with his good arm told her he appreciated the effort. He brushed her cheek with a kiss. "Go ahead, love. I'll clean up."

She ran her fingers through his brown hair. "Leave them for now. I'm going to need moral support. Kylie won't stay quiet about what's happened. We both know it'll come spilling out."

He removed his hand and carried the dishes to the sink. "I'm right behind you."

How did she deserve him? He was strong and kind, and his green eyes were always so steady and tender.

Her wobbly legs didn't want to support her as she stood, nodded, and headed to the living room. Kylie sat snuggled up against Maryanne, who had her arm around the little girl as if she would never let her go. And the funny thing was, Annie believed they did love Kylie. But life got in the way and they let other priorities push contact with their granddaughter to weeks, even months, with no call.

Annie sat across from the sofa and folded her hands in her lap. "Looks like you've got presents, and it's not even your birthday."

Maryanne's light-brown hair brushed a chin line with no sagging skin. She had a subtle tan from their recent trip to the Caribbean.

She leaned forward and picked up the first pink package. "We found this in Turks and Caicos. I think you'll like it."

With a squeal Kylie ripped the paper out of the bag and yanked out a stuffed sea turtle. She hugged it to her chest. "I love it!"

She plowed through the other four bags: a sundress with vivid Caribbean colors, a hammock from Cozumel, an amber bracelet, and a beautiful conch shell. With her booty surrounding her on the floor, Kylie appeared happier than Annie had seen her in a while. It wasn't the gifts though—it was the attention from Lars and Maryanne.

Jon had entered while the focus had been on Kylie, though Annie didn't think anyone else noticed him slip in and sit on a chair against the back wall. His presence grounded her and steadied her for the moment she knew would come sooner or later. If only there was some way to keep Kylie from blurting out the truth, but no eight-year-old knew how to hold back anything important.

Kylie sprang to her feet with the gifts in her arms. "I'm going to try on my dress." She scurried toward her bedroom door.

A reprieve, at least for a few minutes. Annie turned on the light beside her on a table. "How long are you in town?"

Lars answered before Maryanne could. "Two days. I've got a meeting in New York on Friday, so we'll fly out early in the morning."

Maryanne twisted in her seat and motioned for Jon to come closer. "Jon, is your dad here too? I'd love to see him while we're in town."

Jon picked up the chair and brought it around to face the sofa. "He's staying at the Blue Bonnet."

"That's where we're staying too," Maryanne said. "We'll be able to catch up."

"We've been remodeling the old cabin," Jon said. "It's nearly done."

"Are you going to sell it?" Lars asked.

Jon's gaze darted to Annie, and she recognized the question on his face. He didn't know how much to reveal. Maybe blurting out the truth while Kylie was out of the room would be the better option.

She opened her mouth, but Kylie's door slammed, and she pranced down the hall toward them. The sundress fit her well and emphasized the tan she'd already acquired. She spun around for them to see. "I never want to take it off!"

Maryanne tugged a few folds on the shoulder. "It's perfect, just like you. We're going to be here a couple of days, and I thought we might go shopping in Houghton tomorrow if your mommy says it's okay."

"That's fine," Annie said.

Lars rose. "We should probably get to the Blue Bonnet and check in."

"Grandpa Daniel is staying there," Kylie said.

"You call Jon's father Grandpa?" Maryanne's voice held a touch of frost.

"Well, he's my grandpa too." Kylie's face fell and uncertainty crept into her blue eyes. "You know, since Jon is my father."

Lars and Maryanne gasped a collective sound of dismay. Maryanne's hazel eyes went round as she stared at her granddaughter, then swiveled her gaze to Annie. "You've remarried without telling us?"

"Lars, Maryanne, we need to have a little talk," Jon said. "Kylie, it's time for your bath. You can take your seashell into the tub with you."

Kylie's mutinous expression smoothed when he mentioned the shell. She hugged her grandparents and dashed back down the hall.

Annie stood and laced her fingers with Jon's. "This isn't an easy thing to tell you. We've recently discovered Jon is Kylie's father." She moistened her dry lips. "I had no idea until Kylie was diagnosed with celiac disease."

Lars and Maryanne glanced at each other, and Maryanne shook her head as if to clear it. "I don't understand."

"I married Nate a month after Jon and I broke up. I didn't know I was pregnant and never suspected Kylie wasn't Nate's biological child. But Nate will always be her daddy, and I'll make sure she never forgets him. And you know how she loves you. That will never change."

The silence stretched out as the older couple absorbed the news. Annie held her breath, praying they'd understand, but when Maryanne's lips tightened, Annie knew they wouldn't be that lucky.

Maryanne stood and took her husband's hand. "I always wondered about your real feelings. You never loved Nate. Not really. Jon was always there between you."

Annie's chest felt like it had been kicked by a horse. How did she even counter that statement?

/ / /

Jon felt the tension rolling off Annie in frantic waves, and he pressed as much comfort into her hand as he could. Nate's parents stared at them both with matching expressions of disbelief, anger, and grief.

Jon could only imagine how they felt in this moment. "Please don't say anything you'll regret. Annie and I are doing the best we can right now. You have to know I loved Nate like a brother. I would never want Kylie to forget him. From everything I have heard, he was an amazing father."

Lars had been sagging where he stood, but he drew himself up to his full height of six feet. "Like you would know, Jon. You cut him off when he married Annie."

"I did, and I was wrong. Very wrong." There was no real excuse for his behavior, so Jon didn't try to dredge up one. "Nate was one of the best people I've ever met. I miss him every day."

Maryanne shot him a glare of contempt. "Yet you let him think Kylie was his child when she is yours."

Annie made a movement that pulled her hand out of his grasp. "We didn't know, Maryanne. I didn't even suspect." She took a step toward them with her hand outstretched. "Nate tried to help when he saw how much I was hurting after Jon and I broke up, and I let him. We married so quickly, and I never once let myself think Kylie wasn't his. If not for her diagnosis of celiac disease, we still wouldn't know the truth."

"You asked us if anyone in the family had it," Lars said. "It's hereditary?"

"There's a genetic component, and I have celiac disease," Jon said. "When she was diagnosed with the same thing, Annie remembered that Kylie was born a few weeks early. Annie had a DNA test done."

"I didn't expect it to show Nate wasn't her father. We are still adjusting to the truth ourselves. Please don't step away from Kylie. She loves both of you, and she craves time with you."

Lars folded his arms across his chest. "She has another grandfather now. She doesn't need us."

When Maryanne backed away from Annie's outstretched hand, she dropped her arm to her side. "She needs you even more. This has hit her hard, and she needs your stability. Don't punish her for my mistakes."

Maryanne reached for her purse. "We're going now. Lars, I think we should spend the night somewhere else. I have no desire to see Daniel and hear him crow about his new granddaughter."

She marched toward the door with Lars trailing her. Jon started to go after them but thought better of it. They were too angry to listen to any explanations, and he remembered his own reaction to hearing the truth. He hadn't been ready to listen to Annie either. Maybe they would cool off after a few hours.

Annie sank onto the chair and covered her face with her hands. "Kylie will blame me," she said in a shaking voice. "I didn't want it to come out like this. I should have called them right away."

He squatted in front of her and put his hands on the knees of her jeans. He loved everything about her—those big blue eyes and delicate Scandinavian features were etched in his heart. She was thirty-two but still as beautiful as the first time he saw her when he was eighteen. He hadn't allowed himself to think about how she'd loved Nate in his absence, but having the Pedersons show up had brought out that underlying tension he hadn't admitted.

Had she loved Nate more than him? Who would she pick if she had the choice?

He pushed away the fear and gathered his thoughts. "There hasn't been time to even think about letting them know, Annie. Everything has fallen in on you at once. They'll come around, and if they don't, it's their loss."

She uncovered her face to reveal reddened eyes and wet cheeks. "It's Kylie's loss, too, and she's gone through so much. Though they haven't given her the attention I would have liked, they were still a piece of Nate in her life."

He pressed her hand in a comforting squeeze. "I have so many stories about Nate. I'll make sure he's alive in her heart.

We don't need Lars and Maryanne to make sure Kylie has a good life with poignant memories of her daddy."

Annie's blue eyes filled again, and she leaned forward to rest her head against his. "You're a good man, Jon Dunstan. We've upended your life in every way possible, yet here you are still helping and encouraging. I don't deserve you."

His taped ribs ached at the awkward angle, but he didn't stand to relieve the pressure. Not when Annie needed him. "You have that backward. I'm the one who doesn't deserve the two of you." He held her and inhaled the sweet scent of her hair. They'd get through this. They'd already endured so much, and truth was always worth it.

When she lifted her head away from him, he held his bad arm against his body and struggled to his feet. "One of us had better check on Kylie. She's been in the bathtub a while."

"I'll do it."

When she disappeared down the hall, he went into the kitchen and began to load the dishwasher. It was slow going with his arm and aching ribs. Cooking dinner had flared the pain, and he was overdue for some ibuprofen. He paused long enough to find the meds in Annie's cupboard and popped three of them.

Before he resumed the job of cleaning the kitchen, Annie appeared in the doorway. "She's getting on her pj's. I told her she could play on her iPad for a little while." She pointed to the chair at the kitchen table. "Sit while I clean. I can tell by your pinched mouth that the pain is bad."

He didn't argue. Once he was settled on the chair, he watched her swift, efficient movements for a while. Her blonde hair gleamed in the overhead light, and his gaze lingered on the sweet flush of her cheeks. To have a second chance was more than he deserved.

"You're staring," she said.

"Any man would stare when the most beautiful woman in the world was in front of him."

The color in her heart-shaped face heightened. "And you're not a bit prejudiced." She leaned over to put the last plate in the dishwasher.

"Not a bit." He stretched his legs out in front of him and waited for the ibuprofen to ease the pain some. Though he didn't want to tell her about the trouble coming his way, unity and communication were glue for their relationship. She needed to know, and he could use her help. "I got a call from Olivia before dinner. I might be in trouble, Annie."

She turned to face him. "What's happened?"

He told her about Olivia's request and how he'd remembered another possible victim—one of his own. "I'm not sure the police will believe I had nothing to do with this."

Her expression grew fierce. "We can't let her problems spill over into life here."

He hadn't even had to ask for her help, but that was the kind of woman she was. Pulling her into this problem wasn't something he wanted, but their united front felt good.

FOUR

HOW COULD JON KEEP ANNIE AND KYLIE SAFE? HE'D
barely slept after the revelation that Hussert was free, and he
took his coffee out to the deck to watch the sun come up. The
scent of dew on the freshly mown grass blended with the aroma
wafting from his mug, but the sense of contentment he usually
enjoyed was gone this morning.

The men who had taken Hussert out of the hospital confirmed that he hadn't committed his crimes alone. And that
meant the woman and the daughter he loved were likely still in
danger. If Lissa was more involved than she'd admitted, Kylie's
testimony could send her to jail too.

That reality pushed his own problems aside. He could always
find another job, but Annie and Kylie were more precious than
his own life. How quickly life had changed by coming to Rock
Harbor. It had been a roller coaster, but the journey had only
emphasized how empty his life had been without Annie.

He shot off an email to Bree before he had second thoughts
about his idea.

The screen door squeaked, and he turned to see Annie tip-
toeing out with a mug in her hand. Milo followed her, and the

puppy darted down the steps to do his business. Annie's blonde hair, still damp from her shower, flipped up a little on the ends, and she wore her Park Service uniform of dark-green pants and a gray shirt.

He pushed a chair out with his foot so she could sit. "Got a big day at work?"

She put her phone on the table. "I'm going to check in with Mason before I head out to see what's on my desk." She settled on the chair and took a sip of her coffee. "You seem very serious this morning. Did Nate's parents upset you?"

"It wasn't fun. But I'm more concerned about the Hussert situation. It's not only that he's free but that he had help. That speaks volumes about this case being bigger than we anticipated. And I'm worried he may come after you or Kylie."

Her hand lifting her coffee cup paused in midair. "Kylie?"

"I don't believe for a minute Lissa is clueless about what he was doing. That means Kylie could testify against her. She was in Lissa's car after Sarah took her. That makes her an accessory to child abduction. Mason hasn't charged her yet because he was trying to gather more information, but if Lissa's arrested, the other people involved in this could target Kylie too."

Annie set down her mug. "You're right. We'll watch her like a hawk."

"I think she should go with Bree and Kade to Wisconsin Dells for a few days. She'd be away from here and safe with them."

Jon watched the puppy nose through the dandelions while Annie thought through his suggestion. Milo was growing as fast as the weeds in the yard, and he looked more like his sire, Samson, every day.

"I would fret every day she was gone," Annie said. "And this is a family vacation for them. I'd hate for them to have to worry about one more child."

His phone vibrated with a message, and he glanced at Bree's response. She said she'd thought about inviting Kylie but didn't think Annie would agree. Studying Annie's mutinous expression, he had a battle ahead.

"I already asked Bree, and she just answered." He handed her his phone before Annie could marshal arguments against his plan.

She scanned the text. "You shouldn't have asked her without talking to me first."

"You're right, but I'm worried, Annie. This would give us time to figure out who took Hussert and why. It's a good plan, and Bree wants her. She was going to ask anyway. And you know Kylie would love it."

"But there's her celiac disease too. I'm not sure Bree realizes how hard it is to make sure she doesn't ingest gluten. It's everywhere, especially in restaurants."

"Kade told me they're renting a condo and cooking most meals. We can send her gluten-free bread and other food items to make it easier."

Her frown deepened. "You've thought of everything, haven't you?" The way she worded it made it sound like an insult.

"You don't have to decide right now. You can think about it."

"We don't have long. They're leaving tomorrow, and I'd have to get her packed up. And what about Nate's parents? She'll want to see them."

"Dad said they never checked in to the Blue Bonnet. I think they're gone. Maybe they went to Houghton or maybe they headed home."

Her eyes filled with tears, and she stared down. "Without a word to me or Kylie?"

"They feel betrayed. The news came out of the blue."

And so did his own sense of insecurity. He'd thought he'd left the trauma of the past behind until seeing them. How much had Annie loved Nate? More than she loved him now? It was hard to consider that might be true.

She rubbed her forehead. "I know. Let me try to call them." She placed the call, then bit her lip and inhaled. "Maryanne, good morning. I wondered when you wanted to get Kylie for shopping." Her face fell, and she looked down at her lap. "I see. I'm so sorry, but can we—?" She pulled the phone away from her ear and stared at it. "She hung up on me. They're at an airport hotel in Houghton and are leaving in an hour to return to New York."

He winced at the wobble in her voice. "I'm sorry, love. This will hit Kylie hard."

She cleared her throat and nodded. "But a trip with Bree would wash away the disappointment."

Her phone sounded with another message, and she glanced at it and inhaled sharply before she turned it around for him to see.

It was from Dr. Ben. *I called on the DNA to get the early result. Positive. Jon is Kylie's father. Probability 99.99999999%. Congratulations!*

Jon's mouth went dry. Kylie was his own flesh and blood. He'd known the truth in his heart, but now no one could ever challenge it. "I never doubted your word, love."

"But your dad did."

"Not really. He was thinking like a lawyer and wanted to

cover all the bases. No one can ever deny the proof of what we've known all along."

Her blue eyes softened. "I know I shouldn't have let it hurt me."

"But it did, and I'm sorry." He took her hand. "But it's behind us now."

Her gaze searched his. "You're happy?"

"Do you doubt it?" He squeezed her fingers. "Finding you again and having my own daughter is the best thing that's ever happened to me."

She leaned over to kiss him. "I love you."

"I love you more."

She gave his fingers a final squeeze and rose. "I've got to get to town to talk to Mason. Could you have Kylie lay out what she wants to take?"

But her tone warned him she wasn't fully on board and that he'd overstepped his bounds. They would have to feel their way through this kind of thing when it came to Kylie.

/ / /

The coffee in Mason's messy office smelled as strong as espresso, but Annie took a sip anyway to try to wake up after a long night of tossing and turning. "I didn't get another call from Glenn last night. Do we know anything so far?"

As far as she knew, Mason hadn't been able to get a straight answer out of the man before he was taken out of the hospital.

Mason leaned forward and studied the screen on his desk. "You know all of it—he milked the women's shelter of close to a million dollars and funneled it into his political campaign. He tried to kill you and Jon, he kidnapped Michelle Fraser, who could have brought everything down around his head, and he would have killed Sarah if you hadn't gotten to her first. Michelle gave us the evidence of his fraud, and she and Sarah can identify him as their abductor so we can charge him with fraud, kidnapping, and attempted murder. He'll be going away for a long, long time."

"Any identity on the people who took him out of the hospital?"

"We've sent the pictures off for enhancement to see if we can identify them, but it will take a while to get them back. The lab is backed up. Interesting that he called you. He must have had you in his phone."

"He sounded disoriented and confused, too, but that's to be expected with coming out of a coma." She took another sip of the horrendous coffee and grimaced. "What about the BOLO you have out on Idoya Jones?"

The manager of the women's shelter had helped Hussert funnel all that money. Annie suspected Idoya might know more about Michelle's kidnapping and Glenn's other crimes, but she'd vanished.

"We checked with border patrol and there's a picture of her entering Canada. There's been no trace of her yet." Mason leaned back and studied her face. "The one case you haven't asked about is Sarah's."

"How's she doing?" And did Annie even want to know? Sympathy for Sarah after what she'd done was hard to muster.

Mason took a sip of coffee. "She didn't like jail, but no one does. She cried a lot, but she brought this on herself. No one forced her to abduct Kylie—it was her own rage and poor judgment. There are consequences."

Annie had made plenty of the same kind of statements, but it felt harsher coming from Mason. It wasn't like Sarah was a child, though, or even young enough to have acted in the rashness of youth. She was a grown woman and hadn't cared about the havoc and pain she'd left in her wake.

But she was still Annie's baby sister. The one she'd searched for long and hard. The one she'd thought lay in a long-abandoned grave somewhere. Yet she'd shown up here in Rock Harbor, alive and well. At least physically. How much did the horrific details of Sarah's abduction and subsequent life play a part in those poor decisions Mason mentioned?

Probably a lot.

"Have you seen her today? I know Jon dropped her off at his cottage late yesterday afternoon."

"I haven't seen her. I'll admit I'm concerned about her being there alone now that Hussert is out. Whoever helped him get away must be involved. They won't want Sarah testifying against Hussert when we catch him. She's a sitting duck out there by herself. I think you should revoke bail. She'd be safer sitting in jail. And my case would be more secure as well."

Annie gave a slight shake of her head. "I should hate her, Mason, but I find myself pitying her instead. And I shouldn't. She chose to take Kylie of her own free will. But now that the fake contacts are gone and her hair is going blonde again, I see that little girl inside—who she used to be. The baby sister who used to beg me to read to her. I see her watching me all those years ago when I'd sing silly songs. Her childhood was stolen from her."

A muscle in his jaw flexed. "And from you."

"And from me." She nodded. "I don't want her sitting in jail. She's going away for a long time, isn't she?"

"Probably. Her state-appointed attorney is filing a temporary-insanity plea though."

"'Temporary insanity'?"

"She snapped under all the strain. I gotta admit the jury might buy it. She's been full of remorse since we found her."

Annie had seen Sarah's regret from the first moment. All her defiance and bravado had disappeared and never returned.

"If you're not going to send her back to jail, you'd better come up with another place to stash her. Men who are brazen enough to waltz into the hospital and spirit away a criminal like Hussert will figure out where she is soon enough. And she'll go missing too. Maybe permanently this time."

Annie winced at the stark words. It wasn't safe to have Sarah near Kylie, not after what she had done. There was no one Annie could ask to take her.

Her memory jolted back to Max Reardon. He'd always said if he could do anything for her, all she had to do was ask. What if she had him take Sarah to Tremolo Island? He and his staff were the only inhabitants. The place was a fortress. And she could stay in the old Pederson cabin. Maybe it would help her.

"I have an idea." She told Mason about her plan. "What do you think?"

"It's a good idea. Max hates to lose at anything, and he'll make sure she stays safe."

True enough. The man's reputation was important to him. And he had always been good to her. He'd want to help her for Anu's sake as well. Their romance was blossoming quickly.

"I'll give him a call and see what he says."

Mason swiveled in his chair and nodded out his window. "He's down at the Suomi Café with Anu. You should be able to catch him there. And, Annie, thanks for helping out here. I know you're pulling double duty with your own job, but you've stepped in when I needed you. I appreciate it."

"I'm happy to help. We'll solve this case together." She rose, holding the atrocious coffee. "I'm meeting Jon and Kylie there for breakfast anyway."

Having a plan felt like an accomplishment, and she didn't think Max would turn down her plea. Not with Anu sitting right there. But it still didn't give Annie an answer about what to do about Hussert lurking out there somewhere.

FIVE

ANNIE HATED TO ASK FOR HELP FROM ANYONE, BUT she steeled herself as she stepped inside the Suomi Café. The air was redolent with the scent of cardamom, yeast, and cinnamon. She spotted Anu's stylish silvery-blonde bob in a back booth. She sat facing the door with Max across the table from her. The remains of *panukakkua* lay scattered across both of their plates.

Anu spotted her, and her blue eyes crinkled in a smile. "Good morning, beautiful Annie. You seem to be a woman on a mission."

"Could I join you a moment?"

Anu slid to the side. "Of course. You do not even need to ask."

"You're feeling well enough to be out and about?"

Anu nodded. "I refuse to stay inside on such a beautiful day, and Max parked right outside. I only had to walk a few steps." She smiled at Max.

He reached across the table and took her hand. "I only want to be there for you."

This was Annie's opening. "Your help is why I'm here this morning too. You've always told me to let you know if you could do anything for me, but I've hated asking. Now I'm in a corner and need your help."

"Anything." He pulled his hand away and leaned forward with his hands clasped on the table. "What is it?"

His brown eyes and steady manner drew her in. "My sister is likely in danger." She told him about Hussert's escape with the help of three men. "I can't have her around Kylie, and yet I want her safe."

The dimple in his left cheek flashed when he smiled. "I would be happy to have her at the island. That's what you were about to ask, right?"

"You are astute."

"The island is secure, and my guards see any boat that comes our way. There aren't many safe places to come ashore either. And there is plenty of room in the house, or she would be welcome to stay in one of the small cabins." He pursed his lips. "The old homestead was built by your parents. Would you want her to stay there? It might be comforting to be where she spent time as a small child. Has she seen it since she's arrived?"

He'd read her mind. "She hasn't been there as far as I know."

The cabin was from their lives so long ago, when Mom and Dad were alive and the sisters were young and carefree. Before a madwoman changed everything forever.

But maybe it was time they put the ghosts to rest. If there was a chance to bring back the old Sarah, maybe it was in those remembered scenes of their childhoods. Right now Sarah didn't love her. Not really. She had only hatred and revenge in her heart, but the cabin could change that.

"You might be right about the cabin," she said. "Is it habitable? I haven't been in it myself since Sarah disappeared, and the mice might have taken over."

"Not on my watch. My crew cleans it regularly, and I've kept it in order in case you ever wanted to wander through it and remember your parents. While it's not as luxurious as my home, it's comfortable. And all the contents are still inside."

Anu picked up her coffee. "I have been inside recently, Annie. It is nicer than Bree's cabin where Sarah has been staying. She will be quite happy there. I think it is an excellent idea to have her stay there. Though she was young, she might remember more than we think."

Max was watching Annie with a somber expression. Was he able to reach inside and see how torn Annie felt? Memories could be good or bad. Sarah's memories of the night she was abducted were not the ones Annie remembered. Sarah thought Annie could have done more to save her, but if she thought it through logically, she'd know it wasn't true. For example, how could Sarah look at Kylie and think someone her age could do anything to stop a grown woman?

Annie had beat herself up over the years for failing to save her sister, but she'd been helpless and wounded. That knowledge had been hard-won and slow to sink into Annie's heart.

She gathered her composure. "Would it be all right for Mason to bring her out this morning?"

"Of course. I'll notify my staff in case I'm not back yet. Anu and I would like to review the property she's buying from you. I might have some ideas on renovation. Would that be all right?"

"I'd love for her to get your thoughts. Everything you've done on the island has been beautiful."

He smiled at her compliment. "I'm glad she's letting me have some input, though she will probably never live there."

Annie blinked at the statement. They were talking marriage already? If so, why was Anu still pursuing the deal?

The transfer of property was scheduled to occur in a couple of days, and Annie had almost forgotten it in the flurry of events that had rolled in on them all. She'd stop by the title company office to make sure everything was ready. She'd never used that old cabin, and it was going to be wonderful to have Anu as a neighbor.

As she walked out of the restaurant, she texted Mason the okay to take Sarah out to the island. So far Annie had managed to avoid her sister, but was it even the right thing to do?

/ / /

Sarah sat at the bow of the sheriff's boat with the wind lifting her hair. "Annie hates me, doesn't she?" Sheriff Kaleva didn't answer, but then, he didn't need to. They both knew the truth.

The fresh scent of Lake Superior usually energized her, but her sister's continued rejection made her want to crawl in bed and pull the covers over her head. It didn't help to realize she deserved every bit of Annie's disdain. Sarah's actions had brought all of this on her head. It wasn't Annie's fault.

She ran her fingers through her hair, and it made her happy to see it was mostly blonde again. The red was almost gone. When she peered in the mirror now, she saw her sister looking back at her. They had the same Scandinavian features, the same eyes and hair. She was in need of a trim, but it wasn't going to happen anytime soon, not out on Tremolo Island.

Sheriff Kaleva had said very little about why he was taking her out to the island, just that it was for her safety. Typical taciturn Finn. The least he could do was explain.

She swiveled to face the sheriff. "I don't know why I have to stay out there. I won't bother Annie or Kylie. They're safe from me. I know I made a bad mistake, but you don't have to worry about me doing it again."

His weathered face softened a bit. "That's not the problem." A heavy sigh moved his broad chest. "Your kidnapper escaped custody. We're searching for him, but we can't be sure he won't target you again to prevent you from testifying."

Panic fluttered high into her throat. When Jon took her to his family cabin, he'd simply said they were worried about her safety. If she'd known the truth, she wouldn't have stayed out there by herself without anyone else around. "How could Glenn get away? He was in a coma."

"He had help." The sheriff clammed up and squinted toward the approaching island. "You'll be safe here. Max has plenty of security out here, and it's only a few days."

Sarah clenched her trembling hands together in her lap. The fear she'd felt while trapped in that cabin wasn't something she liked to remember. She'd thought all of that was behind her, but she could see how she posed a threat to Hussert. "Is Michelle in danger too? She had to deal with him longer than me, and she has evidence about his other crimes as well."

"We're taking precautions with her as well."

"She could come out here with me. Her mom wouldn't be much protection, and I think she's still afraid of her husband."

"Last I heard, they were working on reconciling. He has plenty of money to hire guards for her."

"I think you heard wrong," Sarah said. "She'd never go back to him. He hurt her."

Mason's gaze swung back to her. "She told you he hurt her?"

"Yes. What if he's forcing her to go back to him? You should check up on her."

"I'll do that." He nodded toward the dock. "Grab hold and tie us up."

She struggled to her feet and reached for a post as the boat bumped against the dock, then clung tight to hold it in place while she slipped the loop of rope around it. Mason secured the stern, then grabbed her duffel bag of belongings before assisting her to the dock's decking.

No one was there to greet them, but Sarah suspected her presence hadn't been something Max was looking forward to. It felt like everyone was against her, and why wouldn't they be after what she'd done? Annie was one of theirs while Sarah was an unpredictable outsider. She might have been born in the area, but she wasn't sure how many knew she was Annie's long-lost sister.

Mason strode ahead of her along the flagstone path toward the huge log home. Mansion, really. It was the largest log structure she'd ever seen, but it seemed cold and forbidding to her. Like it could swallow her up and not even burp. The crazy thought slowed her steps and raised her heart rate even though she told herself she'd be fine out here. The sheriff wouldn't bring her here if he thought she'd be in danger.

Mason rang the bell, and the door opened almost immediately. An honest-to-goodness butler stood in the doorway, wearing a suit and everything. The jacket and tie felt over the top to Sarah, especially out here in this wilderness. Tremolo Island had never been fully tamed. Native timber and thick brush covered most of its many acres, but she still held a few faint memories of how much she'd once loved it.

After staying here a few days, maybe she could learn to be part of this place again.

"Good morning," the man said. "Mr. Reardon is expecting you. This way."

He led the way down a wide hall with a vaulted ceiling that echoed their footsteps. The ten-foot door opened without a sound, and Sarah caught sight of tall windows flanking a massive stone fireplace that reached to the ceiling. Sunbeams touched beige leather furniture that looked as soft as butter.

Sarah couldn't imagine living in a place this beautiful. Max rose from his seat at a large walnut desk and turned toward them with a smile. She'd only seen him a few times, but she'd always been struck by the calm confidence that seemed to ooze from his pores.

That assurance enveloped her now, and for the first time in a long time, she thought she might be able to relax and heal here in this beautiful setting.

SIX

TEARS TREMBLED ON KYLIE'S LASHES. "YOU MEAN
they left without saying good-bye?" She sat on the edge of the
deck with Milo's head on her lap. Her braid needed to be redone,
but Jon wasn't sure he'd be able to do much to help.

He wanted to scoop her up and reassure her, but she wouldn't
welcome that from him, even if his aching shoulder and ribs
would allow it. "I'm sorry, sweetheart."

Her lower lip quivered. "It's because they know you're my real
dad, isn't it? They don't love me anymore."

Angry words about her grandparents hovered on his tongue,
but he bit them back. They'd serve no purpose and would upset
Kylie even more. She'd recognize any deflection as to the reason
for their departure as the lie it was. "Nate is still your daddy.
Maybe we can make them understand that."

Kylie began to sob. "Will I ever see them again?"

He leaned over to put his hand on her shoulder, and at least
she let him without jerking away. "I hope so. It'll take them
some time to adjust to the news. Remember how mad you were
when you heard about it? Can you try to imagine how they feel
right now?"

She moved so his hand fell away. "Especially with Daddy in heaven. It probably feels like I don't love them. But I *do*! They should have asked me how I felt. Grandma said she was going to take me shopping. All my summer clothes are getting too little." She gave a tug on her short top.

Did she have enough clothes to pack for the trip? Did he offer to take her shopping, or did he shut up and let Annie deal with it? All this girl stuff was over his head. It was as bad as trying to roll a log in a river. One slip, and he was in the drink.

"I do have some good news though," he said, testing the waters of her mood. "What would you think of going to Wisconsin Dells with the twins and Davy?"

Her eyes widened, and Milo lifted his head. "For real? You and Mommy are going too?"

He shook his head. "Mommy has to work, but Bree would like you to come along on their trip. Would you like that?"

Did he ask if it would scare her to leave her mom behind? He didn't want to plant doubt in her mind, but he hated the thought of her being homesick too.

She didn't give him the chance to decide. "I'm *eight* now. I'm not a baby. I've stayed at their house lots of times. I'll be with the twins, and it won't matter what house we're in."

He hoped that was true. The first night in a strange house without her mom might be harder than she realized, but he wasn't about to tell her that. They might get a call from her in the middle of the night asking to come home. It was about a five-hour drive, and he could go get her if it came to that.

"We need to pack your things. They're leaving tomorrow. I can help you find clothes that fit. If you need bigger ones, I could take you shopping."

She gave him a scathing glance. "I know what I want to take, and they fit fine. How long will we be gone?"

"A week."

She extracted herself from Milo and scrambled to her feet. "I'll need seven outfits, plus my bathing suit and pajamas. Did you know there are water parks at Wisconsin Dells? I bet we'll go to some of those."

"So I've heard." He started to follow her inside but saw Annie's red-and-white Volkswagen truck pull into the marina's lot. "You can get started, and I'll find a suitcase."

"It's in Mommy's closet. On a high shelf. I should take my iPad so I have something to do on the trip." Her voice faded as she disappeared into the house.

His phone sounded with a message, and he stopped when he saw it was from Mike Willis. He'd been avoiding any decision on what to do about the job offer. There'd been no time to think it through. He read the short message. *I'd like to schedule a time for us to finalize plans for you to join us.*

In the past week he'd wished he could start a business here in Rock Harbor, but he couldn't ask Annie to make that sacrifice—especially not if his investment in the Minnesota practice was never recouped. It would take some time for a private practice to build a patient base, and he hated the thought of putting more burden on Annie.

He shot a quick text back to Mike. *Lots going on here. Give me another week?*

Mike's answer of *Sure* came back quickly, and Jon exhaled his relief.

Jon went down the steps to meet Annie. "How'd it go?"

He opened his arms, and she stepped into his embrace. He

ignored the pain the movement caused and breathed in the clean scent of her before kissing her upturned lips. There was no trace of anger left from the morning. That was one of the great things about Annie—she might get riled, but she never held on to it.

She kissed him back, then pulled away with obvious reluctance and a glance toward the house. "Great. Mason already left to take Sarah to the island. I have to wonder how she'll do out there though. Will she relive the terror of her abduction? Max is letting her stay in our old hunting cabin. We stayed in it a lot when we were little. We girls would fish while Dad was out hunting. It holds a lot of memories."

"You sound a little jealous. When was the last time you stayed out there?"

"I didn't want to be there at all after Sarah was taken, and neither did my parents. We never spent the night again, and I always stayed back when they'd go out to check on the island. And maybe I am a little jealous. I'd like to forget that one terrible day and remember all the good times we had out on the island. It used to be my favorite place."

"I told Kylie about her grandparents leaving. She was upset and cried. She thinks they don't love her anymore."

Annie's brow furrowed. "I was afraid of that. I'll go talk to her."

He started to tell her about Mike wanting an answer, then shut his mouth. She had enough on her plate without worrying about this just yet.

Her phone sounded, and she glanced it. "Unknown." She swiped to answer it. "LEO Pederson, can I help you?"

The color drained from her face, and he clenched his fists. Bad news of some kind, but what?

Her mouth flattened, and she took several deep breaths. "Who is this?" Her fingertips were white where she gripped the phone tightly. "Hello?" She pulled the screen away from her ear and stared at it. "He hung up on me."

"What did he say?"

"That moving my sister wouldn't work, and he'd find her. If I back off searching for Hussert, he might let her live."

"It was Glenn?"

She shook her head. "I don't think so. Glenn was so weak yesterday I could barely understand him. This guy sounded strong and confident. He was using some kind of voice-masking device so I didn't recognize him. I wonder if that means I know him?"

"He must be afraid Hussert will implicate him."

She started toward the deck. "I'm glad Kylie will be out of here. I need to find these guys while she's gone."

He laced his fingers with hers as they walked to the house. That guy had just poked the bear. She'd never give up until she found him.

/ / /

Kylie was uncharacteristically quiet on the drive to Rock Harbor. When Annie and Jon parked in front of Bree's lighthouse home, the little girl unbuckled in the back and grabbed her backpack without her normal chatterbox enthusiasm.

Annie got out of her truck and went around to take her daughter's hand. "You okay, Bug?" Jon took out his phone and waited in the car while Annie took Kylie to the door.

When Kylie glanced up at her, tears were swimming in her blue eyes. "Grandma and Grandpa don't love me anymore, do they? Jon tried to tell me they did, but he was just trying to make me feel better."

"Oh, honey." Annie stooped and embraced her little girl. "They were just surprised. They'll adjust to it and be back to see you."

Annie wished she could feel as certain as her words made it seem. This blow to Nate's parents might not be so easily overcome. The first chance she got, she would call them again and see if she could reassure them.

A booming male voice said, "Well, there's my favorite granddaughter."

She and Kylie turned to see Daniel coming down the sidewalk with his cane. Kylie pulled away from Annie. "Shh, don't tell Grandpa." She scrubbed the tears from her face with the back of her hand and ran to hug him.

He held her to his side and reached into his pocket for a Jolly Rancher. "I stocked up on your favorite lime flavor."

She took the candy and unwrapped it, then popped it into her mouth. "Thanks, Grandpa. Did you hear I get to go to Wisconsin Dells with the twins?"

"So I heard. That should be a fun time." He settled on a bench on the tree lawn and pulled Kylie onto his lap. "I'm going to miss you, little one."

His green eyes, so like his son's, locked with Annie's gaze, and she could see Jon had called him. Annie mouthed *Thank you* to him.

Kylie snuggled against him. "Do you only love me because I'm your true granddaughter?"

"Why, no, Kylie. I loved you before I found out that good news, remember? We had the best time playing at your house way before I ever knew."

"I forgot. Do you love me more now?"

"Let's say finding out you were my own sweet granddaughter gave me permission to love you bigger. That's probably something you can't understand just yet, but when a kid belongs to someone else, we feel we aren't entitled to love them all the way. Someone might take them away or tell us we can't see them. So we protect our hearts a little."

"Maybe that's what Grandma and Grandpa did? That's silly. Mommy and Jon would never take me away."

"No, they wouldn't. So you need to be a big girl and show them you'll always love them. You can be the bigger person and send them a card or text from your iPad. You can let them know you will always love them."

"I could send them a postcard from Wisconsin Dells. Maybe they would like that."

"And you could take selfies to send to them," Daniel said.

"What if they don't answer me?"

Daniel hugged her. "You love them anyway. Time and distance doesn't stop love. And I'll always love you, Kylie. When you go off to college, you can still call me. I'll answer every text and every picture."

She threw her arms around Daniel. "I love you, Grandpa."

He swiped at his eyes and hugged her tight. "You're my own sweet girl. I never dreamed I'd be lucky enough to have a granddaughter like you."

Kylie sprang to her feet as Bree and the family spilled onto the porch with everyone talking excitedly. "I have to go."

"Send me pictures too," he called after her.

Annie managed to snag Kylie for a last hug before she piled into the van with the Matthews family. If Annie could have called her back without hurting her, she would have. A week apart would be endless.

Bree made sure they were all buckled up before calling, "We'll take good care of her."

"I know you will. Have her call me every day."

Bree gave a thumbs-up as the van pulled away. Jon got out of the truck and joined Annie and his dad. He draped his arm around her. "Doing okay?"

She leaned into his embrace. "I'll try to make it through. Your dad was wonderful. He said all the right things."

"I knew he would." He spoke over her head at his father. "Thanks, Dad."

"I hate that they hurt that little girl." His voice was steely. "I've half a mind to talk to Lars myself. Let me know if you need reinforcements."

"I will," Jon said.

Daniel struggled to his feet and grabbed his cane before heading back toward the Blue Bonnet Bed-and-Breakfast.

Jon rested his chin on Annie's head until his phone dinged. He pulled out his phone, and she caught a glimpse of the text. "Mike?"

"He set up a meeting for next week after I put him off. I don't know what to tell him. I'm pretty certain I'll get no money from the practice in Rochester. It will be months, maybe a year or more, before we even know exactly what is happening there. I can't wait that long. I have to support my family."

My family. His words resonated in her heart. "What do you really want to do?"

His green eyes were full of worry. "I like Mike. He'd be a great guy to work with, and he might work with me on the buy-in. But I'd be on call and gone a lot."

"And if you had your own practice here?"

"Less money and more headache to own my own business."

"But you could set your own hours and not be on call. In emergencies the hospital is already used to send patients to Houghton. Even you got transferred to Houghton. Our small hospital isn't really equipped for major surgeries. Would you be wasting your talents to open a practice in Rock Harbor though?"

She knew he was well trained and a good orthopedic surgeon.

He frowned. "Maybe, but being with you and Kylie would be worth it."

She hugged him. "Let's explore the options before you decide. Look at buildings you can lease here. Talk to Mike. I want you to be happy."

Whatever he decided was fine with her. He was staying here with Kylie and her forever. That was all that mattered.

SEVEN

ANNIE STEPPED INSIDE GLENN HUSSERT'S HOUSE AND let her eyes adjust to the dim lighting. "Thanks for letting me check it out myself, Mason."

She was eager to find something—anything—that might help them discover who was behind Hussert's escape. A distraction would help ease the pain of hugging her baby girl good-bye for a week. Kylie had been too excited to do more than endure a quick embrace before she darted toward Bree's lighthouse.

Mason opened the heavy curtains at the picture window, and morning sunlight streamed into the room. "I think we've gone over it well, but another pair of eyes can't hurt. And when we're done here, we need to go check on Michelle if you're game. I want to make sure she's okay. Sarah told me she didn't believe Michelle would willingly try to work things out with her husband."

Annie had a feeling her sister might be right.

Jon stood off to one side as if he was trying not to be intrusive, and Annie beckoned him over. "Look for anything that seems out of the ordinary," she told him.

While he wasn't law enforcement, he'd met Glenn and might spot something that didn't ring true to what they knew about the man. Glenn owned Bunyan Fisheries, he was married, and he was a hunter. Those facts didn't necessarily tell the whole story of who he was, but it was all they had to start with.

Annie spotted a picture on the end table of Glenn with a pretty redhead. "Where's his wife?"

"At work," Mason said. "I let her know we wanted to have another look around. She wasn't thrilled about it."

The house was spotless. The living room furnishings seemed expensive. Leather sectional, nice rug and draperies, the right touches of decor. Annie had heard Glenn's wife was an interior designer, and it showed.

Jon knelt in front of an end table and rummaged inside a drawer that appeared to hold loose pictures. He studied each one before laying it aside on top of the wood surface. Annie knew Mason had checked those pictures, too, so she didn't expect much, but Jon straightened and came toward her with a picture in hand.

"Probably nothing, but check this out."

At first glance the picture he handed her didn't seem odd. Dressed in camouflage, Glenn stood among thick trees with a rifle over one shoulder. One foot was atop a deer, and he wore a big grin. A typical successful hunter picture she'd seen re-created a thousand times over the years.

She glanced at Jon for explanation, and he moved closer to her. "Two questions. The first time we interviewed him, he wore a John Deere hat, remember?"

"Sure."

"What's he wearing here?" He tapped the hat.

"A Massey Ferguson hat." She glanced at Mason. "What yard equipment does Glenn own?"

Mason approached. "He's a big John Deere fan. I don't think he owns anything but that brand. Tractor, big snowblower for the fishery, lawn sweeper. Just about every yard tool you can imagine is in his shed, and it was all John Deere."

Her attention went back to the hat. "The only hat I've seen him wear is a John Deere one, so why the Massey Ferguson hat?"

"You're right," Mason said. "I don't know what it might mean though."

"A competition with a friend?" Jon put in. "I had a buddy who knew I was an Apple fan so he'd give me Microsoft gear."

"Did you ever use it?" Mason asked.

"Well, no."

"That's what I thought. Most of us wouldn't give a joker that kind of satisfaction."

Annie turned the two words over in her mind. *Massey.* Not a common name, not around here anyway. *Ferguson.* A much more common surname at least. She turned over the picture and found three scrawled words in what seemed a male's handwriting.

Your turn next.

She showed it to Mason and Jon. The ominous words shook her. *Your turn.* Someone else's turn to take a deer? Or something more sinister?

"Do you have a list of his employees and friends?" Jon asked. "Massey Ferguson might have some significance."

Annie turned the photo faceup. "Are there are any more pictures of Glenn in clothing or hats with words on them? This one probably struck you because it was so contrary to John Deere, but there might be more that aren't obvious."

"I'll check." Jon went back to the drawer and spread out the rest of the pictures.

While he went through the rest of the photos, Annie and Mason continued to examine the rest of the house. Nothing seemed out of order. She paid particular attention to his office, but nothing jumped out at her.

"Bingo!" Jon called from the living room. "There's a false bottom in this drawer."

She and Mason rushed down the hall to see what he'd found. Jon had the drawer apart with three more glossies spread out on the sofa.

Jon scooped up the pictures and handed them over. "I think the Massey Ferguson one was supposed to be in the false drawer. All the others are pictures of Glenn wearing various promotional items. Look here."

He showed them one of Glenn dressed in a Hawk's tee. "Check out the back."

Swift and deadly.

"Here he is in a King's Camp hat," Jon said.

"And the back?" Annie asked.

"'*This weekend.*' And here's the last." He showed them a picture of Glenn in front of a cabin wearing a Cyclops jacket. "That's the cabin where he held Michelle." He turned it over.

Shoot straight.

They would have to figure out what it all meant. They could start with a list of known associates, but Annie suspected it wouldn't be that easy. The gear meant something important to Glenn and his friends, and none of them would be quick to give up any information.

"Hello?"

Annie turned at a female voice and recognized the woman coming through the doorway as Glenn's wife. She had that creamy skin a true redhead possessed, and a scowl marred her smooth brow. A badge from the top real estate company in town was pinned to the lapel of her camel pantsuit.

"I want you out of my house." Her accusing gaze swung to Mason. "You said you'd be in here only a little while, and it's already lunchtime."

Mason scooped up the pictures and showed them to her. "I have a few questions first."

/ / /

The two hours Sarah had waited for Max Reardon seemed like years. The staff was nice enough and gave her the run of the house, but Max wanted to personally escort her to the cabin where she was going to stay for the week. Sarah had taken a copy of *Jack and Jill* by Louisa May Alcott out to the massive back deck to try to kill time.

She fanned through it, not sure she wanted to dive in, and was struck by a paragraph that lodged deep. *"Our actions are in our own hands, but the consequences of them are not. Remember that, my dear, and think twice before you do anything."*

She hadn't considered the consequences of anything she'd done, and look where it had all landed her. How had she ended up here? She rubbed her head and thought back to the moment when revenge seemed her best option. It had been right after Becky had died, and Sean had come to help her. He'd shown her a picture of Annie with their parents that had been in the paper. There'd been no mention of a kidnapped daughter. It was like Sarah had ceased to be relevant or missed in their lives. And she'd decided to make them pay.

It had been stupid. She sighed and put the book down.

When Max arrived, she'd followed him straight to the cabin, but rounding the final twist in the path brought perspiration to her palms. The scent of dead leaves and pine caused dread to swirl in her chest, and she stood ten feet back, unable to budge.

"There it is," Max said. "Do you remember it?"

"Not really." But was that true? Her pulse chattered like a squirrel, and she wasn't sure she wanted to go in.

"I updated the exterior with a new metal roof and fresh stain. The inside is cleaned, but I left the furnishings."

Something dark pressed in on her, and she didn't understand why that might be. From everything she'd heard, her childhood had been wonderful. She had dim memories of Annie reading her stories and fixing her hair. Why would this place bring so much fear surging into her throat?

"I'll unlock it for you and leave you to wander by yourself." Max carried her duffel bag the final few feet and twisted a key in the door. He stepped inside, set down the bag, then backed out.

He pressed the key into her hand. "It's all yours for now. It's stocked with food, but let me know if there's anything else you need. You're welcome to join us for meals in the main house as well if you'd rather. I have an excellent chef."

"Thank you," she mumbled through numb lips.

Move. Her internal order gave her the impetus to shuffle up the flagstone walk to the front porch. The cabin was small but cute. The porch held two rockers and looked out on a stand of white pines. There was a firepit in a clearing as well as some large pieces of tree trunks cut up to make seats around the pit. The wind sang through the pine needles in an eerie way that sped up Sarah's gait.

She darted past Max and into the house. "Thank you, Max."

"You're welcome."

She could barely wait for him to turn his back so she could shut the door. The latch clicked and muffled the outside sounds. With her back pressed against the door, she closed her eyes for a few moments before she opened them to examine the interior.

Nothing felt familiar. At least not until she walked over to a door on her left and opened it into a tiny bedroom containing a bunk bed. The sight of the Care Bears spreads brought a flash of memory that blurred her vision. Almost in a trance, she entered and touched the worn cotton fabric.

This had been her room with Annie. Sarah had slept on the bottom because she was the youngest. Her mother hadn't wanted her to fall out, so Annie had been designated to climb the ladder. Sarah had cried and begged for the top bunk, but Mom had been adamant. Annie often invited her up for a visit though, and they'd play with their dolls or stickers on that top bunk.

She whirled and dashed from the room before any other memories could assault her. She needed air.

She went out the back door onto a small deck overlooking a tiny patch of grass before the woods encroached. A small path led toward a glimmer of water in the distance. Superior or a small lake? She couldn't remember.

She followed the dirt path into the brush down to a serene pond. Didn't they used to catch frogs out here? After skirting the pond, she followed the narrowing path for a while until she came to a scruffy beach on Lake Superior. A rocky hillside rose to her right and marched around the edge of the water. The only area accessible to the lake was right here in this postage-sized piece of beach. She had a flash of memory that held her still.

Right here was where she and Annie used to lay out on their towels. She could almost smell the coconut oil in the tanning lotion. But this wasn't where she'd been abducted. It was from the dock. She went to her right and walked along the slip of land between the water and the hillside to see where it led.

A scrap of bright color caught her attention up the rocky slope about five feet. The yellow fabric waved in the breeze, and she thought it might be a scarf or a sweater. She climbed over the rocks and grabbed at it. Rocks and sand had buried part of it, and she had to tug it free.

It was a girl's jacket, but that wasn't what froze her in her steps. A large hole gaped in the back and red stiffened the fabric. It couldn't be blood, could it? She raised it to her nose and sniffed. The coppery odor made her shudder.

It *was* blood. And a lot of it.

She turned and scanned up and down the beach for anything that might lead her to the jacket's owner. Nothing. She needed to let the sheriff know about this. But when she pulled out her phone, she had no bars. She'd forgotten the sheriff said there was no cell service out here.

She took off at a run for the main house. Max would know what to do, and he could use his satellite phone to let the authorities know someone out here might need help.

Unless it was too late.

EIGHT

THE REDHEAD TOSSED HER HAIR AND TURNED HER
back on Mason and Jon. "I'll talk to *her*. The rest of you can take
a hike."

Annie exchanged a glance with Mason, who gave her a nod
of encouragement. "Jon and I will wait in the car." He handed the
pictures to Annie, who slipped them into her back pocket.

When the door shut behind the men, the woman exhaled and
tears gathered in her eyes. "I've seen you around. You're a park
ranger, right?"

"That's right. I'm Annie Pederson. I know you're Glenn's
wife, but I don't know your name."

"Candace Hussert." She didn't offer to shake hands but went
toward the kitchen.

Annie followed and found her fiddling with the coffee maker.
Candace shot her a glance. "I need to eat something and get back
to work. Coffee?"

"I never turn down coffee."

The kitchen was like one out of a home magazine with
marble counters, black cabinets, and gleaming brass fixtures.
Annie perched on a leather barstool at the breakfast bar. "Your

home is lovely. I heard you were a designer, but I see you have a real estate badge."

"I stage homes for them. It's fun and different. I've been doing that for about a year." Candace rummaged through the top freezer and drew out a paleo bowl that she popped into the microwave.

"Have you heard from Glenn?" Annie asked.

The coffeepot beeped, and Candace drew down two mugs. "Cream, sugar?"

"Black, please." Annie waited until the coffee was poured to see if Candace would answer the question.

Candace slid a mug across the counter to her. "I haven't heard from him since before he was injured." Her voice wobbled. "I don't believe he did those things, but the sheriff seems to have a lot of evidence."

"People can hold secrets even from the ones they love. And I don't doubt he loved you. When I questioned him about another incident some weeks back, he mentioned you."

Candace swallowed a gulp of coffee and nodded. She set her cup on the counter and turned when the microwaved beeped. "I hope you don't mind if I eat."

"Not at all." Annie inhaled the aroma of the strong coffee and took a sip while she watched the other woman open her meal and grab a fork. From Candace's rushed movements, Annie didn't think she had long to pry information from Glenn's wife, so she had to make the questions count.

The pictures. That should be her focus. "We found some puzzling pictures, and I wondered if you've ever seen them." Annie pulled the photos from her back pocket. "We found these in a hidden compartment."

A puzzled frown crossed Candace's forehead. "We have no hidden compartments. I bought all the furniture."

"I'll show you where we found them after you eat your lunch, but have you seen these before?"

Candace speared a piece of broccoli and chicken and popped it in her mouth. There was only silence as she flipped through the pictures. "They're new to me." She handed them back.

"Look at what's written on the backs. We think what he's wearing and what's on the back might go together into some kind of code."

Candace's face reddened, and she grabbed a tissue from a box in the corner to dab at her eyes. "Why would I help you pin more stuff on my husband? I just want him to come home. He wasn't ready to be out of the hospital, and I doubt whoever took him has the know-how to take care of a coma patient. He'd barely awakened when they took him! This has been a nightmare, and I want to wake up now."

"I wish I didn't have to bother you with this, but I think Glenn is in danger. He called me." Annie told her about the conversation and wished she could offer words of comfort, but this bad dream wasn't going to end for Candace or Glenn anytime soon. "He should still be in the hospital." She flipped over the pictures and pushed them back toward Candace. "Please, anything you might notice would be helpful."

Sniffling, Candace examined each picture and the words written on the back. "He's wearing promotional hats and tees. They aren't his, and I don't know where he got them or what he did with them after he wore them. They're not in our bedroom, and I've never seen them."

So it was likely their guess was right about the pictures being a communication of some kind. "Do the words mean anything to you? Massey Ferguson or the others? Did he have any friends who those words might point to?"

Candace took a couple more bites, and Annie waited for her to think it through.

Candace ate the last of her meal and tossed the container. "The only one might be the Massey Ferguson thing. He has a hunting buddy who buys and sells vintage tractors. He's got several of that brand, probably more than any other type."

A hunting buddy. Annie's pulse increased, but she kept her expression neutral and her tone light. "What's his name? It's probably nothing, but I'll check it out."

"Eric Bell. I don't have an address or a phone number. To be honest, I hated his hunting. It was an obsession, and I felt it took him away from me more than I liked. We both work hard, and I wanted to spend time together on the weekends, but it didn't often happen. He'd get calls even when we already had plans and would leave abruptly. I didn't like it."

Annie rose and gathered up the photos. "I don't blame you. If you walk me out, I'll show you where we found these."

Candace nodded and they went through the dining room to the living room. Annie pointed out the drawer Jon had disassembled.

Candace examined it and frowned. "He had to have done that on his own. It didn't come that way."

For the first time Annie spotted uncertainty in Candace's gaze. She was probably beginning to wonder if she knew her husband at all.

/ / /

While Annie was in a meeting with Mason, Jon wandered down Kitchigami Street past the bank and Copper Club Tavern. This block of Victorian architecture had been restored to its former glory with multiple paint colors and original hardware. He loved the transoms and corbels decorating the storefronts through town.

His shoulder was feeling a little better today. Ribs too. He had a new appreciation for what his patients went through.

The glitter of jewelry in a display window caught his attention, and he paused to examine the pieces. A beautiful sapphire necklace glittered in the sunlight, and the color would match Annie's eyes.

Impulsively, he yanked open the door with Jack Pine Jewels stenciled on the window and stepped inside. The faint scent of a sweet candle wafted in the air, and classical music played softly in the background.

An older woman looked up from behind the display cabinets. Her hazel eyes crinkled in welcome. "Hello, young man. Searching for a piece for your sweetheart?"

Maybe he wanted more than a piece. He loved Annie, and he knew she loved him. The only thing holding him back was uncertainty about his career. What should he do about Mike's offer? There'd been no time to ask Annie her opinion, and he didn't want to make the wrong decision for their little family.

His gaze went to the rings. Nothing was certain in life, and it was senseless to wait for the "right" time.

He approached the display cases. "What do you have in engagement rings?"

She bustled over to the next case and beckoned to him. "Here are the ones we have in stock. How much do you want to spend?"

"I don't know. I just want something nice and unique. Something that suits her."

"You'll be the one who knows what's right. Anything you'd like to take a closer look at?"

He perused the display, but they all seemed alike. Big and bigger diamonds, tiny crescents of smaller ones that glittered in the lights against the black velvet. He'd seen rings just like these on hands throughout his life. Annie deserved something special, unique. Just like she was.

He shook his head. "I don't see anything that looks like her."

She shot a glance toward the back room. "I don't offer this for everyone because our jeweler is getting older and doesn't take on many projects these days, but he could design something just for your lady. Would you like to speak to him?"

"I think so. Is he here?"

"I'll text him." She picked up the phone by the register and turned her back for a minute. "He'll be right here."

She picked up a pad of paper and a pencil. "Let's start out with some basic information. Are there any stones you'd like to see in the ring?"

"Some sapphires to match her eyes. It doesn't have to be the main stone. Just part of it."

A picture of his mom's hand flashed in his memory. "Do you ever redesign vintage rings?"

A stooped man with white hair came into the room. A black apron covered his jeans and tee. "We do that all the time. Do yous have an heirloom you'd like to have redone, eh?" he said in a thick Yooper twang.

Jon hid a smile at the "yous," a traditional Yooper way of saying you or yours. "My mother's ring. It's got quite a few diamonds, large and small both, but I'd like it made into something special."

The woman put down the pad and moved away to answer the phone, and the jeweler glanced at what she'd written. "Sapphires are one of my favorite stones to work with."

Jon's mother had left her ring to him in case he wanted to do this very thing someday. His dad would be pleased, too, and he believed its history would make it even more special to Annie. "Annie has big blue eyes. Sapphires would be great for her."

He pulled out his phone and found a picture he'd snapped of her and Kylie out on the dock. Her hair was wet, which made her eyes stand out even more. "This is Annie."

The man smiled when he saw it. "That's Annie Pederson, Nate's widow, eh?"

Jon's elation deflated at the mention of his friend's name. "Yes."

"I'm glad she's able to move on and be happy. She's a good woman. Good at her job, eh." The man took the pad of paper and pen. "Yous name?"

"Jon Dunstan."

The man cocked a white brow. "Daniel's boy. Daniel bought that ring from my father back in the day. I've seen it many times. Excellent quality stones we can use. I believe I can make something spectacular with it."

"You're Henry Drood?"

"Yous parents have spoken of me, eh?"

"Often. You and Dad both dated Mom."

"And yous father won her hand. But I was compensated when I met my Helen, God rest her soul." He squared his sloped shoulders. "I will make this ring something very special. I know Annie well, and it would be my honor, eh. When can yous get the ring to me?"

"I'll need to have it sent from Chicago. It's in my dad's safe, but I can have it here in a day or two."

An inquisitive expression crouched between his eyes. "There's a rumor Glenn Hussert escaped police custody from the hospital. This is true, eh?"

It would be in today's paper, so Jon wasn't spilling anything he shouldn't. "It's true."

"Terrible thing. I never trusted that man. Or his best friend."

"Who is his best friend? We haven't gotten any concrete names, just those of acquaintances."

"Well, it's his cousin, eh. Joel West."

Where had Jon heard that name? It wouldn't come to him, but he would think about it. Mason and Annie might remember right off. "Strange the sheriff hasn't checked out his relatives."

"They're distant cousins, not first, so not sure how many know. My niece lived next door to Joel's parents, and my daughter used to help her babysit when the boys were young. Glenn spent the night there a lot. That's the only reason I know about the relationship."

Jon followed the convoluted explanation without a problem and couldn't wait to tell Mason and Annie what he'd heard. "Thanks for the information. I'll bring you the ring as soon as it arrives."

But wait. How did he tell Annie about the conversation without revealing where he'd heard it?

NINE

MASON GOT A CALL AS THEY WERE LEAVING THE HUSSERT
home, and Deja Lewis—Mason's new deputy that Annie had yet to
meet—told him Michelle Fraser was in the office. The woman was
in tears and wanted to speak to Annie. Mason had another stop to
make on his way back, so Annie headed straight to see Michelle.

If there was a problem with her husband, why had she come
here instead of going to the Marquette police? She parked on the
street and headed inside where she found Michelle in a confer-
ence room waiting for her at a table. A bottle of tea was uncapped
in front of her, and a pack of cheese crackers was unopened
beside it.

The brunette's brown eyes were red rimmed, and she twisted a
damp tissue in her hands. Her mouth trembled when she saw Annie.
"I know you're wondering why I'm here," she said in a shaky voice.
"But Brandon has his fingers in everything in Marquette. I couldn't
be sure someone wouldn't let him know I had filed a complaint."

This sounded far from a happy couple making their marriage
work. Annie pulled a chair out across from the other woman. "I
can see you're upset. What's wrong?"

"It would be faster to tell you what *isn't* wrong." Michelle
shredded the tissue in her hands. "Brandon has a girlfriend. I

found out he's been seeing her for five years. Five years! From before we were married and all through our marriage. He professed undying love when I was rescued from the cabin, but it didn't take long after I moved back in to find out it was all a lie."

"My sister was surprised you went home. She said he'd been abusive."

Michelle gave a bob of her head. "He was. I stupidly believed him when he said it would never happen again, that counseling would help him. It was such a huge thing for him to agree, and I thought maybe he could change. He's been going, but he still gets so mad."

Annie gentled her tone. "He's hurt you again?"

Without a word Michelle pulled up the sleeve on her quarter-length red top to reveal ugly bruises on her upper arm. The marks were clearly made by someone gripping her very hard. Annie winced and struggled to push down her rage at a man who would hurt a woman.

Michelle tipped her chin up and touched a bruise on the underside of her jawline. "And here. He didn't see enough affection in my expression." She shook her head. "I've left him again. For good this time. But I need a place to stay where he can't get to me. Is there anything you can do to help me?"

"You still have that condo out on Whisper Pike. I don't think he knows where it is, and you'd have the deputies here to fall back on."

"I hadn't thought about that. The shelter paid for it, but I have enough money to keep up the rent."

Annie took a sip of her coffee. "Did you ever hear from Idoya?"

"No. I think she went to Canada. She had relatives there, but I'm not sure where."

"Glenn Hussert was spirited out of the hospital," Annie said. "Has he been in touch with Brandon?"

"Not to my knowledge." Her brown eyes widened. "You think he'll come after me?"

"The sheriff thinks it's possible. You could testify against him. Without direct witnesses, it will be hard to convict him, so Mason wanted to make sure you were safe. If you move into your condo, he'll have a deputy swing by as often as possible." Another thought occurred to Annie. "I have an extra cabin at my place, and honestly, I could use a little help at the resort. Just checking people in and out, renting boats, that kind of thing. Would you be interested? I can't pay a lot, but you'd get food and lodging and a small stipend. And there are people around all the time in the campground. I think you'd be safe."

"That would be wonderful! I love the outdoors, as you know. Can I move in today? I brought my things with me."

"You sure can." It would feel a little strange to have someone else in the cabin where Sarah had lived, but it might be a good thing to push out those memories for now. And Annie would have someone to help out while she was gone so much with the investigations.

"What else can we do to help?" Annie asked.

Her tears dried, Michelle stood. "This is exactly what I need. Can we go out there now? Can I leave my car somewhere Brandon can't find it?"

"I've got an equipment garage at the back of the marina. You can park it there. No one but me uses it." Annie rose and grabbed her coffee. "I'll take you out now."

Michelle followed her out to the marina, and they passed only two cars along the way, both residents of Rock Harbor Annie knew. No one would recognize Michelle's car, a nondescript white Ford she must have traded in her expensive car for. To anyone passing on the street, there was nothing remarkable about it.

Annie reached the marina and drove back to the garage, where she slid open the door to let Michelle in. With the car parked the women walked back out into the sunshine and Annie closed the door and locked it.

She gave a key to Michelle. "I have another one. If you need your car, you can get it out."

The other woman put the key in her purse. "I don't plan to use it. Brandon will soon lose interest in finding me."

"Has he gone hunting much lately?"

Michelle's brows rose at the abrupt question. "He's been gone a lot, but I assumed he was with his floozy."

It had been an impulsive question, but Annie hadn't trusted Brandon from the moment she met him. And a man who would hit a woman might very well hunt her down.

/ / /

Sarah's lungs burned as she ran through the forest. Brambles snatched at her jeans and tee as she hurried in the direction of Max's house. The thick foliage obscured the path in several places, and she had to stop to get her bearings. She reached a clearing and spotted the steep roofline of the house above the pines.

Finally. With the jacket in her hand, she caught her breath before moving to the back deck steps, where two figures sat on Adirondack chairs.

Max, satellite phone in hand, caught sight of her. "I'll call you back." He punched a button to disconnect. His dark brows rose as he studied her. "You appear to be upset, Sarah. Is the cabin not to your liking?"

"It's not that," she wheezed. She bent over and dragged in

oxygen. "Not used to running." When she straightened, she held out the jacket. "I found this along the shoreline near the little beach. That's blood on the back."

Max took the yellow jacket and examined it. "A women's size medium." He turned it over to reveal the blood on the back. "It appears it might be blood. Or paint."

"I smelled it. It's blood."

He nodded. "I should let the sheriff know. Wait here."

Taking his sat phone, he walked to the far end of the deck to place the call. Sarah caught snatches of words like *blood* and *jacket*. She dropped into a chair while he spoke with the sheriff and glanced over at Anu in the other chair. "I hope I didn't disturb you, Anu."

The older woman reached over and took her hand. "You appear quite distressed, Sarah. Is there anything I can get for you? Tea or coffee?"

Anu's calm manner soothed Sarah, and she clung to her fingers for a moment before releasing her. "I'm fine. It shook me up a little to see the blood. I think we need to start a search and try to find the woman."

"You can trust Max to do what is necessary." Anu's blue eyes went more somber. "You were in the cabin first, yes?"

"Yes, but I had to get out of there. It felt claustrophobic."

"I told Max perhaps it was not the best idea to have you stay out there by yourself. Not when you had not been in that place in all these years."

"I was looking at our bedroom. I'd forgotten the quilts. When I saw them, I remembered crying myself to sleep on the bottom bunk and how Annie always tried to make it okay. It made me sad to know she's so upset with me now. And I'm mad at myself for not remembering how often she always took care of me."

Sarah's voice quivered, and she swallowed down the pain. Everything seemed somehow worse since it was her own doing. If not for the way she'd infiltrated Annie's life and schemed for revenge, life might be very different. Knowing Annie the way she did now, Sarah knew if she'd walked up to the door and told her sister who she was, she would have been welcomed with gladness and open arms.

Instead, Annie couldn't trust her around Kylie. And why would she when Sarah had proven how devious she was?

She wasn't aware she was crying until Anu pressed a flowered tissue into her hand. "I am sorry, little one. I see your pain. God sees, too, even better than me since he can feel your heart. Perhaps this experience is to let you find out what really happened twenty-four years ago. You've believed a lie. Maybe it's time to find out the truth."

Annie had mentioned God occasionally, too, but Mother hadn't let that word be spoken when Sarah was growing up in the wrong household. Maybe God was what made Annie and Anu different.

Did she even want to know the full truth? The contrast between her two lives was already stark, and regret could swallow her up. "Annie will never forgive me."

"I believe you underestimate your sister and her desire to serve God. Show her you are repentant and hold tight to a bit of trust. Things will work out in the end, Sarah. You will see."

Could she do it? Could she dredge up all those old, painful memories to get at the truth? How did Becky take her—and why her and not Annie?

Max ended the call and rejoined them. "The sheriff is checking on any missing persons, and I told him I'd have my security men do a sweep of the island."

Sarah stared at the blood on the jacket. "How long will that take? The woman might be out there right now, still bleeding and needing help."

Or dead.

But Sarah didn't want to accept that. In her mind's eye she saw the woman rescued and taken to the hospital. Finding that jacket had to mean something. Like maybe this God Anu had spoken of had put Sarah in a position to make amends for some of her past bad decisions.

She desperately wanted to believe redemption was possible. That someday she could walk down the streets of Rock Harbor with her head high. Right now she kept her head down so she didn't have to see the contempt in people's eyes as she walked past. Bree had told her she imagined that contempt because most people didn't know what had happened. Not fully.

And maybe Bree was right, but it didn't *feel* right. Until Sarah could believe for herself that she would never act in such a hateful way again, she didn't think she could move on. She didn't think she could be part of a normal society when she had done something so despicable. When she thought back to the decision she'd made, she'd been in such a fog of pain and hatred she hadn't been thinking clearly. She loved Kylie, and yet she'd put her in the worst possible danger. What had possessed her to do that? It was like someone else had taken over her body for a while.

She had used the little girl for revenge, and the horror of what she'd done stayed with her every second of every day. She hoped she hadn't done irreparable harm to her niece. Sarah didn't know what it would take to finally be rid of her guilt. Maybe that wasn't even possible.

Guilt that deep had a way of clinging like wet clay.

TEN

THE SMELL OF FRESH COFFEE OVERPOWERED THE underlying smell of stale coffee beans from Mason's ancient brew machine. Annie sat across from the sheriff's desk and glanced through her notes.

Deputy Doug Montgomery and Deputy Deja Lewis entered, and Mason introduced Deja to Annie.

Annie leaned over and shook her hand. The woman's large brown eyes were full of interest and intelligence. She wore her Afro cut close to her head in a no-nonsense fashion. Annie immediately liked her. They all pulled up chairs around Mason's desk.

"Have you ever heard of this Eric Bell that Candace mentioned?" Annie asked.

Mason turned from the small beverage bar along one wall of his office and came toward her carrying two cups of coffee. "After you texted me, I ran a search on him. He lives outside Ontonagon near the Porkies."

The Porcupine Mountains Wilderness Park was Michigan's largest, and a mecca for winter sports as well as hiking and kayaking in the summer. It was one of the last vestiges of wilderness in the Midwest, and residents were drawn to the roaring waterfalls amid its old-growth forests. Solving the deaths of two girls nine years ago in that park was what had kicked off everything Annie had investigated these past weeks.

"Coincidence?" she asked.

Mason set his coffee on his desk and sank into his chair. "Maybe. But I don't believe much in coincidence. My gut tells me he might be involved too."

"Got an address?"

"I'm going to send Montgomery out there along with Deja."

"Would you mind if I went along?" Annie asked.

"Sure. You know the case well, and something he says might jump out at you. Doug, I want you to let Annie take the lead on questioning."

Doug nodded in acknowledgment.

Knuckles rapped on the door. "Come in," Mason called.

Jon poked his head in first. "I hope I'm not interrupting, but I found out something about Glenn you all should hear."

"Have a seat," Mason said. "Coffee?"

Jon lifted the cup in his hand. "I already hit Metro Espresso." He shut the door behind him and came to sit beside Annie.

His glance in her direction heated her cheeks. Alone time with him would be easier to find with Kylie gone for a week. Until now, she hadn't thought about that fact.

"What's up?" Mason asked.

"I ran into Henry Drood when I was out. He asked about Hussert's escape and then mentioned he knew his best friend."

Annie sat up straighter. "Best friend?"

"It's a second cousin, Joel West. I knew I'd heard that name before but couldn't quite pull it from my memory. The guy lives up in Eagle River. Henry said his daughter used to help babysit for West and Hussert back when they were kids."

The name tickled Annie's memory too, and she thought through the investigations. "Wait a second. Isn't that the name of Shainya Blackburn's ex-boyfriend?"

Shainya was a young Ojibwa woman they'd found in trouble in the woods. She'd been terrorized by two guys chasing her. She mentioned breaking up with an old boyfriend who was bad news, and Annie was sure that was the name.

Mason leaned closer to his computer screen. "Let me double-check." It was only moments before he nodded. "Good memory, Annie. That's the guy's name."

"What were all the charges against him?" she asked.

"Drug sales, breaking and entering, poaching. If you remember, he brought out-of-state people in for moose hunting at Isle Royale and a seventeen-year-old girl in the party went missing and was never found. When I talked to the sheriff, he didn't seem to think anything sinister was going on." Mason's gaze collided with hers. "His hunting connection would make sense with what we know about Hussert. I'd turned the incident with Ms. Blackburn over to the tribal authorities and the sheriff up there, so I'll see if he followed up with West. I have to be careful not to step on his toes."

While he called the sheriff, Annie leaned over and took Jon's hand. "What if we go out for dinner tonight? I don't have to be in early with Kylie gone."

His green eyes widened. "We could even go to a movie! Or go swimming in the moonlight."

"Or maybe go to Calumet Theater. I haven't been up there in ages."

"How about I do some research and surprise you while you finish up work for the afternoon?"

The thought of a long evening spent in Jon's company gave her fresh energy. When was the last time she'd had such a long block of time without any responsibilities? Since before Kylie was born. She adored her daughter, but until now, she hadn't consciously realized she needed some time as an adult without anyone asking for something. It felt intoxicating.

"I can't wait to see what you come up with," she said.

Mason put down his phone. "The sheriff talked to West about Shainya's attack, and he had an alibi, but it was weak. The sheriff thought Shainya would have recognized him if he'd been one of the two who chased her, so he dropped it. But he said West was cocky and belligerent, and he wouldn't be surprised if he was involved somehow."

Annie turned to Jon. "Did Henry know anything else about Hussert or West?"

"He said they'd been best friends from childhood, but that you seldom saw West down here. Usually Hussert went to Houghton. And they were hunting buddies."

"I think we should have a talk with him," she told Mason. "It's two o'clock. We could take a run up to Houghton and see if we can track him down."

"Before we do that, let me see what properties are listed in his name. Maybe he's got a large tract of land where the men hunt." He jiggled his mouse and went back to perusing his computer. "Looks like he only owns a place in Houghton."

"Where's he work?" Jon asked.

Mason consulted his notes again. "He owns an outfitters store. Outdoors West."

"By himself?" Annie had to wonder if Hussert had joined him in that venture.

Mason went silent as he researched the question. "Looks like he owns it free and clear. No outstanding loans, and the corporation is only in his name."

"He still could be behind Hussert's escape. But if so, where did he stash him?"

"Glenn needs medical care," Jon pointed out. "Does West have any connections to nurses or physicians? Glenn could die without some intense support."

"Maybe West wouldn't care, if it was all about keeping Glenn from testifying," Mason said.

"I think it would have been more than that," Jon said. "As his cousin, West would probably want him to survive."

It made sense to Annie too. "You're turning into a crack investigator, Jon. Good work."

His eyes glinted with promise as he smiled back at her, and she couldn't wait to see what he had planned for the evening.

/ / /

Eric Bell lived in a neat bungalow with a million-dollar view of the Porkies. The lush green foliage on the mountain slopes drew Annie's eye for a moment as she walked with the deputies toward the yellow front door. She didn't expect to find him home on a Thursday afternoon.

After getting no response at the door, she led the way across the gravel drive to the big barn on the other side of the driveway that housed his vintage tractor sales. There was only one vehicle in the parking lot, so she hoped they'd be able to have a private conversation with the man. The sliding barn door stood open to let in the summer breeze, and the windows had screens. Inside, the place smelled of oil and old hay. Rows of vintage tractors were parked along the walls, and she spotted several Massey Fergusons.

A red-haired man in a green plaid shirt and jeans lifted a hand in greeting. "Be right with you, folks." He appeared to be in his late thirties.

He handed an older man in bib overalls some kind of part and ushered the guy to the door before he stepped to where they stood examining a tractor. "What can I do for you?"

Annie took out a pen and pad of paper. "I'm LEO Annie Pederson, and these are Deputies Montgomery and Lewis. We have a few questions for you."

The man's smile faded, and a frown crouched between his brown eyes. "Okay."

"We understand you are friends with Glenn Hussert?" Annie said.

"Yeah, so what?" Bell yanked a greasy red bandana from his back pocket and bent over to wipe a smear off a tractor.

"Three men took Hussert out of the hospital around two o'clock Tuesday morning. Would you happen to know anything about that?"

Bell stuffed the bandana back in his pocket. "We're just hunting buddies. That's it."

He didn't seem worried about Glenn at all. Maybe because he knew all about it? Annie pulled up the picture she'd taken of the photo they'd found of Glenn in the Massey Ferguson hat. She showed him the front and back of the picture. "Why would he wear that hat when he was a big John Deere guy?"

"No idea." But he didn't look at her.

He wasn't a good liar. "I think you do. The words on the back, 'Your turn next.' What did he mean by that?"

"Look, I already told you I don't know anything about the picture or Glenn's escape. Unless you've got a warrant, you can get out of here. I have work to do, and you have no right to hassle me. Glenn was a hunting buddy, nothing more. I'm sorry he's in trouble, but it's not my worry."

Annie handed him her card. "If you remember anything that might help us find him, please give me a call."

He grunted and threw the card in the trash. "Out." He pointed at the door.

Annie lifted a brow and glanced at the deputies in case they had any other questions, but Doug shrugged and moved to the exit. Deja followed him.

While they hadn't gotten anywhere, Annie was sure Eric Bell knew more than he said.

ELEVEN

JON SAT ON A PARK BENCH AT THE END OF JACK PINE
Lane. Children squealed on the merry-go-round, and Milo lay
at his feet with his head resting on Jon's shoe. The blue sky had
that color of late afternoon with a few lazy clouds floating past.

It hadn't taken long for Jon to hatch a plan for a romantic
evening with Annie. If only he already had the ring, but there was
no rush. They had their entire future ahead of them.

He'd found a charter boat and had arranged a chef to bring
steaks and a grill on board to cook for them. The only thing he
lacked was music, but he could connect a speaker to his phone
and have some of their favorite songs playing. Would she be dis-
appointed they weren't going to a movie? The dinner cruise would
take several hours, and he hadn't wanted to cut that time short on
such a beautiful night.

"I didn't expect to see you here."

He glanced up to see his dad leaning on his cane. "Dad."
After scooting over to make room for his father, Jon patted
the seat beside him. "You probably need to rest after that walk.
Thanks again for reassuring Kylie."

"Glad to reassure my little girl."

His dad's recovery from the stroke had been slow and painful. Dad put his weight on his cane as he eased onto the bench.

"I'm glad you came by," Jon said. "I wanted to talk to you."

"I already know you asked for your mom's ring." His dad's sly smile told Jon he approved. "It's on its way."

Jon should have known the housekeeper would immediately call his dad. "I should have told you first."

"Your mother left it to you. It's your property, and you don't need my approval, even though you have it. I'm delighted with the prospect of having Annie for a daughter. And Kylie is a dream come true for your old man. Your mama always wanted a girl, you know. I wish she were here to enjoy that lovely little granddaughter of ours."

Jon's throat tightened. "Me too, Dad. And Annie doesn't know about the ring. I ran into Henry Drood. He's going to design something special with the stones."

"I can't wait to see what Henry comes up with. When do you plan to pop the question?"

"I'm not sure. I assume it will take a while to design the ring." He forgot to ask Henry how long it would take for him to create it. "Um, Dad, just so you know—the paternity test came back. I'm definitely Kylie's father. Ninety-nine percent certainty."

"I never doubted it, son. I'm glad you have confirmation, especially now that there are legal questions."

"What should I do about Nate's parents? I have a feeling this is going to escalate."

"I could speak to them. We've always been friendly. Or you could give them a call in a friendly way and let them know the proof has come. Try talking to Lars. He isn't as volatile as Maryanne."

Jon gave a jerky nod. "I'm glad to have it settled for all of us as I make plans to stay in Rock Harbor."

"And then what?"

"What do you mean?"

"Partnership? Private practice here in Rock Harbor? New house or living at Annie's? What are your plans?"

His dad wasn't usually so nosy. Their routine was he quietly waited for Jon to offer information, not go digging for it. "Is there a reason for the questions?"

A smile lifted the side of his dad's lip that didn't droop from the stroke. "Maybe." He chuckled. "I should tell you my news, then you'll understand. I asked Martha to marry me last night. We're not getting any younger, so we plan to tie the knot next week."

"Next week? Dad, that's crazy. You've only been dating a few weeks."

"I've known her for years, Jon. And we're no spring chickens. We both know we want to be together, and I'm not about to live in sin with her."

Jon glanced away, unable to deal with the reference. "I only want your happiness."

"And Martha makes me happy. I'd like to think I do the same for her."

Jon didn't doubt it. He'd seen the girlish blush on the older woman's face often enough. "Where will you live?"

"Martha is going to hire a manager for the Blue Bonnet, and we'll move out to the cabin when it's done. It's small, but it will suit us fine. And it's not far from my granddaughter."

"Sounds like you have it all figured out."

Jon couldn't put his finger on the underlying cause of his alarm. Was it that he thought Dad would forget Mom? He didn't think he was selfish enough to begrudge his dad a new life after losing her. Mom wouldn't have wanted him to be alone the rest of his life, and she'd been gone nine years. It was time. Dad's stroke had been a wake-up call that time was a precious commodity.

"I'm not going to meddle any less in your life," his dad said. "You're important to me, Jon, and always will be. Marriage won't change that."

His dad had shone a light on the discontent swirling in Jon's heart. The two of them had always been close, and he hadn't wanted to think that might end. Of course it wouldn't. He was a jerk for even thinking his dad would change toward him.

He leaned over and hugged his dad with one arm. "Congratulations, Dad. I'm glad you found Martha. She's a wonderful woman. I think she's even managed to put a few pounds on you."

His dad rubbed his belly. "I wish you were wrong about that. The wedding will be the Sunday after Bree and Kade get back. Martha wouldn't hear of letting Bree miss out."

"Does Naomi know?" Martha Heinonen and her daughter were as close as he and Dad.

"She's telling her right now. That's why I decided to take a walk. I didn't want to sit and worry about whether Naomi might talk her out of it."

"Naomi likes you. She'll be happy for her mom. Martha has been a widow for many years. Naomi probably thought her mom was never going to find someone."

His dad leaned down to rub Milo's head. "I hope she's happy about it. I should take this little guy home with me for the week so you and Annie don't have to worry about him."

"Would Martha mind?"

"What do you think? She's got search dogs running in and out constantly."

"Okay, if you're sure." Jon shot off a text to Annie telling her

Milo was going to the Blue Bonnet. "What can I do to help with the wedding?"

"Just show up with a smile and bring your new family. It will be the start of a new life for all of us."

Jon was never more sure that he wanted to marry Annie than he was in this moment with his dad as they both envisioned a new nuclear family. A wife and daughter. The reality of it took his breath away.

/ / /

Trees crowded the road as Annie drove toward Houghton. She thought through what they knew about Joel West. "I wonder if we should speak to Shainya Blackburn before we see West. She might have heard from him since they broke up, and maybe she saw him with Glenn."

"Give her a call," Mason said. "We're still twenty minutes away. You have her number?"

"I've got it." Annie pulled to the side of the road, scrolled through her contacts, and placed the call.

Shainya answered on the third ring. "Hello." Her tone indicated caution and curiosity.

Annie put the call on speaker. "Hi, Shainya, this is Law Enforcement Officer Annie Pederson. I hope I'm not disturbing you."

"Annie." Her tone brightened. "No, not at all. I almost didn't answer because I didn't recognize your name at first. You came up on my phone as LEO Pederson. I always think of you as Annie."

"I'm glad you answered because the sheriff and I have a few questions about your ex."

"What's Joel done now?"

"How long did you date him?"

"Two years. I realized he was wrong for me three months in, but I kept thinking he'd change for me. Why do women do that? No one changes, not really. Live and learn, I guess."

Annie had seen way too many friends go down that same path. "Listen, did you ever meet Joel's cousin Glenn Hussert?"

There was a gasp before Shainya answered. "I nearly called the sheriff after I heard about Glenn's involvement in fraud and abduction. I thought the sheriff might roll his eyes at my call though."

"Sheriff Kaleva would never do that. He's always glad for any information. What did you want to tell him?"

"Joel and Glenn are as thick as thieves. They seem to talk in a secret code too. Sometimes what they say to each other doesn't make sense."

Annie's thoughts went to the pictures with the hats and tees. "Do you have any examples?"

"One time they were talking about going hunting on Saturday, and Joel told Glenn he was bringing cookies. I packed his food and knew there were no cookies, so I had no idea what he meant. There was always a lot of that kind of doublespeak."

Cookies held no magic information for Annie, but the doublespeak mention reinforced her suspicion the pictures had some other kind of meaning. "How often did you see Glenn?"

"Every week. We'd be out getting pizza, and he'd show up like Joel had told him where to find us. Or we'd be at my house, and he'd stop by to call Joel outside to talk."

"Did they go hunting a lot?"

"Almost every week. That was one of the things we fought

about all the time—his time with Glenn was always more important than being with me. I got tired of it. The first time he hit me, I thought it was a fluke and he'd never do it again. When he broke my nose, I knew he was never changing. That's when I left."

"I'm sorry you went through that." Annie could forgive a lot of things, but physical violence wasn't one of them. She had zero tolerance for that kind of thing.

"Did they always hunt in the same area?"

"Oh sure. They guard it like it's the location of the crown jewels, but Joel forgot one of his guns once and had me bring it to him."

Annie's pulse raced. "Where was it?"

As Shainya explained the location, Annie's elation ebbed. It was the area where they'd found Sarah and Michelle. The cabin was out there, but the deputies had checked the surrounding area several times without discovering anything.

"Did either Joel or Glenn own any other property or hunting tracts?"

"Well, there's Joel's warehouse. He has his taxidermy setup there."

"In Houghton?" They were on the outskirts of the city now, and Annie dug a pen and paper out of her bag for the address.

"Actually, no. It's in Chassell."

A little farther, but not much. "Do you have an address?"

"Let me check. I know where it is, but I'm not sure of the address."

Annie heard rustling before the chimes of a computer booting up. She clicked the pen open and shut a few times while she waited. Maybe they should head there before seeing Joel. If they found something suspicious, they might get more information out of him.

"Here it is." Shainya rattled off the address, and Annie wrote it down.

"Thanks, got it. Do you think Joel might have been one of the men who took Glenn out of the hospital?"

"There was a fuzzy picture in the paper from the parking lot camera, and I recognized Joel."

Annie gasped and glanced over at Mason, who had raised his brows. "You're just now telling me this? This is huge news, Shainya."

"I assumed you already identified him since you called asking about him." Her voice rose a decibel defensively.

"How do you know for sure one of the men in the picture was Joel?"

"Several things. The slope of his shoulders and the way he stood. And then there's the hat. I gave it to him for his birthday."

"Stormy Kromer caps aren't uncommon," Annie said. The iconic Yooper hat was usually a Mackinaw plaid of black and red with earflaps. While it was a winter cap, she'd assumed the guy wore it to disguise himself when he spirited Glenn away.

"This one is. They usually have only that little string tie in the middle to untie the earflaps. I took off that tie when I got it and replaced it with leather shoelaces. Joel always complained he couldn't get his fingers around the string."

A detail none of them had noticed. "Are you willing to testify that the man is Joel based on what you saw?"

Shainya's answer came quickly. "I know it was him, Annie. No doubt in my mind. I'll say the same thing in court. Just don't tell him I'm testifying, okay?"

"I won't," Annie promised. "Thanks for your help."

As she ended the call, she hoped it was enough for an arrest.

TWELVE

ANNIE SUGGESTED THEY GO TO CHASSELL FIRST, AND
Mason agreed. While she drove on to the small town, he shot off
texts to deputies and other personnel about Shainya's identification
of Joel's newspaper picture.

They had probable cause to bring Joel in for questioning at
least, and maybe enough for an arrest. With somewhere to look,
the few prints they'd picked up in Hussert's room might pan out
to belong to Joel. And with questioning, they might find who
else had helped transport him out of the hospital. And where to
find Glenn now.

Was he even still alive? It had been a dangerous move to take
him out in his poor condition. But maybe that was part of their
plan. They didn't want Hussert to talk.

Annie parked at the address, a green-metal pole building on
the outskirts of Chassell. No other vehicle was in the small lot
overtaken by weeds.

She opened her door and got out. "Doesn't seem like this
place gets much traffic."

Mason climbed out and followed her to the metal door.
Weeds pushed up through the cracks in the pathway and creeped

onto the concrete. The grass was eight inches high and hadn't been mowed for a while.

There was no bell but Mason pounded his fist on the door. "Sheriff Kaleva," he called. There was no sound but the caw of some crows on a scraggly oak in the yard. "Let's try around back."

Annie followed him around the side of the building, then took a step back at the stench of something rotting. Flies swarmed a fifty-five-gallon metal drum, and she shuddered at the mass of fur and other animal remains in it. "Nasty."

Mason repeated the knock on the back door, but the place appeared empty. While he yelled his name again, Annie wandered up the far side where a few dusty windows opened up in the metal siding. Standing on tiptoes, she managed to peer past the fly-speckled glass into the dark interior. It was too dim to see much, but she thought it seemed empty. She'd need a flashlight and a ladder to see better.

She returned to find Mason on the phone. When he ended the call, she lifted a brow his direction. "What's up?"

"I called for a warrant for this property and his house in Houghton."

She glanced at her watch. Just past four thirty. "Are we waiting on them to arrive?"

"Yeah, I want to see what they find." He fished out his keys. "You can go on back, and I'll catch a ride with Montgomery." He flipped on his flashlight and shined it into the window. At his height Mason was able to examine the interior from a better angle. "Nothing in this main room. I see some doors to other rooms though. We'll check them out. Get on back for your date," he said. "I'll wait on my team."

From the knowing glint in his eye, he must have seen her

surreptitious glance at her watch. She wanted time to get dressed up a little, and if she left in the next fifteen minutes, she'd get home a little after five. She'd have enough time to do her hair and makeup. It was adequate time, but just barely.

She nodded toward the back of the lot. "I want to check out the shed first. Maybe it's unlocked."

"I'll come with you."

She and Mason went to the weathered utility shed that crouched along a back alley. It was as dilapidated as the other building, and it stood ajar, giving them probable cause. She glanced at the sheriff.

"Be my guest," Mason said.

She nudged the door open the rest of the way with her foot and stepped inside, pausing a few seconds to let her eyes adjust. The place smelled of grass and dirt. An old lawn mower was in the back corner. Hooks holding yard tools lined one wall. Another wall held fishing poles and nets. It was surprisingly well organized considering the building's disrepair.

Before she started to examine anything, she pulled out a pair of Nitrile gloves and handed some to Mason as well. She spotted an old metal chest under the window and stepped over to open it. It wasn't locked, and the rusty lid squeaked as she forced it open. Inside she found charcoal sketches. Had West been an artist? He had to have drawn these.

Mason squatted beside her to peer into the chest too. "Maybe he commemorated his trophies this way. Nice buck." He removed the sketch of a twelve-pointer and stared at it. "Looks like the Porkies in the background."

She spotted the Lake of the Clouds and nodded. The sketch

had been framed in cardboard, and as she started to lay it aside, a piece of paper fell from between the edges of the cardboard. It was a black-and-white photo of a man lying on the sand near what appeared to be Lake Superior. He was on his stomach with his face turned away from the camera. Dead?

She flipped it over and gasped before showing it to Mason. *I took my turn.* "The back of the picture in Glenn's house was a little different."

Mason nodded. "It was *Your turn next.* I'll have this picture examined to see if there is any way to identify the victim."

"You think he's dead?"

He nodded and touched the picture. "Might be blood at the back of his head."

Annie had thought he'd been in the water and his hair was wet, but Mason was probably right.

"Yo, Sheriff."

Mason turned at the call from outside. "Coming. I think the search warrant has arrived. You get out of here and enjoy your evening."

She nodded and went to her truck. A teenager on a skateboard stopped and glanced her way. "Hi," she said to him. "Do you know Joel West, who owns this property?"

"Sure. He's basic, but he hangs out sometimes." He glanced toward the basketball court. "Takes us to play basketball."

"Have you seen him around lately?"

"Couple days ago. Came here with some fam and took away most everything."

"Did you speak to him?"

"Nah, he was in a hurry."

"Did you overhear him say where he was going?"

"Getting some other dude and heading for Canada. Least that's what one of them said."

Another dude. Glenn?

/ / /

Jon adjusted the collar of his Hawaiian shirt as he went up the steps to Annie's door. A gull landed on the deck and peered at him with black eyes before flapping off toward the water. A guitar twanged somewhere in the RV park, and the scent of barbecue chicken came from the same direction.

He'd debated about how much to dress up, but they were going to be on the water, and he didn't want to look like a dork in a blazer and slacks. He ran his damp palms over his khaki shorts, then raised his hand to knock on her door. Before his fist fell, Annie opened the door with a bright smile.

She wore a blue sundress that matched her eyes, and her blonde hair curled around her head. Strappy white sandals with a bit of a heel lifted her closer to neck level with him. Her light scent floated his way—something sweet like vanilla.

He grasped her hand and pulled her closer. "You're beautiful."

"You look pretty good yourself." She stepped into his embrace, and he kissed her.

She fit perfectly in his arms like she always had. Like she was an extension of him, two hearts forever entwined. Kind of flowery, but that's how he'd always felt.

She eased her arms around his waist when he pulled back. "We could just stay home and enjoy being alone."

There was nothing he'd like better, but he couldn't wait to see her reaction. "I want to show off my gorgeous girl tonight. And I think you'll like what I have planned."

"Michelle is doing a great job. I can leave without worry." She tucked her hand into the crook of his elbow, and they went down the steps to his car.

He helped her into the low-slung vehicle and went around to his side. "Did you hear from Kylie?"

"I did. She's having a terrific time." Annie smiled. "How far are we going?"

He started the engine and pulled out of the parking lot. "Not far."

"Can I have a hint?"

Maybe he should have told her to be prepared to get wet, but the water wouldn't hurt her cotton sundress. "You'll see soon enough. How'd your investigation go today?"

"We didn't get far, but Shainya identified one of the men who took Glenn out of the hospital."

The recounting of her afternoon provided the perfect distraction until he turned in the drive back to the Rock Harbor marina where the charter boat awaited them. He spied the catering truck in the lot and hoped things were ready on the boat. He didn't think Annie had noticed as she described what they'd found in Chassell. He might be able to whisk her to the boat before she got wind that it was a catered dinner cruise.

He parked as far from the catering van as he could. "We're here."

She gaped out her window. "We're going out on a catamaran? What a great evening!"

He'd been second-guessing his choice as he drove here, and her enthusiasm was a shot in the arm. "Yep."

He got out and opened her door. The strains of Tim McGraw's "Live Like You Were Dying" floated above the lapping of the waves against the hulls of the boats. The ambience was just right.

He offered her his arm. "This way, my lady."

By the time they walked out on the dock and stepped aboard the boat, the scene was set. A white tablecloth covered a table at the starboard rail overlooking the water. Tim McGraw continued to play through the speakers Jon had brought over earlier, and a serving table laden with food separated them from the grill where the chef was preparing to cook their filets. Tiny white lights swung above their heads as Jon escorted Annie to their table and pulled out her chair.

She tucked the skirt of her dress under her and settled on the chair. "How did you pull this together so fast? You only had a few hours."

He glanced over the table to make sure all his instructions had been followed. Trenary toast and thimbleberry jam from The Jampot waited for her to dig in. "I was motivated."

She leaned her chin on her hand and sent a smile his way that made him lean over the table and kiss her. "What was that for?" she asked in a whisper as the song flipped to "I Like It, I Love It."

"Tim says it better than me," he said.

"Are you going to defer to Tim McGraw all evening?"

"Maybe. I'm not that eloquent." He reached across the table and took her hand. "But I'm always going to be here, Annie. I'll never let you down again. I'd rather die first."

The teasing light in her eyes ebbed, and she squeezed his fingers. "Let's not talk about dying. I believe you, Jon. The past is behind us. Let's focus on the future."

"Dad's getting married. He told me today."

She caught her breath. "Oh my goodness, what wonderful news! I'll bet Martha is over the moon. Naomi too. Does Bree know?"

"I'd guess Naomi called her after her mom spilled the beans."

"I wondered how you met Henry. He and your dad were good friends, weren't they?"

He'd have to tread carefully here or he'd spill the beans. She couldn't guess he'd been in the jewelry store. "So Henry told me. I remembered his name, but it had been years since I'd seen him." Best to steer the conversation back to his dad and Martha. "They're tying the knot as soon as Bree is back. Dad doesn't want to wait. I think his stroke reinforced how brief life is, and he doesn't want to waste a minute of the time he has left."

He'd give anything if he had that ring in his pocket right now and could tell her he didn't want to waste his time with her either. Maybe he should do it anyway. She'd be glad to wait on a ring. Annie had never been materialistic.

The boat's engine throbbed under his feet before he could spill the words he longed to say, and he was glad for the interruption. The day he proposed needed to be memorable in every way, including the ring he slipped on her finger. They had time.

THIRTEEN

WITH A FULL BELLY, SARAH LOCKED THE CABIN'S LATCH
behind her and glanced around the small space. Anu had pushed
for her to move into the big house, but Sarah didn't want to lose
the opportunity to recover any snippet of memory she might still
find floating around in her head.

The old lamps cast a yellowish glow on the log walls and floor.
She wandered over to the sofa and touched its rough surface.
Corduroy maybe? It was worn slick and shiny in several places,
probably from her father's thighs. In the kitchen she found a plastic
colander, and she had an image flash of snapping green beans into
its tan bowl. The dishes in the cupboard were gray Arabia dishes
with a navy stripe around the edge. Their familiarity was instantaneous, and she could almost smell her mother's pasties.

She hadn't expected anything to be familiar.

She peered out the window into the dark back lawn. After
dinner Max had given her a jubilant smile after a call on his satellite phone. His men had found the woman and taken her by boat
to the hospital. She was going to be all right. Sarah had wanted
to ask if the woman knew who had found her jacket and asked
for help, but that seemed self-serving, so she kept her mouth shut.

Her eyelids were heavy, so she went to the larger bedroom where her parents had slept. No way could she sleep in her little-girl room. If only she'd stayed in her bed that long-ago night, she would have grown up here. Mother would not have had a chance to grab her.

But was that even true? When Annie recounted the abduction, it sounded like Mother had known there were two girls and came prepared to take one of them. Sarah knew firsthand how determined Mother could be. If she hadn't found them that night, she would have hidden in the shadows to seize the chance when it came.

Maybe it had been fate.

The door creaked when Sarah pushed it open and entered her parents' room. A light beside the bed cast a homey glow. The faint scent of perfume still lingered in the air and drew Sarah to the dressing table. Her mother had worn something with *white* in the name. There was a half-empty glass bottle of The Body Shop White Musk. She uncapped it and took a sniff. It brought images of hugs and kisses, soft warm arms enfolding her, and a woman's voice.

Sarah went to the closet and touched the clothes inside. Her dad's flannel shirts and jeans, her mother's twill slacks and sleeveless tops. The clothes didn't trigger the nostalgia Sarah had experienced with the perfume and kitchen items. On impulse, she opened the bureau drawers until she found one of her mother's nightgowns. She shed her clothes and pulled it over her head.

She and her mother were much the same size, but the nightgown held no scent of her mom, only the staleness of wood from the drawer. There were clean sheets on the bed, and she slipped between them with a sigh.

She snapped off the lamp beside her and lay there with her eyes open as the tree limbs danced in the wind and moonlight cast shadows in the room. Now that she was in bed, she couldn't rest, not knowing what had happened the last time she was here. What had possessed her to wake her sister and coax her into going to the dock? It would have been a fair hike for two little girls. Knowing that now painted Annie in a different light. She had indulged her little sister. Not many big sisters would have crawled out of bed and gone traipsing through hordes of mosquitoes in the night.

They'd been fearless back then. Now fear was Sarah's constant companion. Did Annie wrestle with hidden demons, too, or had her idyllic upbringing left her unbothered by shadows?

Where was Annie now? Did she ever think of her sister, or had Sarah killed every bit of love in her heart for that little girl so long ago?

There would be no sleep until she answered some of the questions. Sarah threw back the sheet and climbed out of bed. She went back to the living room and slid her feet into her sandals, then stepped out onto the porch. Though her phone had no signal, it still told the time. Nine thirty. She set off in the direction of the dock where Mason had dropped her off.

When she saw the gleam of moonlight on the water, she checked her phone again. An eight-minute walk for an adult. Annie would have held her hand, and it would have taken two little girls longer to get here. Ten minutes, maybe fifteen? Had Mother been watching from somewhere, or had she been in the boat the whole time waiting?

Nothing made sense about what had happened twenty-four years ago. She'd come out of nowhere, hadn't she? They'd been there a little while, but not that long. It was such a strange fluke that they would have gone out that night. It had never happened before, at least not that Sarah remembered. Could someone have planned it all along? Her uncle Clive maybe? If only she could remember more, but a five-year-old wouldn't have noticed much.

It was unlikely the truth would ever be known about what happened that night and why. But Sarah decided then and there she would dig and find out what she could. She might come away none the wiser for it, but she had to try.

/ / /

What a perfect evening. Annie stood at the boat's railing and leaned into Jon's embrace as he stood behind her. They gazed out at the moonlit water without speaking. The stars twinkling overhead and the sound of the waves lapping at the hull of the boat added to her contentment. They weren't that far from the shore, and the lights of a shoreline cabin flickered on.

"What a fabulous dinner," she said finally. "The filet was perfect."

The chef had prepared grilled asparagus, corn on the cob, fresh salad, and cheesy potatoes as well. Strawberries dipped in chocolate were the perfect dessert, and now she was too stuffed to eat another bite.

And she had Jon here all to herself. Perfection.

If she could only relax and not worry about Kylie. She'd always been the one to care for her daughter, and she found it impossible not to fret.

The sound of another motor rose above the sound of the water, and a bright headlamp shining their way nearly blinded her. Bright-blue lights flashed as well.

She shielded her eyes with her hand. "Who on earth is doing that? Coast Guard maybe?"

A voice amplified through a bullhorn shouted, "Coast Guard. We are boarding."

"Guess that answers the question," Jon murmured in her ear.

This shouldn't take long. Any boat on the water was subject to boarding to ensure papers were in order and no smuggling was going on. She'd been stopped a time or two over the years, though they always backed off when she displayed her identification.

The blinding light prevented her from seeing much detail of the men in the patrol vessel, but the catamaran dipped a bit as two men came up the ladder. She turned her back on the patrol and focused her attention on the boarding officers.

She dug in her purse for her credentials. "I'll handle this."

Jon caught at her arm. "I don't like this, Annie. I've never known the Coast Guard not to ask a few questions before boarding, like what was the last port of call and what is our destination."

He had a point. She pulled her gun from her purse and the weight of it helped steady her. "You're right. This isn't usual behavior."

The captain stepped from the wheelhouse to intercept the men boarding. In the dim lighting she saw the first man step aboard. He was not in uniform and carried an assault rifle. From here it appeared to be an HK416. Lots of firepower. Her measly SIG Sauer .45 wouldn't be a match for his. A ski mask covering his face convinced Annie they were in trouble. This wasn't a Coast Guard checking credentials.

She caught Jon's hand as the boarding man jabbed his rifle into the captain's belly. "Come with me. We need to hide so I have a chance at these guys." Jon gestured to the ladder to below deck, but she shook her head. "We can't let ourselves be trapped." She spotted a metal cabinet and dove behind it with Jon. "Text Mason. I think we're close enough to shore for you to have a signal. Tell him to call the Coast Guard."

Peering around the edge of the cabinet, she held her gun ready. What did the men want? She'd never heard of any pirates out here on Lake Superior. With her blood roaring in her ears from adrenaline, she didn't hear the words the man barked at the captain as a second man joined them.

They argued for what seemed an eternity, but Annie couldn't hear well with Jon's bulk blocking her.

He gripped her forearm. "They're looking for you!" he hissed the words softly in her ear.

"What?" That made no sense.

"They said they wanted the female ranger-cop turned over to them, and they'd let everyone else go."

She gave a slight shake of her head, then peered around the cabinet again. Neither man looked familiar. Even if they had, their ski masks would have obscured a clear ID on them.

Wait, Shainya had mentioned a modification to the hat she'd given Joel. She tried to examine the hats on the men, but there wasn't enough light to see well.

"Can you snap a pic of them with your phone?"

"The flash will get their attention."

"If they're asking the captain to turn me over to them, they might want me alive, so I don't think they'll shoot. I'll aim for their legs if they come this way."

"Okay, get ready." Jon leaned around the other side of the metal cabinet and aimed his phone toward the two.

The light flashed from it, but the man in the back seemed to be the only one who noticed. He whipped toward them, and his rifle came up. Jon had already ducked back, and Annie didn't think he'd spotted their location. He'd reacted too slowly.

The guy jabbed his buddy with his elbow. "I saw a light. Toward the back of the boat. Maybe it's the ranger."

The first guy seemed in charge, and he barely glanced away from the captain. "Check it out." He stuck a finger in the captain's chest. "Where is she? We know she's here."

"I don't have a park ranger aboard. Just a couple on a romantic dinner cruise. You've stopped the wrong boat."

The captain's strong assertion and steady gaze was having an effect on the leader. He took a step back and pulled out his phone. The other guy raised his rifle as he took a step in the direction where Annie and Jon were hidden, but the gun shook in his hands. He didn't seem too eager to explore on his own.

The leader spoke into the phone with a hushed voice that didn't carry to where Annie crouched. Was he calling for verification or more backup?

"Did you hear from Mason?" she whispered to Jon.

He held up a finger and nodded, which she took to mean they should stay quiet because the other guy was approaching. She dared a quick glance around the cart and saw him five feet away. She could easily take him out at this distance, but she hoped the leader might call him back.

The wail of a siren came faintly to her ears. There must have been a Coast Guard boat in the area. The approaching man's head snapped toward the sound, and he squinted in the dark toward the boat lights heading their way.

"We'd better get out of here!" he called to the leader. "I think it's a police boat. Or the Coast Guard."

The leader put down his phone and gestured to him. "Go, go!"

They both dashed for the ladder and disappeared over the boat's railing. Annie leaped to her feet and rushed for the ladder as well. She needed some way to identify the men, but she saw no registration numbers on the boat's port side.

As it sped off into the night, she slammed her palm against the railing. Who were they, and what did they want with her?

FOURTEEN

THEIR EVENING HAD COME TO AN UNEXPECTED END.
Jon noticed Annie's hands trembled a little as she paced the lot in the marina. At least they were all in one piece with no one injured or worse. It felt appropriate that clouds had blotted out the moonlight just as the night's events had overlaid their fun time together with the threat of violence.

Mason ended a call on his phone and took Annie's arm, forcing her to stay in one place. "Let's have a seat on the benches. Do you need some coffee or something stronger?"

She waved off his concern and sank onto a bench overlooking the lapping waves. The scent of fuel overpowered that of the lake. "I'm fine."

Jon stood behind her with his hands on her shoulders. The tension radiating through her muscles to his fingers was palpable, and he rubbed his thumbs over the tightness. "It's all over."

Mason took out his pen and notebook. "Okay, go over everything you heard. Let's start with you, Jon."

Jon recounted the initial boarding and how the guns and masks had clued them in to hide right away. "Annie was getting out her gun and didn't hear the leader demand to know where to find the female ranger. It had to have been Annie they were looking for."

"Huh," Mason said. "Why would gunmen be searching for you, Annie?"

"Could it have to do with Glenn's escape? Maybe his men are trying to make sure I don't testify. And I received that weird voice-distorting call that warned me to stop digging."

Mason tapped his pen on the page. "Your main area of focus has been investigating Glenn's friends and acquaintances. Maybe someone wants to stop that."

"They came prepared with big assault rifles," Jon said. "They knew their stuff and were quick to run when they heard your siren."

"Were there any identifiers you could give me on them?"

Annie moved restlessly under Jon's hands. "One was six-two or so. He wore a hoodie and a ski mask so I can't even tell you the hair color, but he was thin, not bulky at all. Big feet. The other guy was about six foot and more slender. Same ski mask though. It had to be hot wearing that stuff. And he wore some kind of hat, but I couldn't tell if it was the one Shainya mentioned. Let me see that picture you took, Jon."

He handed her his phone and she enlarged the photo. "I think that might be the hat. Can we have Shainya take a look?"

Mason nodded as she talked. "I'll shoot it over to her phone. How about as their boat approached? Any details?"

"It was too dark, and their lights were blinding," Jon said. "They threw on floodlights as they reached the catamaran. The captain handled things well. He tried to calm the men while we prepared to take on the attackers. They had heavy firepower with their guns though. It might not have turned out so well if you hadn't come so quickly."

"Good thing you had a chance to let me know." He put his pen and pad away. "This isn't your investigation, Annie, not really. You have a daughter to raise, so I'm letting you take a step back."

Jon knew how that offer would end. The woman he loved didn't seem to know the meaning of retreat. When her shoulders tensed, he gave a gentle squeeze.

Annie shook her head. "I want to see this thing through to the end. You need my help, Mason. This is a big web of crime. We don't know where it's going to lead, and you need as many of us poking around as possible."

"I'm not saying you haven't been an asset, but in the end, it's my job—not yours."

Her chin came up. "I'm not quitting. I'll continue poking around on my own if you lock me out of the investigation."

"I'm not doing that, but I want you to think about Kylie and all you have to lose here."

"I'm not living my life in fear. When it's my time, nothing I do will change what God has set in his Book of Life. How many times does the Bible say 'Fear not'? Enough times that we know God doesn't want us to cower in our homes. And I'm not going to do it. What kind of example would that be for Kylie? I want to model courage, not cowardice."

Her impassioned speech softened Mason's granite expression. "Just know I won't think less of you if you decide to back away." He put his pen and notepad back in his pocket. "The captain didn't recognize the men or the boat either. All we can do is keep on with our investigation and follow through on finding Hussert. Maybe once we trace this all the way back, we'll know why tonight happened."

Jon didn't say anything until Mason walked to his SUV and

slid inside. He removed his hands from her shoulders. "I'll take you to the Blue Bonnet, love. I don't think it's safe at your place. Those guys might decide to finish the job." He heaved a sigh. "So much for our romantic evening. We'll be spending the rest of it thinking over everything that happened."

She rose and tucked her hand into his elbow. "It's early enough we could watch a movie and eat popcorn while we decompress. We can hang out in your room and avoid the other guests. I can sleep on the living room sofa if all the guest rooms are taken."

"I think there's a single down the hall that's rarely rented." Snuggling with her on the sofa held definite appeal, but Jon stifled a grin as he led her toward his car. She'd be interrupting the movie every few seconds with ideas about what to do next in her quest to get to the truth. One of the hazards of loving an investigator. But that was all right with him. More than all right. Her persistence was one of her best traits. It meant she'd hang in there with him even when he messed up.

Look at where they were now: The love she had for him when they were teenagers had never really gone away. Persistence was good.

/ / /

Annie was adorable wearing the oversized gray sweats Jon had loaned her to sleep in last night. Her blonde hair was mussed when she came down the steps of the Blue Bonnet and headed for the coffee bar Martha always had set up. Milo ran to greet her.

She spotted him standing in the doorway to the parlor and yawned. "I hope you've made coffee. I barely slept last night."

"Well, we didn't even get to bed until close to three. But yes, coffee is ready." He handed her his mug and led her toward the kitchen where he could get another one for himself.

They'd watched a movie before starting to talk about the men who boarded the boat again. That had woken them both up. Mason would have the picture Jon took of the men sent to Tech to see if it could be enhanced. Maybe they'd find identifying details in it. He'd already heard back from Shainya, who believed the thinner man was Joel West.

Martha bustled from the dining room with a plate of muffins she put on the table. "You must be starved. I've got thimbleberry and blueberry muffins. Gluten-free, of course." Her sidelong glance at Jon followed her smile. "I'm learning all kinds of new recipes these days."

"The best I've ever tasted." Jon selected a thimbleberry one.

Annie opted for blueberry and bit into it. "Ooh, still warm. I'll have to get your recipe so I can make these for Kylie."

Jon could already see he was going to like having Martha around, and it wasn't just her cooking. The older woman knew how to surround him with love and approval without smothering him. And Dad was thriving from her attention.

He spied the ring on her finger and took her hand. The pink stone was huge and stunning. He was no gem expert, but he thought it was tourmaline. "Dad did you proud. It's beautiful."

Martha beamed and color flooded her cheeks. "I told Daniel I was too old to need an engagement ring, but he wouldn't hear of skipping it. He picked it out himself, and it's so perfect. I don't know how he knew I love pink tourmaline."

He suspected Dad had consulted with Bree and Naomi. Dad had always touted the need for research with everything in life. "He's a smart guy." He released her hand.

"Did I hear someone say my name?"

His dad made his way into the dining room, but in spite of his slowness, Dad's gait and strength seemed to be improving. Living in this big bed-and-breakfast had forced his muscles to work more.

Jon poured his dad a cup of coffee. "I was admiring Martha's ring. Good job picking it out. Did you hear us come in last night?"

"Couldn't help but hear you. It was like a herd of elephants wandering the house. I thought about getting up, but I figured you needed your rest since it was so late." His green eyes landed on Annie. "And then Annie is here too. What happened?"

Jon gestured toward the dining room table. "I'll tell you over breakfast."

They settled at the table, where Martha had set out a display of scrambled eggs, bacon, and muffins. His dad and Martha ate their breakfast while Jon told them about the men boarding the boat.

His dad wiped the butter from his fingers on a cloth napkin and pulled out his phone. "Let's list possible reasons for this. It's always good to lay out different scenarios and see where they lead. Your top suspect?"

"Glenn's associates," Annie said immediately. "They have to silence me or I'll testify against Glenn on the kidnapping charges. We're already fairly sure one is Joel West."

"But Glenn is missing, so why the urgency?" Martha asked.

"Good question." Jon exchanged a glance with Annie. "He's bound to be found though. They can't hide him forever."

"This is the Upper Peninsula," Martha reminded them. "Do you have any idea how easy it is to disappear up here? Men can hide out in the woods for years. Or sneak across the border by boat into Canada. Even with Samson's help, it took Bree a year to find the downed plane that finally brought Davy home to us all. The possibilities are endless."

"Any other reason besides the investigation into Glenn that someone could be searching for Annie?" his dad asked. "What other cases are you working on, Annie?"

She put down her mug and frowned. "There have been a few missing hikers, but I haven't gotten anywhere. That's all I can think of right now."

Jon hated to bring up another possibility, but it had to be said. "Your sister abducted Kylie. That investigation is still ongoing."

"But she was apprehended and will be tried. Kylie was returned safely, and it's over."

"Is it really?" He held her panicked gaze. "What if there was more to it than we know? Yes, I know she said she did it out of anger, but what if someone else was involved? Maybe she didn't want to implicate that person."

"If that were true, why try to silence me about something I don't even know?"

"I don't know. I'm just trying to think of all possible explanations. These guys were rich enough to afford a nice boat. Does that mean something?"

A frown formed on her brow. "I have no idea. Glenn had amassed quite a lot of money with his scheme, but it appeared he was using it for his election. He owned a fishery, so I'm sure he has more than one boat. My money is on the idea that the men are connected somehow to Glenn."

"So we have to focus on finding him," Jon said.

"Easier said than done. We do know that Joel West was one

of the men who helped Glenn escape. And if he was on the boat last night, he's clearly here and not in Canada."

"If Shainya is correct," Jon said.

Annie's phone sounded. "Kylie is sending me a FaceTime request." She turned away to answer the call.

At this point Jon didn't know who was behind the attack on the boat, but he had to figure out how to keep Annie safe. Her living alone with Kylie out there wasn't the best situation. He'd stayed a few nights when he was first injured, but he couldn't stay there now with their little girl out of town. It wouldn't look right, and the temptation might be too great for them to handle.

The ring would be here today since he'd had it overnighted. He could just up and marry her, ring or no ring. His dad was jumping right in with both feet. Jon could do the same.

FIFTEEN

SARAH PAUSED TO FAN AWAY THE MOSQUITOES SWARM-
ing her face. "We should have waited for the sun to drive the
mosquitoes away." Mist hung in the humid air, and the scent of
the lake mingled with the wildflowers under her feet.

Anu had awakened her early to go for a hike along the shore,
and the foliage was still damp. The older woman didn't appear to
be winded or in need of a break.

Anu paused to adjust her sneaker and to retie the bandana
around her head. "It's out now, and the skeeters will be gone soon.
Did you sleep well?"

"Not really." Anu's open expression and the concern in her
blue eyes prompted Sarah to expand her comment. "It was weird
being back in that cabin, you know? Were you here back then?
When I was abducted?"

"Oh my, yes, Sarah. The entire community turned out to
search for you. There was a manhunt that went on for months. We
wanted to bring you home even if the news was very bad. Your poor
parents grieved so much. Your mother was never quite the same."

Sarah settled on a large rock by the water and tossed pebbles
into the gentle waves. "You knew her well?"

Anu picked a wildflower and sniffed it. "Very well. She was an expert rug weaver. I sold her rugs in my store just as I sell Annie's now."

"Did you know my cousin's family?"

Anu eased down onto a boulder and pulled out her water bottle. "Nearly everyone in the region has been in my store, so yes, I knew Sean and his uncle. His parents, too, of course."

"Uncle? I didn't know Mother had a brother. I only ever met Sean."

"The family had a most painful falling out many years ago. Sean's father, Clive, was a most distasteful man, and he would cross the street to avoid speaking to his brother Mort. And Mort ended up changing his name."

"I was thinking about the abduction last night." She told Anu about timing how long it took to walk to the dock. "My memories of that night are unclear, but I remember Mother coming out of the shadows and grabbing me. Like she'd been lying in wait. But how could she know we would be there? We didn't sneak out of bed and go see the loons every night."

Anu tucked a strand of silvery-blonde hair behind her ear, and a frown appeared on her brow. "That is a most interesting observation, Sarah. Do you know who was in the cabin that night? Anyone except your parents?"

"I don't remember anyone else, but I was only five. Annie might remember."

Sarah couldn't let it go. There was some detail they were missing about that abduction. What if it had been planned? Who would have planned it? And why?

"I wish I could talk to Annie about it all. She hates me now."

Anu stooped down and retied her sneaker. "She is hurt, my dear. Give her time."

"Since she won't speak to me, could you ask her if anyone else was there that night?"

"I will do this for you. I will go back to my house later today and see what she remembers." Anu rose and picked up her water bottle. "We must finish our hike. I would like coffee and breakfast."

They turned to retrace their steps, and Sarah heard a noise. Like crying or an animal. "Did you hear that?"

Anu tipped her head to one side and nodded. "A dog?"

"Maybe."

The sound came again, and Sarah plunged off the trail into thick foliage. "Go ahead and I'll catch up," she called to Anu. Sarah fought her way through brambles and heavy brush until she broke through into a clearing. From here she couldn't see the water or Anu, and she wasn't sure how far she'd come.

"Hello?" she called.

A whine came from her left, and she went that direction. A forlorn golden retriever sat tied to a tree. The animal looked neglected and much too thin. When Sarah glanced around, she saw a half-collapsed tent and the remains of a fire. The dog had no food and an empty water dish.

"Anyone here?" She walked to the tent and ducked inside.

The interior held a sleeping bag, a backpack, and several canned food items. Inside the backpack she found women's jeans and tees as well as a pair of size-seven sneakers. She exited and looked around the campsite. A bag of something swung from a high tree, and she retrieved it by letting down the rope tied nearby. Inside, she found dry dog food. Someone must have been trying to protect it from any stray animals.

She dumped food in a pile near the dog, then poured what water she had into its bowl. The poor thing drank thirstily, then gobbled up the food almost in one gulp. Its tail thumped on the dirt, and she knew she couldn't leave it here.

She rubbed its ears. "Where's your owner?" Her fingers found a tag on the collar around its neck. Scout. That could be a male or female name.

The dog's dark eyes stared back expectantly. Sarah knew how it felt to be trapped and helpless. She couldn't walk away from this situation. Kneeling beside the tree, she fought with the knot and managed to untie the animal.

"Let's go, my friend. We'll see if anyone at the big house knows who you belong to and what has become of her."

Could Scout belong to the woman whose jacket she'd found? The one Max's employees had taken to the hospital? If so, why hadn't she asked someone to care for it? The answer to those questions weren't to be found out here in the woods, but Max would know what to do to reunite this dog with its owner.

/ / /

The worry on Jon's face stayed in Annie's thoughts as she left the Blue Bonnet and hurried down Houghton Street to the downtown area. He'd promised to pick her up in two hours at Mason's office, though she didn't hold out a lot of hope that the sheriff had figured out who had launched the attack last night.

"Annie!"

She turned and saw Anu waving to her from the door of her shop. Though Mason was expecting Annie, she detoured to see the older woman.

A smiling Anu embraced Annie at the doorway to Nicholls' Finnish Imports. "Good morning, *kulta*. I hear the children are having a wonderful time in Wisconsin Dells."

"Kylie FaceTimed me this morning, and she had quite a lot to say. They're going to a water park today. And they bought fudge last night after dinner. Everything important." Annie laughed as she remembered her daughter's excitement.

But her laughter was tinged with worry about the water park. What if Kylie fell off a water slide?

Anu gestured to the door behind her. "Do you have time to come in?"

"Not really. I need to talk to Mason." She didn't tell Anu what had happened on the boat.

"I shall make it quick then. I spoke with Sarah this morning. Out on the island, some of her memory appears to be coming back. She mentioned how strange it was that Becky Johnson seemed almost to be waiting for you girls. Do you remember it that way?"

Annie took a step back at the sudden question. It wasn't something she'd consciously thought about, but as soon as Anu asked the question, Annie remembered how quickly the woman had appeared on the scene when they reached the dock. And it was late.

"Sarah might be right."

"She wonders if it had been planned by someone. Was anyone else staying on the island when you were there? Do you remember or were you too young?"

Annie struggled to push back the curtains of time and pull

out such long-forgotten memories. It wasn't until recently she'd even remembered much about that day. The horror of the attack on her and the abduction of her sister had veiled the other events of that week for so long. Was anyone else there? What had happened that morning and the day before?

"Let me think about it. Is Sarah doing all right out on the island?"

"She was a little upset to see the bedroom where the two of you had slept. The flood of memories seemed to be unexpected." She handed Annie a small red notebook. "She wrote down everything she could remember about Becky and her family. It might be helpful sometime."

Annie took the notebook and stuffed it in her backpack. "I haven't been in the cabin since she was taken. I'm surprised it's all still there. I assumed Max would have hauled it all away and redone it for guests. I gave him permission to do whatever he liked with it."

"He cleaned it up, but that was all. It is a good, tight cabin—otherwise the rodents would have destroyed everything over the years. Max said it was dusty but intact."

The thought of everything just sitting as they left it tugged at Annie's heartstrings. Her parents' things would still be there. The dishes and tableware would be the ones she ate meals with all those years ago. Even their toys would be in the closet.

She might have to check it out herself. Maybe it would bring back memories. But to do that, she'd have to be prepared to face Sarah, and she wasn't quite ready for that. Not today.

She gave the older woman a quick hug. "Thanks, Anu. I need to run. I'll let you know if I remember anything."

Annie crossed the street to the jail. Maybe Tech found

something in the photo Jon took. The receptionist sent her to the war room, where she found Mason with his two deputies and several forensic techs.

Mason beckoned to her from the whiteboard at the front of the room. "I was about to call you. You don't look any the worse for wear this morning."

"I'm fine. Martha stuffed me with muffins and coffee so I'm set for the day." She slid into a seat on the front row and exchanged pleasantries with the rest of the group.

"I was about to get started. The first order of business: We didn't get much more detail about the photo of the men who boarded the boat. Shainya is sure the one man is Joel, so at least that gives us something to go on."

Annie focused on the things Mason had written on the board. It was a list much like Daniel had insisted they create this morning. Mason had underlined Sean Johnson's name, which she found interesting since he was dead and couldn't be behind what they were dealing with.

She pointed to the board. "Sean Johnson?"

Mason turned back to the board. "Hear me out." He drew lines with the marker between Sean's name and those of Lissa Sanchez and Glenn Hussert. "We know he was connected to those two. And those two are connected to everyone else in some way. What if all this spirals back to Sean? Maybe what's happening now is something Sean originally put into play. If we follow Sean first, maybe we can uncover what's really going on. I admit it's a long shot, but now that we have extra help, we can afford the personnel to explore the possibility while some of the rest of us dig in to people like West and Bell. And I'd like you to consider staying in town until we sort this out."

Annie caught her breath at the idea that it all might lead back to Sean. And if so, did her sister's presence here lead them somewhere closer to the truth as well? She dug in her backpack and pulled out the red notepad. "Sarah sent this to me through Anu, but I haven't read it. It's everything she remembered about Becky and the Johnson family."

Mason took it and flipped the cover open to scan. There were two pages. He handed it to Annie without commenting. She scanned through the pages.

Becky was raped by her brother Mort when she was fifteen, which was the reason for the estrangement in the family. Their dad smuggled drugs in and out of Canada. Their mom left them after that, and Becky went to live with Clive and Sean. She had a baby from that attack, and the baby was stillborn. She got a job in a nursing home when she was sixteen and eventually moved away. She had diabetes and wouldn't take her medicine, no matter how much I reminded her. I found her in a coma and called 911, but she was dead when they got her to the hospital.

Clive beat Sean from the time he was little, and he hated his dad. Becky once found him torturing a rat and ran to tell Clive about it. When Sean got beaten until he was unconscious, Becky blamed herself and vowed never to tell on him again. He could get her to do just about anything after that. She was always a little afraid of him.

When Annie finished reading, she glanced up at Mason. "A lot of violent dysfunctions in the family."

"And threads of why Becky would do something like taking

Sarah. She probably wanted to replace the baby she'd lost. Serial killers usually start out torturing animals. I'd say we're on the right track with focusing on Sean."

And Annie would have to talk to Sarah about all of this. At least her sister was trying.

SIXTEEN

WHEN THE TEXT CAME THROUGH WITH OLIVIA'S NAME, it was a stark reminder that Jon had done nothing yet about the problem back in Rochester. *Please help me.* The sun streamed through the parlor of the Blue Bonnet and washed out his screen, so he walked into the shadows nearer the fireplace.

He had to ask the investigator to exhume Tessa Abston's body. It was the right thing to do. Annie was going to check out what the situation was in Minnesota, but with everything going on here, he was sure she hadn't gotten that done. He didn't want to prod her when someone seemed to be after her. He needed to handle this himself.

He stared at the number Olivia had texted again. It was the same detective he'd called when the news first broke. Ken Perry. The guy had been a suspicious jerk when they'd talked last. Would his attitude have changed any?

Sighing, Jon placed the call, and it was answered on the second ring. "Detective Perry."

The gruff voice sounded the same, like he'd just puffed a pack of cigarettes. "Detective Perry, this is Dr. Jon Dunstan."

"I wondered if I might hear from you. Rats fleeing a sinking ship and all that. I'm recording this conversation as I did the last one."

Jon tensed and paced the parlor. "I don't know what you're referencing, Detective. Has something happened?"

"We arrested your former boss, and she tells me she's ready to implicate everyone else."

He should have taken care of this sooner. The delay wasn't going to look good. Should he hang up and get an attorney?

No, he had nothing to hide.

"Olivia called me and wanted me to testify for her. I told her I couldn't do it. But talking to her made me remember a patient I lost unexpectedly. I was called in after a car crash and was in surgery for hours. Olivia went to see a patient for me, and the patient died that night. The death was very unexpected, though she'd found out the week before she had pancreatic cancer."

"When was this?"

"A year ago."

"Why didn't you call the police then?"

"I didn't suspect anything like murder. No one would have. But now with everything that's happened, I have to consider the possibility that Olivia did something to her. Would an autopsy show a drug like that now?"

"I doubt it, but I'll ask the coroner. I suspect it would be too instantaneous to lodge in bone or hair. Hang on, let me ask. He's across the hall."

Jon rubbed his head and listened to the faint sounds coming through the phone.

The detective returned. "No go. It would be impossible to detect now. Convenient."

"Look, I didn't have to tell you about this case. I knew it would raise your suspicions, but I had to ask about it, okay? I care about my patients. I thought Olivia did too. I still find it hard to believe she'd do something like that to people she supposedly cared about. What about liver assays? Would there be enough to check there?"

"The coroner says no. You seem to know a lot about investigations."

"My girlfriend is a law enforcement officer for the Park Service. She works closely with the sheriff, and I've been tagging along with her some. You can talk to Sheriff Mason Kaleva and check me out."

"I will do that."

Was it Jon's imagination, or was the detective's tone a tad warmer? "Look, I know you have to do your job, but none of the rest of us knew about her activities."

"You're sure about that?"

There was a warning tone Jon didn't like. "I argued about Olivia's innocence with you last time we spoke. I now know I was wrong. So no, I guess I can't vouch for the others. But as desperate as she was when she called me, I think she was the only one and is trying to get some of us to vouch for her. I don't know what drove her to do it. That's something you'll have to take up with Olivia."

"Is that all you have to say?"

"That's it. I had hoped none of it was true."

"Didn't we all. Thank you for calling, Dr. Dunstan."

The call ended, and Jon thought the detective calling him "doctor" might have been a sign he believed him. But time would tell.

A flash of movement caught his eye, and he spotted a mail truck pulling into a parking space in front of the bed-and-breakfast. He bounded to the door and met the woman before she could ring the bell. He quickly signed for the overnight delivery and shut the door.

His hands trembled as he opened the box and stared at his mother's ring. It was a lovely set with top-quality diamonds, but it didn't suit Annie. Henry might have already started on the ring since he was familiar with these stones.

He grabbed his keys and headed for the door.

/ / /

By the time Sarah took care of Scout and made it to the big house, Max and Anu had left to get Anu to work on time, and Sarah spent the next couple of hours bathing the golden retriever, during which she determined the dog was a male. She gave him copious amounts of water and fed him again. By lunchtime, he was a different canine.

But where was his owner? She fixed a peanut butter sandwich in her small cabin, then went to gather the belongings at the campsite. The dog whined and didn't want to follow her into the brush, so she left him by the water and went to where she'd found him.

There was no sign of the tent or his water dish. No backpack or anything else. The only sign the woman had camped here was the way the grass was beaten down. Maybe Max's employees had gathered them up for her.

Sarah went back to the big house to ask to use the satellite phone, only to be told Max had taken one of them and the other was out with one of the groundskeepers. The employee had taken a four-wheeler, so it was hard to say where he might be on the island.

With Scout in tow, Sarah wandered down to the dock to sit in the sun and wait for Max's return. Squirrels chattered from the oaks along the shore, and gulls swooped down to taunt the dog, who didn't seem to care. The fresh scent of the water and the warmth of the sun made her drowsy, and she lay back on the deck and closed her eyes.

It was about one when she heard the rumble of an approaching boat and sat up. She recognized Max's sleek yacht and dangled her legs above the edge of the water as she waited for him to come ashore. He might know the answers to her questions without using the phone, but she hated feeling so cut off from the world.

Not that she had anyone to call.

If she tried to contact Annie, she'd be unlikely to take the call. And Sean was dead. Bree was on vacation. That didn't leave anyone in her address book, so it was a moot point.

Max came toward the shore, and Sarah stood to intercept him. The dog barely lifted his head at the movement before he plopped back and closed his eyes.

Max's smile always lifted her spirits. "You look chipper today." He offered her a water bottle dripping from the cooler.

She took the bottle and uncapped it. "Thanks."

His gaze went to the dog sleeping behind her. "Where'd the pooch come from? It's skinny."

"I found him at an abandoned campsite. I think he might have belonged to the woman your workers found and took to the hospital. He was tied up, and it's hard to say how long he was without food or water. His name is Scout."

Max winced and went past her to stoop and pet the dog. "I've always liked goldens."

"He's a sweetheart. Listen, we need to figure out how to get him back to his owner. Could I use your phone to call the hospital and let her know I've found him? What was her name?"

"Actually, I'll call for you. One of my guys can take the dog to her." He retrieved the phone from his back pocket and placed the call.

When he turned his back on her to walk a few feet away, she sidled that way too. After all she'd been through with the dog, she wanted to make sure he got through to his owner. She couldn't make out the woman's last name.

"Oh, she's gone already? This is Max Reardon, and my men brought her to the hospital. We found her dog and wanted to return him to her. Could you give me her contact information? A phone number or address? Yes, I'll hold."

He wasn't looking at Sarah as he dug out a tablet with a stylus and prepared to take down the info. It appeared they were getting somewhere. He jotted down something and ended the call. She quickly stepped back a few feet and knelt to pet the dog so Max didn't know she had been eavesdropping.

She thought she saw irritation on his face as he moved back to her side, but when he smiled, she decided she was mistaken. His genial expression was the same as always.

"They didn't have a number for her but I have an address. I'll have the dog returned to her."

"What about her belongings? I was going to pack them up for her, but they were gone."

"I had my men see what they could find. I'm sure they discovered the site like you did. When did you find the campsite?"

"Just after lunch."

His long stride moved toward the house. "I'll have Dennis deliver everything along with the dog."

The thought of not seeing Scout again hurt her heart. "Could I go too? I'd like to make sure everything goes okay."

He frowned and shook his head. "You're supposed to be in hiding out here. We don't know where Hussert's friends are, but we know they are after your sister too. She barely escaped yesterday."

Sarah put her hand to her chest where her heart had stuttered. "Is Annie okay?"

"She's fine, but two men boarded a boat she was on last night. They were looking for her and they had assault rifles. They meant business. If someone happened to see you with Dennis, your location would be blown, and we'd have to find somewhere else to hide you. In good conscience I can't allow you to go."

It wasn't what she wanted to hear, but she understood the logic of his argument. "Okay. When are you taking him?"

"Not until tomorrow. We have a storm rolling in." He nodded to the sky out over the water where black clouds loomed. The scent of rain freshened the air. "It's supposed to be bad."

She'd have one more night with the dog. "I'll take him with me so I'm not alone tonight."

"Of course. Feel free to come back for dinner at six."

"Thank you." She didn't want to make any promises. The little cabin was beginning to mean a lot to her.

SEVENTEEN

THOUGH THE BACK ROOM OF THE JEWELRY SHOP WAS spotless, it reeked of a rotten egg smell. Jon waved his hand in front of his face and shook Henry's hand as he stood from his jeweler's bench, which looked more like a desk. "What died in here?"

Henry gestured to some jewelry on the desk's surface. "Liver of sulfur for a nice patina on the silver ring I'm working on. Yous get used to it. Did you get the ring, eh?"

"I have it right here." Jon handed him the velvet-lined box.

Henry opened it and touched the engagement ring. "Exactly as I remember it. The diamonds are lovely. Let me show yous what I have in mind."

Sorting through a stack of papers, he produced a pencil drawing of a ring. "This would be the large diamond in the middle of yous mother's set. In a heart shape around that, I'd put small sapphires around the larger stone, then more diamonds in a second row. Matching sapphires along the wedding ring would be spectacular."

"It's perfect for Annie. When could you have it completed?"

Henry tipped his head to one side. "Do I detect anxiety in yous voice, young Jon?"

"Yes, I guess so. You already know Glenn has escaped, but there's more." He told the older man about the boarding of the boat the day before. "I don't like the idea of her and Kylie alone in the cabin."

"That was very brazen of the men. I can see yous is worried. And yous think being engaged will alter Annie's behavior? She's in law enforcement and very capable. Every man wants to protect the woman he loves, but she may take it as yous don't trust her to be the smart professional she is."

Jon hadn't thought of how Annie might take his concern. "She's an excellent investigator."

He bit his lip and thought about it. Knowing Annie's ability didn't lessen his worry, but she was a better shot than him. She had a natural ability to see things others might miss, and her protective instincts were more finely honed than his. She'd been a mom for eight years and was used to protecting Kylie. But still, didn't two people on their guard make a stronger team than one? He'd been the one to hear the men boarding the boat were after her.

Henry patted Jon's arm. "I can see yous are still torn. I can have this ring done in three days since all the stones are right here in my shop. Would that work for what yous have in mind?"

"So quickly? I appreciate it, Henry. And you're right—she's unlikely to be swayed by my worry. Maybe part of it is that I'm ready to share my life with her. I want us together forever. I nearly lost my life, and she's been in constant danger since I got back to town."

Henry set the ring box on his bench. "None of us know the length of our days. I will call when the ring is ready."

Jon passed him his business card. "Here's my number."

"And I will pray for young Annie's safety."

"I appreciate that more than you know."

Walking out, Jon realized his anxiety stemmed from his own lack of prayer about the danger. God knew the number of each of their days, and his worry showed a great lack of trust. What was that scripture? Something about worry being unable to add an hour to life. He'd have to look it up.

And do better himself.

He turned onto Houghton Street, and as he neared the jail, he spotted Annie exiting the building. "Hey!" He broke into a jog and reached her in moments.

The shadows in her eyes ebbed when he held out his arms, and she walked into his embrace. "I missed you," she said.

He kissed her before replying. "You seemed upset. What's wrong?"

"You always seem to know." She told him about her sister's comments. "I need to walk around in that cabin, even though I don't want to."

He tucked a strand of blonde hair behind her ear. "There's time to do that later, love. What happened twenty-four years ago isn't significant when you're in the middle of trying to protect yourself and Kylie from the maniacs on the loose right now."

Her blue eyes stayed troubled. "Mason is going on the assumption that things are tied to Sean Johnson somehow. He was Becky's nephew. What if Sarah could tell us something about him that would help us crack all of this now?"

That was a stretch, but he could see Mason's reasoning. And Jon recognized the determined expression on Annie's face. She wasn't one to leave any stone unturned, even if she found a creepy-crawly under it. In this case, that creep was her sister.

Though he'd seen Sarah's remorse, he wasn't ready to trust her yet, and he didn't want Annie to let her guard down either.

He put his hands on her shoulders. "When do you want to go out to the island? I'll go with you. We can stroll through the old cabin while you see if you remember anything about that night. And if you do it with Sarah, something she says might spark something in your head and vice versa."

She leaned on tiptoes and kissed him. "You are the best. Do you have time to go right now?"

"Sure do."

And on the way he could tell her about the call with the detective in Minnesota. He wasn't sure if he'd done the right thing, but it was over now and there was no going back.

/ / /

Annie wiped damp palms on her khaki shorts and forced herself to take a deep breath. At the other end of this walkway, she'd confront her sister again, and she was not ready. Not even close. The storm in her heart felt more turbulent than the one brewing out over the water.

Jon walked beside her, and he pushed stray branches out of the way along the narrow path to the small cabin where she'd spent many idyllic days as a child. The scents of the island—pine, moss, and dead leaves—stirred her trepidation. Some of her earlier memories were anchored on this island.

The path opened in front of them, and the cabin came into view. Roses flanked the path here, and their sweet fragrance nauseated her. Someone had attacked her the last time she'd been on the island, and she was thankful for Jon's steadfast presence. The green metal roof gleamed in the sunlight, and the freshly stained cedar logs gave the cabin an updated feel. She glanced around but didn't see Sarah. Maybe she was inside.

Jon squeezed her fingers, then released her to step to the door. He rapped his knuckles on it. "Sarah?"

No answer. He peered in the window before trying the knob. "I don't think she's inside."

"Should we find her first?" Annie would rather have had a chance to inspect the cabin by themselves, but Jon had a point about the two of them being able to bounce memories off one another. "There's a pond out back between here and Superior's shore. Maybe she's sitting out there." She and Jon walked around the side of the cabin into the back, and she spotted the path. "The pond is this way."

Her pulse throbbed in her throat. This was harder than she'd thought it would be. Any minute she expected to see her smiling mother or her dad come striding up from the big lake. Mom used to lie out in her one-piece blue suit on the tiny beach that opened up this way. And Dad would usually catch walleye for dinner. She would beg to help clean it, and he'd cook it over the charcoal grill in the picnic area he'd constructed by the pond. That area was gone now, lost to the ravages of storms and weather.

Jon took her hand when she didn't move. "Want me to go look for her?"

Annie shook her head. "I can go too. Just remembering." She cleared her scratchy throat and forced her feet to move along the pebble path. The shrubs were trimmed and neat instead of spilling across the path the way they'd been so many years ago. Everywhere she looked she found evidence of Max's care for the property. There was a new tire swing along the way too. She and Sarah had spent many hours in one during their childhood.

The sound of a dog's happy bark carried over the squawks of the gulls overhead, and she spotted a golden retriever leaping into the air to catch a Frisbee. The bright-orange disc looked like one she and Sarah had when they were little. The same one?

The rest of the red dye in Sarah's hair had faded, leaving only the blonde shade matching Annie's. Sarah's happy, carefree expression caught Annie's attention. The island had been good for her. Or maybe it was the dog.

The golden saw them first. It gave an excited bark and, tail wagging, ran toward them. Sarah's relaxed posture changed, and her smile dropped off. She came toward them but said nothing, as if she was waiting for Annie to explain their presence.

Annie knelt and petted the beautiful dog. "Did Max get you a dog?"

"No, I found him. He belongs to a woman who was injured out here. Max didn't know about the dog when he had his caretaker take her to the hospital. Scout will have to go back to her tomorrow. I wish I could keep him." Sarah looked down and clenched her hands together.

With a final pat Annie rose and put her hands in her pockets. "Um, Anu told me you wanted to talk about the night you were abducted. I don't remember much about that week, and I thought we might walk through the property and the cabin together. Maybe we will remember something."

"You think it's a crazy idea, don't you? That someone planned to take one of us all along—that it wasn't an impulsive decision."

"I hadn't thought about it, but after Anu told me about your theory, I realized there were a lot of unanswered questions about that night. I wish we'd had the opportunity to ask Sean about it."

"Sean?"

"He was related to Becky, right? Maybe she said something to him about how it happened. He knew you were Sarah Vitanen."

"Yes, he did."

"And now the family is gone."

"Not everyone. I heard Sean has an uncle who is still alive. He has Alzheimer's, but we—I mean, you—might catch him on a good day."

Annie hadn't remembered the man. "What was his name?"

"Mort Jones."

"Not Johnson?"

"Anu said he changed his name after a big blowup in the family."

Which would be why they hadn't realized he existed. Annie started to text Mason before she remembered there was no service out here. "Ready to take a walk through the place?"

Sarah swallowed hard. "If you say so."

Annie hadn't stopped to think about how hard this all was for Sarah. Her life had changed even more than Annie's that night. New compassion for her sister began to stir in her heart. Maybe she could figure out a way to forgive her.

EIGHTEEN

SARAH'S HEART RATE STILL HADN'T RESUMED ITS calm rhythm at the sight of her sister. She hadn't expected Anu's intervention to result in Annie's sudden appearance. And she'd been so calm and nonconfrontational.

Don't expect too much.

Her internal warning failed to tamp the slight hope rising in her chest. She led them to the back door and into the cabin. "When were you here last?"

"That night," Annie said. "I saw the exterior a few weeks ago, but I haven't been inside since your abduction."

Sarah sympathized with the huskiness in her sister's voice. She'd felt disoriented last night too. "You probably remember where everything is better than me."

Jon walked into the main area and plopped on the worn sofa with the dog. "I'll keep this guy occupied while you walk through. The fewer distractions, the better."

Annie wandered to the closest cupboard and opened it to reveal the stacks of plates. "I don't remember much really. It's all a blur. I've been trying to remember what went on that week. Were we here for vacation, or was there some other reason? I'd assumed it was vacation, but you're right—Becky seemed to be lying in wait for us. Almost like someone was watching us sneak away and told her."

"But that was before we had cell phones. Not that it matters since they don't work here."

"We had walkie-talkies. They worked for closer range."

Sarah vaguely remembered hiding in the bushes with Annie and listening to their mother call them on the walkie-talkies. Could someone have been watching them and relaying the information to Mother?

She trailed after her sister toward their bedroom. Her steps slowed as Annie opened the door. The glimpse of the Care Bears spreads on the beds made her feel dizzy and light-headed. Annie appeared to be just as reluctant because Sarah nearly ran into her when she stopped abruptly.

"Sorry." Annie's voice quavered, but she took a halting step forward. "I'd forgotten how we loved the Care Bears. Did you find the ballet shoes you got for your birthday? They should be in the closet."

Sarah stepped into the room after her sister, and the closet beckoned irresistibly after the mention of the slippers. Mother used to snap at her for whirling around the room and trying to stand on her toes. The habit had soon been trained out of her with pinches and sharp words.

When Sarah opened the closet, the stale air rushed out, but there was the hint of another odor. Baby powder maybe? Several brightly colored hair scrunchies lay on the floor. Little girl clothes hung on the rod. Small flared jeans, smiley face tees, and a stack of bright board shorts took her back to the nineties.

She picked up the ballet shoes sitting beside the small pink shorts. "They're here. Remember our jellies? They're here too."

Annie sat on the lower bunk and touched the cover. "They were comfortable. I don't remember what time it was when you woke me. Do you remember?"

Sarah glanced at the clock on the bedside table. It had stopped now, but she saw the glow from that night in her mind's eye. "It was a little after midnight."

"Do you know why you woke? Did you hear a sound or anything?"

It wasn't common for her to awaken. She normally slept straight through the night, especially back then. Did she have to go to the bathroom? Without making a conscious decision, she crossed the room and sat beside her sister, then leaned her face into her hands to think. What happened that night?

"We'd played *Candy Land*," she said as a memory rushed in. "I won."

"I let you. I always let you win."

Sarah should have known her sister would have done that. Annie always protected her and tried to make sure she was having a good time. She'd been like a little mother. How had she forgotten that? Maybe it had all been driven out by the new life of excessive discipline and harsh punishment.

Sarah lifted her head. "You slept in my bed with me that night."

Annie's fingers clutched a fistful of bedding. "I'd forgotten. You thought you heard a Windigo scratch at the window. That's it! I remember you waking me to tell me there was a Windigo outside."

"I don't remember, but maybe that's why I was so afraid the first time I came back in here."

But Annie had been afraid of the Windigo. She'd come home from school and told Sarah about the fifteen-foot-tall monster who ate humans. It had sunken red eyes in a stag skull and it liked little girls to fill its hungry belly. At least that's what Annie had said.

"Do you remember anything else after I woke you?"

"Just that you wanted to go see the loons. They had chicks, and you thought we'd see lots of them. I liked the loons back then, too, so it didn't take much to convince me," Annie said. "Well, I was afraid we'd get in trouble, but I wanted to see them too. I thought we could run down there and be back to bed without Mom and Dad hearing us. We grabbed some bread from the kitchen and sneaked out the back door."

"I remember Mother came out of the shadows in a boat, but I don't remember what she said."

"She said there were two to choose from. And she sounded so *cheerful*. Every time I remembered the tone of her voice, I shuddered."

Sarah had heard that tone all too often when Mother decided she needed to be locked in a closet as punishment. She shuddered too.

"Back to the loons. Why did you want to go so badly? Do you remember? We'd seen them just before dusk. It's not like loons are rare around here."

Sarah closed her eyes, then popped them wide when a memory came to her. "Someone told me about the chicks. He said they carried them on their backs, but we'd never seen that."

"No, we didn't. Do you remember who told you?"

"It was an older kid at the marina playground the morning we left." Sarah scrunched her face up as she thought. "Annie, I think it was Sean. His dad was working on the pavilion."

The huge revelation made her want to vomit. Had Sean helped orchestrate her abduction?

/ / /

The storm had held off, and a picnic after the traumatic day was what they both needed. Jon was surprised they'd pulled it together as quickly as they had. He removed fish from the grill as Annie set the corn-and-tomato salad she'd prepared on the table. The spread included sweet potato fries she'd whipped up in the air fryer too.

If only he had that ring ready. He suspected he was going to see missed opportunities to propose over the next few days while he waited.

He hadn't fully made up his mind whether to wait or to propose without a ring. How did a guy even do that though? The ring was the chocolate on the strawberry. It wouldn't be the same without it.

He served her the nicest piece of fish with perfectly crisped edges. "What's next in your investigation?"

She ladled salad onto her plate and his. "I'm going to take a hard look at Sean and his associates, going back as far as I can. Mason hasn't discovered anything, but he focused on the last couple of years. I think we need to go back further than that."

"What did you make of Sarah's memories of Sean telling her about the baby loons? Could his dad have been involved in the abduction?"

Her blue eyes held sorrow. "It could have been a coincidence that Sean told Sarah about the baby loons, but it *feels* deliberate. Coupled with Becky being ready to snatch one of us, I can't rule it out. And if he would do something like that at ten, what would he have been capable of as he got older?"

He salted the fries and dipped one in ketchup. "Speaking

of investigations, I spoke with the Minnesota detective this morning." He told her about the menacing text from Olivia and his call to Ken Perry. "Once he heard my girlfriend was a LEO, his attitude changed. He talked to the coroner about another autopsy and was told it wouldn't show. So I won't ever know if Olivia killed one of my patients."

"I'm sorry, Jon. That has to be hard."

"Have you heard from Bree and Kylie?"

"Bree called after Naomi told her about your dad and Martha's upcoming wedding. She was ecstatic. I think she was almost ready to jump in the van and head back north to participate in the plans. She was almost giddy. Kylie promised to FaceTime me tonight on her iPad."

"Do you think they're rushing into this?" He dropped the casual question to gauge her reaction to a quick wedding.

"Why wait? They've known each other a long time. I hope you don't mind the mention of Nate, but his death taught me how precious time can be. When you know, you know." She reached across the table and took Jon's hand. "Nothing could convince me we shouldn't be together. We've come through so much in this past month. A lifetime, really. But it's only made us stronger together."

His fingers tightened on hers. "I hoped you'd feel that way." Now was the time.

But as he constructed his first sentence to launch into a proposal, her gaze went above his head. "It's Deja."

The deputy came toward the house in a brisk walk. She reached the steps and held out a paper. "I'm so sorry to have to disturb you with this, but it's part of the job. You're being served, Annie. The Pedersons are suing for custody of Kylie."

Annie sprang to her feet and snatched the paper from Deja's hand. "You can't be serious!" She tore into the envelope and read the first page before showing it to Jon. "I can't believe this. They barely pay any attention to her. It seems insane."

"They were angry when they left here," Jon said. "Maybe they'll reconsider when they've had time to cool off."

She skimmed the first page again. "This is dated yesterday, so they put it in motion right away. You might be right. They may regret it even now. I should probably call them. I told them they could see Kylie any time they wanted. Our relationship won't change their access to her."

Deja retreated. "Well, I'll let you hash it all out. Sorry to be the bearer of bad news."

Jon called out a thanks as the deputy went to her car. He and Nate's parents had been friends a long time. Their reaction two nights ago had stunned him, but maybe losing Nate had scarred them in a lot of ways.

He steered her back to their dinner. "I could try talking to them."

"Maybe." She sank onto her chair. "I can't believe we have to deal with this on top of everything else."

He'd lost his moment. Asking her to marry him now would be stupid when her thoughts were consumed with what to do about this new wrinkle. But maybe it was for the best. If he held his tongue for a few days, he'd have the ring in hand.

The bigger problem was how to convince her to let him stay or to move to town for now. She'd need to be here for the renters and the boaters. She had Michelle, but it was hard to say for how long. And Michelle was new—she couldn't handle all the problems that might come up.

NINETEEN

WITH A LAST SWIPE OF THE SPONGE, THE KITCHEN sparkled. Jon closed the dishwasher and started it. "How about ice cream in town for dessert? I think the storm will hold off long enough. And, Annie, I'd like you to consider staying at the Blue Bonnet for now."

She had expected this conversation all day. Worrying about what might happen next was not in her nature. "I'll be fine here, Jon."

His green eyes were troubled. "But you're alone." He held up a hand of protest. "I'm not saying you're not competent. You are an amazing law enforcement officer. Smart, fast, resilient. But that doesn't mean you'll be safe. Too many LEOs die in the line of duty every year. I don't want you to be one of them."

"'Safe'?" She lifted a brow. "Safety isn't my first priority. If it was, I wouldn't wear this uniform. I'm here to aid and protect others. To preserve our wilderness area. None of us know how many days God has written for our lives. We have to do the job before us and not worry about that. A Christian doesn't worry about safety. We're already safe with our eternal home prepared for us. On this earth, we do what God has put into our hands. For me, that's law enforcement. It's justice. That's my priority."

"Taking ordinary precautions isn't wrong. You wouldn't run out in front of a car or leap over a cliff."

"You jumped off a cliff to save Kylie," she reminded him.

The lines between his eyes eased. "And I'd do it again to save her."

"And I do my job to save people too."

His chin jutted out. "But a little care couldn't hurt."

"Kylie isn't in the house, so I can sleep with my gun on the nightstand. That's taking care. I'll arm the alarm system after you leave. I'm surprised you're not asking to stay with me."

His gaze raked over her, and he stepped closer to run his thumb over her lower lip. "I'm not sure I'm strong enough to resist temptation. Our wedding night can't come soon enough for me."

Warmth spread in her chest, and her mouth went dry. "Me neither," she whispered.

She told herself to back away, but instead, she moved close enough to feel the way his heart pounded in his chest. His lips came down on hers, and she closed her eyes as his arms pulled her closer. This was where she was supposed to be. Who needed safety?

It seemed he retreated too soon, and she made a small noise and tried to pull him back, but his hands moved to her shoulders in a slight push. A flush stained his cheeks, and his eyes were heavy lidded.

"See what I mean?" A crooked smile lifted his lips. "You're way too tempting. Come on, work with me here. The Blue Bonnet?"

She wanted to indignantly reiterate all her earlier arguments, but she knew love drove everything he said. If she loved him—and she did—she should meet him halfway. What did it cost her to agree to stay in town a few nights? Nothing but a little gas driving back and forth.

"Okay, but only on one condition."

"Name it."

"We stop for a turtle sundae and I can get the biggest one in the shop."

"Done."

"I'll get some clothes." She beckoned for him to follow her to the bedroom where she tossed items from her dresser and closet into a backpack. "I'll take enough for three days. I hope we find Glenn by then and locate the core group associated with him."

"Three days? You think you can do it that quickly?"

"I'm going to try. If I run out of clothes, I can wash them or come back for more." She zipped the backpack. "You realize I'll need to come check on things here and make sure the cabins are all right. I've got maintenance on the roofs happening on some of the cabins. I'll need to oversee that and pay the contractor. The world doesn't stop because two guys are after me, Jon. I can't walk away from the business here."

"Maybe you should give it to Sarah."

His words hit hard, and she set the backpack on the floor. "Just because I talked to her today doesn't mean I want her heavily intertwined in my life. I'd have to teach her this business from the ground up. That would take months. I'd need to live here with her and show her how everything works."

"A temporary situation."

"One I'm not ready for. At least not yet." She tossed in her sound machine, then grabbed the handle of the backpack and went to the door.

He stepped out to block her path. "Don't be upset with me, love. This is for your own good. If you didn't see how much she regrets what she did, then you're blind."

She fisted her hands. "You want her around our daughter?"

He flinched and shook his head. "I don't think she would do it again."

"I didn't think she'd do it in the first place! But we nearly lost Kylie because of my sister. And that also meant you nearly died. I won't be quick to forgive and forget. The ripples from her actions are still ongoing. Glenn's buddies are after me because of her. Her plot enveloped us all in a whirlpool of danger and betrayal that is still unresolved."

He reached toward her, and she took a step back. "Maybe I should just stay here."

"Don't, love." His soulful eyes pleaded with her for understanding. "You're right. We can't trust her yet. But I have to admit the way she looked at you tore at my heart."

"When?"

"In your old bedroom. She fought tears the whole time. Being back at the cabin brought back a lot of feelings for her. If she could go back and change what she did, I think she would."

"Well, she can't!" Annie stepped around him and marched down the hall.

Thunder rumbled in the distance. They needed to get to the Blue Bonnet before the storm hit.

She'd give anything if she could erase what Sarah had done, but it was still too fresh.

/ / /

The sea of green trees passed quickly by the window as Annie drove her Volkswagen truck toward Baraga. First thing this morning she'd gotten a tip via a text from Shainya that Joel West was hiding out in a cabin outside the city limits. Annie had called Mason, and he'd told her to call for backup if she found him. Annie planned to ask some questions while she waited for a deputy.

Jon consulted the map on his phone. "Take a right on Baraga Plains Road. It's about half a mile."

Her thoughts ran with possible scenarios. Would he come to the door without suspecting why they were there? He might not even be involved, and this would be a wild-goose chase. Or would West face them down with a gun?

"You're quiet this morning," Jon said.

"I want answers, and I'm afraid West isn't going to cough them up when we find him. If we find him. He could have skated out by the time we get there."

He put down his phone. "Or he may spill everything when you put the pressure on him. Where's your usual optimism? You've got this, Annie."

"Oh, so now you have confidence in me when last night you wanted me to hide and wait?"

"I never said to do that!"

She chuckled. "Got you. I'm just a little discouraged today. We've been following Sean's trail for over a month. For a while we thought we had him pegged. Buried and forgotten. Now it appears much of what's going on in the area swirls around him and his influence. I'm not sure what we'll uncover next or how many layers we're going to find."

"Sarah's memories really threw you yesterday."

"Yeah. I don't like remembering that time, and here I am digging deeper into events that I should have forgotten by now."

"It made you strong, love. Stronger than any other person I know. You'll get to the bottom of it." He pointed. "Whoa, I about let you miss it. It's this house."

She braked in front of a narrow drive that backed into a thickly wooded forest. Tall weeds poked through the gravel, and branches nearly covered the opening in some places. "Doesn't look like anyone is living here."

"He might have just arrived when he fled his house and business. In fact, what if we park out here along the road and walk back? He might have done the same so no one knows he's there."

"Not a bad idea." She pulled onto the shoulder of the road and shut off the engine. "Let's circle around back and try not to be seen."

A flock of birds took flight when she stepped into the ditch by the shoulder and entered the forest. There was no fencing around the property, and the trees grew so closely together here it was easy to get disoriented. She stopped a few times and figured out where they were going.

Jon trod a few feet to her right, and he gestured to her. "I hear music," he whispered.

She heard it now too. Johnny Cash crooned "Sunday Morning Coming Down," and the music came from behind the house. Trying not to snap any twigs under her feet, she veered away from the house and moved past it to stand in the woods thirty yards from the backyard.

A rickety deck clung to the back of the cabin, and a rusty

metal yard chair held a man in his late twenties. He had a full beard and wore a denim shirt and jeans in spite of the heat and humidity of the day. The bag on the deck next to him was from McDonald's, and he popped the last bite into his mouth. Once he swallowed, he belted out the words of the song blasting out of his phone.

Time to move. She texted Mason first, then while West's voice helped drown out the sound of their movements, she and Jon rushed from the shelter of the woods and got to the broken-down steps before he realized they were there. The song ended, and he reached behind him.

Annie whipped out her gun. "Freeze! I'm park service law enforcement, and I have a few questions for you. No hasty moves. Stand up with your hands in the air."

He complied, and Annie nodded for Jon to disarm him. Jon pulled a revolver from a holster behind him and stepped back.

"What do you want?" His tone was mild in spite of his gruff appearance. Intelligent hazel eyes studied her. "Do I know you?"

"I don't think we formally met on the catamaran you boarded Thursday night."

His eyes widened. "You're the ranger?" His gaze darted away, and he took a step back.

He'd just admitted they were looking for her. She motioned to the chair. "Have a seat. I want some information. How well do you know Glenn Hussert?"

He settled in the chair and propped one boot on the other knee. "Glenn and me go way back. We're cousins."

"Hunting buddies?"

"Sure, we go out sometimes. With a hunting license, of course."

"You have any other friends who join you?"

"Sometimes." His cautious tone told her he wasn't sure where this was leading.

"Sean Johnson?"

"Not since he's dead." He snickered as if he'd made a great joke.

Annie didn't smile. "Did Sean come with you a lot?"

"Some. Not every time."

"What was your usual quarry?"

"Deer, moose, squirrel, rabbit. You name it, we took it and ate it."

Could they have been hunting campers? They'd suspected something heinous was going on for some weeks, but they had no proof. Maybe these guys were out for a little "fun" and chased lone hikers, but did they do something more than that?

"You have any records of the illegal moose hunts?"

"They got seized when I was arrested for it. Never returned them." He yawned. "If that's all you got, I'd like you to leave. This amounts to police harassment since I've done nothing."

The faint sound of a siren wafted through the trees around the place. He must have realized what she planned because he leaped from his chair and dove off the edge of the deck.

She brought her gun up and yelled, "Freeze!" The man ran like the wind, and she went after him, but he disappeared into the trees. She and Jon split to search for him, but he was gone, leaving only the shivering of leaves in his wake.

TWENTY

AFTER A QUICK LUNCH AT THE SUOMI, JON WATCHED Annie go into the jail to consult with Mason about what they'd learned from Joel West. Jon wandered across the street to a park bench and sat down. Sparrows flocked around his feet in search of scraps, but he had nothing to give them. The aroma of flowers hanging from baskets on the lampposts mingled with the freshness of the air after the storm last night.

He pulled out his phone and contemplated playing *Pokémon Go* so he had something to trade with Kylie when she got home, but he wasn't in the mood. His thoughts swirled with plans for the future.

His decision about his future continued to nag at him. Mike wouldn't wait much longer.

His phone vibrated with a text from Henry, and Jon blinked at the unexpected message of *It's done*. Already? Henry had just started yesterday morning. He must have worked long hours yesterday.

He jumped to his feet and hurried down Houghton Street to Jack Pine Lane and turned toward the glimpse of blue lake. When he opened the door to Jack Pine Jewels, Henry looked up from behind the counter and smiled. Dark rings rimmed his brown eyes, and his white hair was mussed as if he hadn't combed it this morning.

"Did you even sleep last night?" Jon asked when he reached the display case.

Henry glanced at his watch, an old Seiko. "Naw. I was too excited about the way the ring took shape. It is even more beautiful than I'd hoped. See what you think." He reached into the safe and retrieved the velvet box.

Jon took it and lifted the lid. His breath caught as sunlight caught the faceted diamonds and sapphires. The heart shape perfectly expressed how he felt about Annie. The matching wedding ring curved into the shape and snugged against the gold.

"I've never seen a more beautiful ring." He managed to take his eyes off it long enough to reach out and shake Henry's hand. "I can't thank you enough. I never expected it to be finished so quickly."

Henry gave a happy sigh. "I was inspired. Let me know how that proposal goes, eh. Pictures would be appreciated."

"You bet. How much do I owe you?"

Henry moved to the register and named the price, which was worth every penny. Jon whipped out his debit card and paid for it, then thanked the jeweler again. He stopped in a convenience store and grabbed a cherry Popsicle before he wandered down to the water. He sat on a boulder overlooking Lake Superior and ate his frozen treat.

Gulls landed nearby and he told the closest one, "You wouldn't like this." Its black eyes disagreed with his statement.

How should this proposal go down? Over a romantic dinner? A walk along the water at dusk? What were some of their favorite things to do over the years? Surfing had been at the top of the list when they were younger, but they hadn't had time to go much this summer. Annie was in her element out on a boat, but that might be an awkward place to get down on one knee.

He stared out over the Big Sea Water. Lake Superior had dominated their lives in so many ways. It would be appropriate to have it as a backdrop. He'd first kissed her on its shores, and much later Kylie had been conceived within hearing of the lake's waves.

He opened the box again and stared at the ring. He'd loved Annie for so long, and it seemed a dream that they were finally going to start their lives together. The ring couldn't be on her finger too soon for him.

But when and where? His gaze went out over the water again. Maybe keeping it simple would be best.

Pictures. He'd seen pictures of proposals on social media, but how did someone go about doing that when you wanted the moment to be in private? What if he set up a hidden camera and recorded a video? He could have still photos lifted from it. That would work.

A smile curved his lips as he anticipated her reaction when she saw the ring. Would she be willing to get married quickly or would she want time to plan something fancier? Her wedding to Nate had been hasty. Jon wanted her to have whatever she wanted, but he hoped she'd be as eager to be with him as he was to be with her.

Tomorrow would be epic.

/ / /

Mason blew out a breath and leaned back in his chair. "So you're saying you think Sean and his father had something to do with

Sarah's abduction? That's a stretch, Annie. He would have been, what—ten?"

"Probably about that. But he would have likely been doing only what his father asked him to do. It shows what the family was capable of though. I'd like to talk to Mort Jones."

"He sure slipped under our radar in Sean's investigation. That name change was fifty years ago. Not sure what you think you'll get from Mort since he hasn't had contact with them in decades. And he has Alzheimer's."

"Maybe he has good days and bad days. I could ask the staff at the memory center to call if he seems coherent."

"You can try." Mason reached for the phone and placed a call.

Annie listened to his request about Mort, but it was clear the man likely couldn't tell them much. Even if Sean's uncle came around enough to question, there was no guarantee he knew anything about his sister's abduction of five-year-old Sarah. Maybe all that information had died with Becky and Sean. Was Annie even on the right track? Proving Sean and his father were involved in the abduction didn't help their investigation of what was going on here now.

Deja poked her head into the office, but she paused when she saw Mason on the phone. Annie gestured for her to join them, and she came into the room.

When Mason hung up, Deja didn't wait for permission to speak. "We have another missing tourist, Sheriff. A woman by the name of Ella Anderson. She disappeared in the Kitchigami Wilderness three days ago."

Annie's jurisdiction. "Last seen?" She took out a notepad to jot down details.

"She rented a kayak on Monday here in town and left the Kitchigami Wilderness Tract boat launch. Her brother said she called in on Tuesday and Wednesday mornings, but he never heard from her after that. He tried to call several times."

"Can we get the last ping from her phone?"

Mason reached for his phone. "I'll get that started."

Annie chewed the tip of her pencil. "Did her brother say what her destination was with the kayak?"

"She was going to try to paddle out to that little spit of land near Tremolo Island. It's uninhabited, but she wanted to spend Wednesday night there and paddle back on Thursday. But she never checked in."

"No cell service out there," Annie told her.

"No, so he didn't worry at first. He thought maybe she decided to stay an extra day, but when she didn't get home by nine this morning, he got worried. She was supposed to help prep for a wedding anniversary party for their parents tonight. The cake was ready an hour ago, and she didn't show to pick it up."

This sounded ominous. "You have a picture? Have we found her vehicle yet?"

Deja handed over a picture of a smiling blonde with large, dark eyes. Young, too, late teens most likely. "Her car is in the lot by the boat launch into Superior. No sign that anyone has tampered with it. And of course, no one has seen her since she left on her kayak Monday."

Annie rose. "I'll go out and see what I can discover."

Mason hung up the phone. "The process to get the phone records is started. The nurse at the memory care unit said Mort doesn't have many good days anymore, but they happen when least expected and don't last long. She suggested you stop in every morning for a while. The clouds in his mind are more likely to part for a few minutes then."

"I'll try that. Did you talk to the detective in Minnesota, put in a good word for Jon?"

Mason nodded. "He wasn't ready to back off Jon, but he was impressed that Jon asked him to look into the patient who died. I think Jon will be okay when this is all over."

"If only he'd get his investment back, but I think that's a lost cause."

"Yeah, the detective said the other doctors were splintering, and he expected the practice to file for bankruptcy. Sorry, Annie."

"It's okay. We'll make it." She thanked Mason and exited the building, then glanced around for Jon. She didn't see him at first until she caught sight of him walking her way from the north. He'd probably been on the beach. She lifted a hand in greeting and headed to meet him.

With the wind in his hair, he looked happy and carefree. She stepped into his embrace, and he kissed her as if he'd missed her in the two hours she'd been gone.

He pulled away with a reluctant smile. "All done with Mason?"

"Yes, and there's news from Minnesota." She told him what Mason had said. "But you'll figure out what you want to do. We'll be okay."

His green eyes flickered, but Jon managed a smile. "I have you and Kylie. That's all I need."

"You're right." She kissed him. "We also have a missing kayaker. I need to head out to the boat launch and have a look around. We might need to take the boat out and see if we can find her. I pray she hasn't overturned out there." That was always a worry in the lake's cold water. Hypothermia could set in very quickly.

"Want to go now?"

"Yes. I'll drive in case we find her kayak." She led the way to her parked truck. "You know, I never heard the name of the woman Max found on Tremolo. What if it's the same woman?"

"Was she heading there?"

Annie opened her door and got in as he went around to the passenger side. "She was going that direction to camp at a small island, but a current could have sent her on past and over to Tremolo." She handed him her phone. "Would you call Max and ask the woman's name?"

"Sure."

She drove down Houghton Street and out of town as he placed the call and left a message. "No answer?"

"Nope."

"Hopefully he'll call back right away." She drove out to the Kitchigami Wilderness Tract and parked beside the woman's pickup, a ten-year-old blue Dodge. "That's her vehicle."

The truck was unlocked, and Annie checked the registration. Ella was eighteen, nearly nineteen. A quick search of the truck and the surrounding area didn't turn up any evidence. Not that Annie had expected any. She retrieved the keys to the park boat from inside her office and headed for the dock.

Before they got out of cell range, she called the hospital where Max's men had taken the woman and asked if they had a patient by the name of Ella Anderson. They had no record of her, so Max must have found a different woman.

Annie feared the worst for Ella as she and Jon boarded the boat and headed out into the lake. The storm last night had been fierce, and if the Anderson woman had been in the kayak coming back this way, she could have drowned.

TWENTY-ONE

THE BRISK WIND LIFTED ANNIE'S HAIR AND BLEW IT
into her eyes. She steered the boat through the waves left over
from last night's storm and squinted at the light bouncing off
the water.

She reached into a storage bin and extracted binoculars that
she handed to Jon. "See if anything catches your eye out there."

He scanned the horizon. The uninhabited bit of land Ella
had been heading for was just ahead and to the west of Tremolo
Island.

She pointed it out when it first came into view. "See if you
spot a kayak or any bright clothing on the beach. It's a rough
landing spot without much sand to pull up on."

He nodded but remained silent as they approached the area.
She didn't see anything out of the ordinary with the naked eye
either. She cut the engine and moved to drop anchor. "I need to
go ashore and see if there's any sign she was out here. An old fire,
footprints, anything."

"If she was here, last night's storm would have washed away
a lot of the tracks."

"I know, but just in case she's still there, I need to search." She threw out the inflatable raft and got it ready. When it was fully inflated, she dropped it overboard by the ladder and descended.

When Jon started after her, she held up her hand. "No, I can do this alone. It won't take long. The place is tiny. It's a lousy spot to camp, and I'm not sure why she chose it. Not much cover from the wind, and there isn't even much firewood."

She saw the objection gathering in his eyes and pushed off from the boat before he could try to change her mind. He needed to get over his constant worry about her. Her job was never going to be behind a desk where she was completely safe. But even then, was anyone completely safe? A roof could cave in while she sat at a computer. A tornado could lift her right out of her chair. Life would never be safe. It wasn't meant to be.

Her arms ached from fighting the waves when the raft bumped the rocks on the sliver of beach. A gull squawked at her when she nearly stepped on it as she jumped out and pulled the raft ashore. Once it was secured, she scoured the area for any proof Ella had made it here.

She found evidence of a fire in the middle of the tiny island, but it was impossible to tell how long ago it had been lit. A couple of beverage bottles lay strewn nearby, one a soft drink and the other water. She found so sign of a kayak being dragged ashore, but last night's storm would have washed away the disrupted sand.

If Ella had ever been here, she'd left no sign of her presence.

Annie decided to circle the island as close to the water as possible in case the current had brought something ashore. She picked her way through the rocks and sparse vegetation. On the east side of the island, she spied a small glint of something gold in the weeds. She reached into them and picked up a necklace with a small, round charm dangling on it with the engraved letters *EA*.

Ella Anderson?

Annie's gut clenched at the possibility that she might have to tell Ella's brother she was never coming home. Annie knew all too well how hard news like that hit. Her gaze wandered over the rolling waves to glimpse the Tremolo Island dock in the distance. A tiny figure sat on the side with her feet dangling.

Sarah.

How did Sarah stand going out there where her life had changed forever? Annie fought with the fear and terror every time she went to the island.

Fear.

She'd just been condemning Jon for his constant worry and fear for her when she was neck-deep in it herself. All these years she'd let fear control her. When it came to her job, she charged in without worry, but when it came to her sister, she shut down in a quicksand of fear and doubt.

It was at the heart of her unforgiving attitude toward Sarah. Annie feared losing Kylie, and she feared trusting Sarah ever again. How could she ask Jon to let go of his fear when she hugged her own to her chest? But how did she get past it? How did anyone get past that lump in the throat and the pressure in the chest that fear brought?

She'd always believed in trusting God, but when it came to her giving up something she'd clung to for protection, she'd been unable to do it. Did God expect her never to have fear? She didn't think that was possible.

A verse in Psalms she'd learned as a child came to her.

"When I am afraid, I put my trust in you."

Not *if* but *when*. Everyone had fear. All her fears were grounded in the love she had for others. For Kylie, for Sarah, for her parents and Nate. Losing Nate and her parents had been horrible, and the experience had only reinforced her fears of losing others she loved. Especially Kylie.

But she had to turn from that fear and trust God to do what was best. If she kept up the walls of fear around her heart, she'd never get past living this way. Of being afraid every second her daughter was away from her. These past few days had left her sleeping poorly and waiting for every call from Kylie or Bree.

Her gaze lingered on her sister's distant figure. She had to start by forgiving Sarah and giving her a second chance. Not with Kylie but with Annie's own heart.

It wouldn't be easy, but she had to try.

/ / /

On Sunday before church Jon had set up the movie camera in a nearby oak tree. His trial run of a minute was successful with a clear line of sight and intelligible audio, though there'd been a boat accident just west of the dock. He'd been afraid there would be activity out there and he'd have to scrap his plan, but the Coast Guard had towed the boat away and rescued the occupants. Everything was ready.

He and Annie had both changed clothes, and he'd grabbed the food from the fridge inside the cabin where he'd stashed it.

Everything was in order, except for his racing pulse.

Annie had covered the old table with a white cloth, and she decorated the top with wildflowers and real china.

He set the containers on a nearby bench seat. The aroma of fish and chips mingled with the fresh scent of Lake Superior. "I thought we'd have a Finnish feast today."

She looked beautiful in the patriotic sundress she'd changed into. Her hair was up with a few blonde tendrils touching her high cheekbones. She'd kicked off her shoes, and her nail polish matched her dress.

She peeked at the containers. "From the Suomi?"

"I talked them into cooking up some fried vendace and chunky fried potatoes. The Finnish version of fish and chips. We'll have squeaky cheese with thimbleberry jam for dessert."

"Perfect Independence Day food. We can see the fireworks from here later." She nodded toward the house. "It looks nearly finished. What has to be done before you can move in? Or is your dad going to move in?"

"He and Martha are going to move in. I could live with them, but that feels awkward. I'll need to find another place to live."

Should they eat first, or should he end this torture of waiting to pop the question?

If he proposed now, the food would be cold. He grabbed the white containers and opened the fish. "I guess we'd better eat while it's hot."

He put generous servings on both plates, then set bottles of tartar sauce and ketchup closer to her chair as she moved around the end table to have a seat. She'd dropped into place before he had a chance to pull her chair out for her. He was already failing at the romantic gestures.

A fish splashed out in the lake, and the sounds of laughter mingled with blaring music from a passing boat drifted toward them on the gentle breeze. A few clouds floated across the blue sky above them and added to the perfection of the day.

Annie squeezed tartar sauce and ketchup onto her plate. "I'm starving."

"Me too." And the sooner they ate, the sooner he could get that ring on her finger. He took a bite of fish. "Wow, that's good. Did you try it?"

"The Suomi makes the best fried fish ever. How are you eating it though?"

"I twisted a few arms and provided the gluten-free flour. They used fresh oil so it wasn't contaminated. Molly pulled a few strings for me as soon as I started eating at the Suomi, and I promised her a free appointment for her knee problem."

"Molly knows how to keep her customers happy." Her gaze wandered to the container of squeaky cheese and the jar of thimbleberry jam from The Jampot in Eagle Harbor. "Would it be crass to have dessert before I'm done with the meal?"

"I won't judge you. I'm eyeing it as well."

He pushed the food closer to her, and she scooped a spoonful of jam onto her plate before dipping a piece of cheese in it. She closed her eyes and moaned. "Heavenly. It's been ages since I've had it this way."

They demolished lunch, and he had some squeaky cheese and jam himself. "You can have the last piece."

She leaned back and shook her head. "I'm stuffed. It's all yours."

He ate the last of it just to get the food out of the way so he could proceed to the real reason they were out here. When Annie got a text, he pulled out his phone as well. His camera control app was already open, so he discreetly clicked on the video. Now for her to finish what she was doing, and it was go time.

She made a huffing sound. "Mason found the boat that boarded us the other night. It had been stolen and was found this morning. Someone set it afire and it sank. No prints off that thing."

"These people mean business. Mason needs to up his manpower and find them."

"He's already hired a new deputy and is working hard at it." She set her phone down. "There's nothing we can do right now. I don't want to go to the nursing home to see Mort today in case the staff is having special events. Let's enjoy our day and hit it again tomorrow."

He fingered the ring box in his pocket and rose to hold out his hand to her. Her brows lifted, but she took his hand to rise from her chair. "Are we going somewhere?"

The table and chairs were in the way of the camera, so he led her closer to shore and facing the camera slightly. This staging for pictures was getting old. Maybe he shouldn't have monkeyed with it.

His mouth was dry, and he swallowed before dropping to one knee. Somehow the ring box was in his hand and open. He held it out wordlessly at first, then gathered the words he'd thought about saying. "Annie, when I first met you, I was mesmerized by your beauty. That same day, we were in town for ice cream, and you saw a little girl crying on the sidewalk. You ran over to see what was wrong, and she'd gotten lost. By the time we found her house, you'd given her your ice cream and asked me to give her the Snickers bar in my pocket. Remember that?"

She gave a wordless nod, so he was encouraged to continue.

He lifted the ring box a little higher. "I think you are the most amazing person I've ever met. Smart, determined, kind, and compassionate." Her eyes filled with tears, and she put her hand to her mouth, but she still hadn't said a word. "You're a wonderful mother and the best companion on life's adventures I could ever hope to have. I threw away a chance with you once, and I don't ever want to live without you. I know I don't deserve you, but I love you with everything in me. Will you marry me, Annie?"

She slipped the ring on her finger, then swiped the moisture from her cheeks and threw herself toward him. He was on his way to his feet to catch her when she barreled into his chest. The force of her impact pushed him back, and he clutched her to keep her from falling, but they were too close to the edge of the dock.

He teetered on the edge for a few heart-stopping seconds before they both tumbled into the cold water. The shock of the frigid waves drove everything else he wanted to say out of his head.

He pushed toward the surface with one foot and came up to see her laughing and flinging her wet hair out of her face.

She threw her arms around his neck. "I think you need me to marry you to keep you in line."

The press of her warm lips against his made him forget about the cold water trying to drag them down.

When she pulled away, lights danced in her blue eyes. "That's a yes in case you weren't sure."

TWENTY-TWO

ANNIE COULDN'T TAKE HER EYES OFF THE MAGNIFICENT ring on her finger. She turned it this way and that in the sunlight streaming through the cabin's windows. Jon wanted her to look at the engagement video frames and pick out some pictures, but it was hard to take her attention off the beautiful promise on her finger.

Jon touched her chin with his fingers and gently turned her head. "Check out this one, Annie."

The smile in his voice touched her. He'd put so much thought into this. When he told her how he'd overnighted the ring and had this planned so meticulously, she realized how much he had wanted the day to be special for her. And it was.

She scooted her chair closer to his at the table, then tilted the screen so she could see better. The resolution was sharp and clear, much better than she'd been expecting. Tears flowed as she watched the video through to the end where she couldn't help but laugh at how ridiculous they appeared falling into the water.

Jon pulled the band from her hair to let down the wet locks. "I'm going to tell our kids you tried to drown me."

"'Kids'? You want more?" She tried to make the question sound casual, but her pulse sped at the thought of another baby.

"Of course. The sooner the better. Kylie needs a sibling."

"She has asked for one often." She turned her attention back to the laptop to avoid thinking about how much Nate had wanted another baby.

Jon's hand covered hers. "You okay? Your smile went away."

"Nate always wanted another baby," she blurted out.

The sparkle in his eyes faded, and she squeezed his hand. "That was a dumb thing to say."

His gaze lowered to their linked hands. "You loved him."

She leaned over and tipped his chin up so she could gaze in his eyes. "Yes, I loved Nate, but not like I love you. Like I've always loved you. You're the love of my life, Jon. It's amazing and wonderful we got a second chance. That doesn't often happen."

His smile came, but it was a little crooked. "I might need to hear you say that some even after we're married."

"I'll say it all the time."

"I messed up so much. I don't deserve a second chance, but I'm thankful you gave me one."

"Just remember that while I'll mention Nate sometimes, it doesn't mean you aren't first in my heart. You have always held that spot."

"I'll try to remember." He leaned over and kissed her. "I need to call Nate's parents and get that stupid lawsuit settled. Things have been so crazy I haven't done it."

"I've thought about it too. Maybe they've cooled off by now, and when they heard we have proof you're her father, they will realize the lawsuit is futile. Maybe we can do it tomorrow. I don't want any unpleasantness to spoil our day." She turned back to the computer. "Let's see what else we got."

"We can go through this frame by frame and grab some of the best ones for still photos," Jon said.

He advanced the video little by little, and they picked out eleven pictures as they evaluated expressions and stances. In the final few seconds of the clip, she caught a flash of something she didn't recognize in the water. It was red, which wasn't a normal color for fish.

She put her hand atop his. "Hang on. Can you blow that up?" She pointed out the red blob in the water behind them.

"Sure, hang on." He made a few keystrokes, and the picture expanded.

She leaned closer and pointed. "Move the screen to the left."

He complied and shook his head. "I can't make it out. Maybe it's something from the boat accident this morning."

She stood and moved toward the back door. "Let's go see."

They had taken off their shoes to let them dry, so she went down to the yard and walked straight in at the water's edge. The waves were shockingly cold when she waded into the current. The dock was to her right, and she stopped to orient herself to where she'd seen the bright color.

"I see it." Jon's head submerged, and his bare feet kicked up as he dove down. She barely breathed as she waited for him to surface.

A gull landed on the dock and then another. And another.

His head broke the surface of the water, and he gasped. "It's a woman. Get me a rope. There's one in the shed. Can't tell much yet, but you'd better call Mason."

"He won't want you to disturb the site. Come on out, and I'll call him." She hurried back to the kitchen to grab her phone.

A woman. Ella Anderson or someone else? She grabbed her phone and called Mason. She went back outside as it rang through.

"Annie?" Mason's voice held impatience, and she thought he might have been hoping for a day off too.

"Mason, we found a body off the dock at the Dunstan cabin. A woman."

"On my way. Don't touch anything."

The call ended. Like she'd touch it before he got there. Not when it was clear the poor woman was already gone. She dropped into a chair on the back deck to let the sun warm up her cold skin. They'd draped their towels from earlier across the chairs, and she held out one for Jon.

He shook the water from his hair and clothing and came toward her. He toweled off. "Mason on his way?"

"Yes. He'll bring a forensic team, so we need to stay away to prevent contaminating it any more." Her gaze lingered on the dinner table they'd left out. "We probably obscured some evidence already."

He squatted in front of her. "Not the way I hoped our day would go. I mean, you said yes, but I hate that we'll always remember this day attached to something so awful."

She leaned forward and cupped his face in her hands. "I love the way you care for other people. We'll never forget that proposal."

"When all the hoopla dies down, we need to talk about when and where."

"We will," she promised. "We will."

/ / /

Sarah hugged herself in the darkness of a thick grove of pines. The thin light of the moon did little to illuminate where she stood. She had taken the dog out to do his business, and the blackness of the night creeped her out. The heavy scent of pine added to her distress in some way she couldn't identify. Had there been the smell of pine trees when she was taken? Maybe coming to this island had been a mistake.

A branch snapped, and a man's voice floated through the trees. "The boss will be mad."

The gruff voice brought Sarah's head up. She couldn't see the man and didn't recognize the voice, but something about it lifted the hair on the back of her neck.

She sidled that way and peered through the spruce needles into a small clearing that let in the moonlight. The two men standing there were unfamiliar to her. The closest one wore a plaid shirt that stretched across his shoulders. A glint in the other one's hand appeared to be a gun.

"You think I care what that old gasbag has to say?" The gunman snarled. "And anyway, he's gone. He'll never know."

"She's protected."

"Says who? No one will know if we have a little fun."

"She'll tell."

"Not if she's never found. We can take a dinghy out and scuttle it. Everyone will think she and the pooch drowned. Come on, those fireworks got me fired up."

Sarah stifled a gasp and took a step back. *She and the pooch.* Were they talking about *her*?

"If you don't want to join in the fun, I'll go without you."

"Sounds like you've thought of everything. I'm in. The boss won't be back until tomorrow. We have the run of the place."

Where could she hide? And what about Scout? He was likely to give her away with a whine or a bark, but the thought of leaving him to the mercy of those men felt wrong. They might shoot him.

She backed away and glanced at the slight trail that led back to a cave she'd seen. Could she gather spruce branches and hide the opening? It might not even save her. Those men had likely worked here a long time and knew where to find all the nooks and crannies. But not trying wasn't an option.

Wait, maybe she could go to the big house. The housekeeper and butler were likely still there. She could hide in one of the closets. Maybe she could get a gun. They'd have the satellite phone too. They'd be able to call for help.

But Sarah wasn't sure how to get to the house with the men on the main path. She got so easily disoriented in these woods, especially at night. The cave would have to do until she was sure they were out of the way. Then she'd make a run for the big house.

She moved as quickly and quietly as she could, but it felt like every movement caused a small twig to snap. The noises sounded impossibly loud to her ears, but she hoped the men were making enough sound on their own to cover hers. Along the way she began to fill her arms with pine boughs. The groundskeepers had been working on trimming the past couple of days, and she had plenty of them by the time she reached the cave.

She shoved the dog inside, then knelt and backed in herself and laid out the boughs as she went. It was only three feet high, but it opened up and widened out the deeper in she went. The opening appeared mostly closed when she was done, but she could see glimmers of moonlight through it in places. That shouldn't matter though. It was completely dark inside, and the men couldn't see her.

Barely breathing, she waited with her hand on the dog's head. When his ears pricked and he gave a small whine, she shushed him. They must be out there. Was there anything in here she could use for a weapon? Since it was too dark inside the cave to see, she felt around with her hands, praying she wouldn't touch a snake or a spider. There was nothing that made her bite back a scream, but she found the right size rock to use as a weapon. She hefted it in her hand. Perfect.

Voices floated past the pine boughs. "She has to be around here somewhere."

"She probably took the dog out to pee. We could circle back to the cabin and wait for her."

"I think she overheard us and is hiding."

"What if she went to the big house?"

The leader's chuckle held a dark, mirthless note. "I hope not. We'd have to kill them all."

The other guy snorted. "And how would you cover that up?"

"I'd figure it out. Come on. Let's go to the cabin and wait."

The sound of their footfalls through the rocks came as a welcome relief, and Sarah let out the breath she was holding. She couldn't go to the big house without putting everyone else in danger. What was she supposed to do? Once daylight came, they'd see her makeshift hiding place with no trouble.

The boats.

The leader had mentioned scuttling one. What if she took it out herself while they were waiting at the cabin? The boathouse was off toward the big house. She should be able to sneak in there and get one out, then row for the mainland. It was her only hope.

TWENTY-THREE

ANNIE SWATTED A MOSQUITO AND RAN FOR JON'S CABIN
with him behind her. Her insect repellent must have worn off.
Tonight's fireworks had been spectacular and had lasted for an
hour. The pesky insects were making a feast of her skin.

She flicked on the light as she entered, and Jon shut the
door behind him. The place smelled of lumber and new paint. "I
should have checked on things at the marina today."

"Got a call from Michelle?" Jon asked.

"No, it's just that the Fourth is often hectic."

He crossed the kitchen and embraced her. "She would have
called if they needed you. It's after eleven. Are you tired? It's been
a crazy day." A lopsided smile lifted his lips, and he took her
hand, turning it so the ring caught the light. "I hope you're as
happy as me."

Her gaze lingered on the ring and the way the sapphires
nestled close to the diamonds. "Too happy to be tired."

The remaining items from their picnic were inside. Jon had
set up the table and chairs in the living room, and a red-and-
white cooler perched on the new granite counter in the kitchen.

Jon pulled her into an embrace and rested his chin on

top of her head. "If you're not tired, could we talk about the wedding?"

She hadn't had a moment to think about it with the discovery of the body. Mason would probably have more news tomorrow on the poor woman's identity, but she didn't expect him to find much forensics or DNA evidence. They'd both been suspicious the woman was associated with the boat accident. It was the likeliest explanation for how the body had ended up off the dock.

She pulled away and grabbed his hand to lead him to the chairs. "Let's sit and discuss it."

Instead of letting her move to another chair, Jon settled on one and pulled her onto his lap. "Stay close. I can tell what you're thinking by how you tense and move. If you plan to wallop me for my suggestions, I want a little head start."

She chuckled and settled against his broad chest. His hair and skin smelled of lake, underlaid with his cologne. "I will take all suggestions into consideration. This is your wedding too. And it's your first."

When he tensed, she realized how crass that sounded. She shouldn't have reminded him that she'd been married before. Not today, especially when she'd already unsettled him with a remark about Nate wanting more kids. She hadn't realized he was still a little uncertain of how much she loved him.

She straightened and turned to gaze into his eyes so he understood what this meant. "It's a dream come true to get to spend the rest of my life with you. My first wedding was a quick event, barely a blip on the pattern of life. This will be a ground-shaking celebration of what I've wanted since I was a teenager. I love you so much. Thank you for loving me. Thank you for so quickly picking up the reins of being Kylie's father. Not many men would have."

His pupils expanded, and he inhaled. "You don't know how much I needed to hear that right now, love." His gaze searched hers. "What would you say to a quick wedding? I don't want to wait any longer. I want us to be a family. I want to see you across the breakfast table every morning and pull you close every night in our bed. I can't wait to see both our names on a checking account and to plan a life together. We have so many decisions. Like where we will live and where I will work."

Her pulse rocketed up at his admissions. "I want that too. We don't need a big, fancy wedding, though I'd like our pastor to marry us. I don't want another justice-of-the-peace wedding."

"Neither do I. This is too important, and it's forever." Indecision lit his green eyes. "It's Sunday. How quickly could you be ready?"

"You mean, like this week?" She hadn't been expecting something this fast, but when she looked into his face and saw how much he wanted her, it weakened any qualms she had about what might seem to others as rushing into it.

"I'd marry you tonight if I could."

"We have to wait for Kylie to get back. She'll be home Thursday. How about the Saturday after your dad's wedding? I'd like our friends to have enough notice to come. People like Anu, Kade and Bree, your dad and Martha. Not many. Just those we love."

He nodded. "I admit I'd like it sooner, but I can wait thirteen days. Kylie would be upset if we went ahead without her. Think she'd be a flower girl?"

An image of their daughter dressed in pink and carrying roses lodged in her head. She wanted a perfect day so badly. "I'll start the search for a dress. If she wants to wear the dress, she'll do it."

"I've been thinking about the future with my job too. What do you think I should do? Let me lay out the options again. I could open a practice in Rock Harbor, but it will be tight financially for a few years. It will take everything I've got and then some to scrape together enough to open an office. The second option would be to work out of the hospital. It probably would cost much less. The third choice is to work for Mike at Houghton Orthopedics. I like him and I think we'd get along well. I'd have to be on call some, but that comes with the territory of an orthopedic surgeon."

There was a lot to consider. "The money isn't a big deal to me. Which option would give you more time with Kylie and me?"

He answered as if he'd thought it through. "If I open a practice here in Rock Harbor, I'll get called out for emergencies in the night. It might not be often, though, since it's a small community. And I could refer people to Houghton just like happens now. At the Houghton practice it would mostly be Mike and me rotating on calls, and there would be more accidents up there, especially with the college kids out skiing. Winters might be hectic."

"Let's stay here and give back to our community. I don't need a lot of money, Jon. I just need you."

He pulled her close for a kiss, and she knew it was the right decision.

/ / /

Sarah's heavy eyes finally closed for what seemed like only a few minutes, but when she popped them open, she realized dawn was nearly there. The light had that quality where the sun could begin to break over the eastern horizon at any minute.

And she was still trapped inside this cave. She leaped to her feet and listened. The birds were beginning to sing, which was another sure sign of impending daylight. There was no sound to indicate the men were lurking out there, so she cautiously moved the pine boughs out of the way. Once the top half were down, she poked her head out. Nothing stirred but wildlife. She removed the rest of the branches, then patted her thigh to call the dog to her and stepped out into the rocky area surrounded by forest.

She took a deep breath of fresh air to exhale the musty smell of the cave from her lungs. The boathouse was to her left, just before she would get to the big house. Were the men even now lying in wait? Her heart was trying to leap out of her chest, and she eased through the trees toward her destination. If only she could call for help, but she was on her own out here. Mason would come if he knew. Or Bree if she was nearby. But Sarah was going to have to save herself.

The dog padded along beside her, and she marveled at how quiet he'd been all night. It was almost as if he'd realized how frightened she was. And she was still more scared than she'd ever been in her life. Her imagination was able to fill in the gory details of what the men had planned for her, and she couldn't let them catch her.

The boathouse was only a stand of oak trees away now. She could see its outline through the leaves and brush. If she got away from this place, could she make it to safety? It would depend on the big lake. Some days it was placid and golden, and other days it raged like a wolf. She hadn't seen its temperament yet today.

The back of the green boathouse grew closer through the trees, and she paused to orient herself and check out the lay of the land. The edges of darkness had softened with the coming dawn, but no one was stirring on the grounds yet. The boathouse had a back door she spied from where she stood, and after a careful examination of the clearing, she made a break for it. The door was unlocked when she twisted the knob, and she practically fell into the darkness of the interior.

The dog whined and squirreled around her feet. "I'm okay," she whispered.

It reeked of motor oil and gasoline. After a few moments, her eyes adjusted to the darkness, and she spied several larger boats rocking in the waves. She didn't dare take one with a motor. The noise would be sure to attract attention. There was a rowboat in the corner, but it would be hard to maneuver out of the boathouse by herself. Two kayaks were hanging on the back wall. Maybe she could manage to get her and Scout to safety in it, though she wasn't the best at handling one of those.

It appeared to be her only option though. With effort she lifted down a kayak and carried it out the back door toward the water. The sound of the waves had dread clutching at her throat. The waves were much bigger than she'd hoped.

She glanced down at Scout. "Ready, boy?"

He gave a huff of approval and licked her hand. She set the boat in the water and lifted him into the front seat area, then waded in. The cold shock made her gasp, and she quickly climbed into her seat and grabbed the oar. She struggled to get the kayak turned around in the waves to face the mainland. This was not going to be easy.

She splashed cold water on her arms and legs as she rowed, but at least the kayak moved forward and not back to Tremolo Island. She made it past the dock and squinted. She was still too far to see the mainland, but her arms burned as she rowed with all her strength toward the sun peeking over the horizon. As the boat moved farther away, the waves turned to big rollers that picked them up and dropped them down the troughs of water. The dog hunkered in his seat and whined.

"It's okay, boy." But was it? Fear squeezed her in a vise, and she had a terrible feeling she'd jumped from the frying pan into the fire.

A huge wave soaked her with cold water and filled the seat around her. Were they sinking? Was it even possible to sink a kayak? She knew they could be overturned, but she hoped it would stay afloat.

She peered through the dim light. Was that an island or a spit of mainland ahead? Examining it, she decided it had to be that tiny island she could see from the dock. It could be a safe haven for them to rest. She aimed the bow of the kayak toward it and renewed her efforts to make headway in the huge waves. Her lungs burned, and her arms felt wooden by the time the hull of the kayak bumped sand. She could barely stand to stagger out of the boat to grasp the side with fingers numbed by the water.

She dragged the boat onto the shore, and the dog jumped out. She fell to her knees and embraced the golden's warm fur. They'd made it, but they were sitting ducks here. She had to gather enough strength to hide the kayak in case the men came out here searching for her.

It wouldn't take long for her theft of the kayak to be noticed. All she could do was pray Max sent someone out for her— someone who wasn't those two men.

TWENTY-FOUR

MORNING WAS GENERALLY BETTER WITH ELDERLY patients, but Jon thought it seemed a lost cause as he walked with Annie toward Mort Jones's room at Rolling Hills Adult Living Center. The walls of the memory-care unit held memorabilia from the forties and fifties like old signs and army uniforms from World War II and displays of kitchen items. An old red jukebox played an Elvis tune that would have had Bree, a rabid Elvis fan, singing along.

Even the scents seemed designed to enhance memory in the residents. He smelled evergreen and candy cane near an old-time Christmas scene and a hint of pumpkin pie. Much nicer than the stench of urine and feces he'd expected. This was a nice place, well-kept and clean.

A nurse directed them to a community room and told them Mort was putting a puzzle together. When they entered the room, a tiny white-haired lady rose and came toward them with a smile.

She took Annie's hand. "I knew you'd come to see me today. I told my roommate my daughter would be here any minute. I waited on breakfast for you, and I'm hungry. Let's eat."

Annie gave a helpless glance at Jon, and he nodded. "I'll talk to Mort," he said.

Annie didn't have a mean bone in her body, and he knew she couldn't resist the elderly woman's childlike trust. She went through the door with the old woman, and he glanced around the room. His gaze locked on a man who looked just like Sean's father. It had to be his brother. Mort Jones sat at a folding table by himself with puzzle pieces spread out on the surface. He stared blankly at the wall and not at the table. Not a good sign.

Jon approached and put his hand on the man's frail shoulder. "Mind if I join you?"

Mort didn't respond, so Jon pulled out a chair and sat across from him so he could gauge his expressions. "You're Mort Jones, aren't you? I'm friends with your nephew, Sean, and I knew your brother."

"He never talks," a male voice said behind Jon.

Jon turned around to see a portly guy in his eighties. The guy's wispy white hair covered a bit of his scalp, but his beard was lush and full. His hazel eyes were alert and clear, at least for now. Jon had hoped to find Mort in a similar state, but it hadn't panned out.

The man folded his arms across his sizable belly. "In the three years I've been here, I've never heard old Mort say anything. Of course, he didn't say a whole lot before he got the dementia."

"You knew him before?"

"Sure did. Worked for him. I was the crew boss on one of his construction crews. Collected a paycheck from Mort for over forty years."

Jon gestured to the third seat. "Would you mind answering some questions?"

"I'd like to do anything other than stare at four walls and wonder how long it will be today before I forget my name." The man went around the table and pulled out a chair. The loud squeak it made on the floor made everyone jump except Mort. "Name's Abraham. I don't like to be called Abe."

Jon put a puzzle piece onto a matching one to see if it would engage Mort. No response. "So, Abraham, I assume you knew Mort's brother and nephew?"

"Clive and Sean. Two peas in a pod for sure. Both tricksters. Couldn't trust either one not to play a mean joke on you. Oh, they fooled lots of people, but not me. I saw them pull too many cruel stunts."

"What kind of cruel stunts?"

"Once Sean gave me a sandwich with crude oil mixed in with peanut butter. Took one bite and spit it out. That kind of thing isn't funny."

"No, it's not," Jon agreed. "Did you ever meet Clive's sister?"

Abraham scratched his beard. "What was her name? Brenda, Barbara . . ."

"Becky," Jon said. "Becky Johnson. She was the baby. Twenty years younger than Clive."

"Becky, yeah, that was her. Standoffish. My son asked her out once, but she shot him down. Clive and Sean usually went to her place. She hated Rock Harbor and wouldn't come visit them much after she became a mother."

That was the time period that interested Jon. "You ever meet the little girl?"

Abraham's big head swung side to side. "Nope. She showed up once before she became a mom, and that was the only time I laid eyes on her for the next twenty years or so. Can't remember exactly. I think that little girl being snatched upset her. She was crying and carrying on that weekend. Never knew what it was about, but Sean told her to leave and get out of town. Big blowup, but I never did figure out what it was about."

Jon had a suspicion Becky had admitted taking Sarah, and Sean and his dad helped her get out of town undetected. Given Sean's mean streak, Jon was beginning to believe Clive and his son helped stage the abduction. It all made hideous sense.

He felt Annie's presence before he saw her. Her hands rested on his shoulders, and he tipped his head back to smile up at her. "Just having a nice talk with a longtime friend of Mort's."

Her blue eyes brightened. "I can't wait to hear all about it." She squatted beside Mort. "Hello, Mr. Jones. I'm Annie. Annie Pederson. I knew your nephew, Sean. Did he or your brother ever mention me?"

Mort had been staring blankly, but he lowered his gaze to settle on Annie's face. "You're the other girl. The one Becky left behind."

Every line of Annie's body tensed. "That's right," she said in a soft, soothing voice.

"I told Sean it was wrong to help Becky with that whole thing. Those boys always were boneheads." He touched Annie's cheek with a crooked index finger. "Pretty girl, pretty girl, all the pretty girls. She wanted a pretty girl."

Annie tried to ask more questions, but he continued to babble about pretty girls and soon lapsed into silence again. While they didn't know the details, it was clear Sean and Clive had been involved in Sarah's abduction.

/ / /

"At least now we know for sure Sean helped his aunt." Hand in hand with Annie, Jon walked toward Lake Superior.

"I guess it doesn't matter, not really. We can't change the past." She shaded her eyes with her hand and pointed. "I think the building is this way."

Jon nodded. They'd stopped to show Annie's ring to Anu, and she mentioned a place to lease for Jon's practice. So they'd walked down to see it and meet with the Realtor Anu had called.

Storm clouds built in the western sky, and the scent of ozone from the flickers of lightning mingled with the flowers blooming in the tree lawn. "We've got waves ahead of the storm," he said. "If this place works out, I'll be able to hear the water."

"I thought you might like that. Anu said it was almost at the end of the street here, just after the jeweler's." Annie's eyes went wide. "Can we stop and show Henry the ring on my finger?"

It touched Jon to see how much the ring meant to her. "You bet. He'll be so happy you love it, and it will take a few minutes for the leasing agent to get here."

It was after nine, so they were open. He held the door for her, and they stepped inside. Henry was putting pieces into the display case, and he straightened when he saw them.

His smile broke out, and his gaze darted to the hand she held out in front of her. "Ah, yous said yes," he said in his heavy Yooper accent. He wiped his hands on his black apron and came around the end of the display.

"The beautiful ring cinched it," she said. "I can't believe you created it so quickly. And it's such a perfect design."

"Yous delight makes this old man very happy. When is the exciting day?"

"Saturday, July seventeenth," they said in unison.

"Less than two weeks," Annie added.

"No wonder he wanted it done quickly. Now yous can find something to complement the blue in your eyes and in the ring."

"I'd love a goldfinch necklace." Annie told him about how God had sent a goldfinch to comfort Kylie as she was waiting for rescue from the cliff's edge. And how Jon had saved her knowing it might cost his own life.

"Yous got a good man there."

Annie's expression turned speculative. "Did you ever hear Sean and Joel talk about hunting?"

Jon hid a grin. He should have known Annie would take the opportunity to quiz Henry herself.

Henry went back behind the display case. "Me and Sean used to play poker together, and he mentioned it. Those boys were crazy about hunting and fishing like three quarters of the men in the U.P."

"There have been several deaths of missing hikers in the past few months, maybe longer. And we've had reports of men chasing some women hikers, almost as if they were using them for a hunting sport. My gut says they might be related. One of the women who was chased was Joel's ex-girlfriend, so that brings it in a little closer. You ever overhear anything that sounded off?"

Henry ran a hand through his white hair. "That's a terrible thing to think about. I haven't been around Joel since he was in his late teens and early twenties. There was nothing like that back then, and nothing Sean said that would make me think he was that kind of man."

Henry was in a position to overhear things. Maybe they should talk to all the shop owners, especially the outfitters. "You hear any chatter around town about something like that?" Jon asked.

"I've heard men talking about their shoots. Nothing that stood out as strange." He pulled at his ear. "Though now that I think about it, two guys were standing outside smoking a couple of weeks ago. It was a nice day, and I had the windows open instead of the air on. I only recognized one of them. Eric Bell. You might not know him."

"We know the name," Annie said in an eager voice. "What did you hear?"

"Eric said something about the quarry that got away. The word *quarry* struck me as odd. Most men would have said *deer* or *moose* or whatever they were hunting."

A shudder ran down Jon's back. That word sat wrong with him too.

"Eric is already on our radar. I'll tell Mason. Thanks, Henry." Annie touched her ring. "And thanks so much for this."

"I enjoyed doing it, Annie." He turned to grab another box of jewelry and went back to work.

When Jon and Annie stepped back into the sunshine, he took her hand. His assumptions about their morning might need to be reassessed. "You still want to go look at property with me, or do you need to talk to Mason?"

She glanced at her watch. "Let's go. It will give Mason time to drink all his horrible coffee, and there won't be any left to offer to me."

Jon chuckled. "We can stop at the coffee shop and get you some real stuff so your hands are full."

"Not a bad idea."

They walked on down toward the water. The roar of the growing waves increased, and whitecaps threw themselves against the rocky shoreline. There wasn't much of a beach at the end of the street with the incoming storm, just a thin layer of sand.

Jon gestured to a freshly painted storefront. "This must be it."

"And there's Fiona." Annie waved at the stocky brunette unlocking the door to the building.

Jon hadn't met Fiona Edwards, but she owned several properties in the downtown area. She'd been the driving force behind the revitalization of the Victorian architecture. In her forties with carefree curly hair and no makeup, she didn't strike him as a real-estate mogul but as a soccer mom.

"Jon Dunstan." They shook hands, and he liked her easy smile and firm grip.

"I've heard a lot about you from my dad, Ben Eckright."

That raised her higher on his list too. "Your dad is a gem."

"He is," she agreed. "Come on in, and I'll tell you about the place."

Within minutes he knew the place was perfect. There was a great area for a waiting room and four exam rooms as well as an office and multiple places for supplies. Patients would have to get X-rays and tests at the hospital, but they were used to that aspect of small-town life. And because Rock Harbor needed an orthopedist, she pitched him a price half of what he thought he'd have to pay.

It would all work out.

TWENTY-FIVE

QUARRY. THE WOMEN WHO HAD SURVIVED MEN CHASing them had mentioned that word, and Annie shuddered every time she heard it. It brought back the memory of Sean calling the girls he'd murdered "quarry." Was he the mastermind behind everything? He was dead and useless to them for information.

Mason's coffeepot was blessedly empty, but Annie carted in a cup of coffee from Metro Espresso to be on the safe side. She settled in a chair and pointed the other chair out to Jon as they waited for Mason to get off the phone. Jon had his phone out with his weather app on the screen. Rain lashed the window behind Mason's desk, and the building shook with thunder.

Mason ended the call. "We have an ID on the body you found yesterday. It's Ella Anderson."

Annie sagged against the seat back. "Oh no. Cause of death?"

"Pending an official autopsy, it appears to be a gunshot wound to the back of the head. Almost execution style." He rubbed his forehead. "I have to notify her family. She was only eighteen."

"The Coast Guard should know who owned the boat that crashed offshore of my dad's cabin," Jon said.

Mason nodded. "It belonged to Eric Bell."

Annie absorbed the news. They'd suspected him all along. "Saturday was Ella's parents' wedding anniversary. It won't be a day they like to remember now."

"No."

"How many dead tourists does this make?"

He leaned back in his chair. "Depends on how you look at it. I suspect Sophie Smith and Penelope Day could have been the first victims."

She absorbed the horror of that scenario. "This spans nearly a decade then, and we have a serial killer or group."

He nodded. "Those two plus Christopher Willis and Grace Mitchell, though Grace died in that ATV accident. I count her because of what she told Michelle about being chased. In addition to that, we have two confirmed survivors who were chased: Shainya Blackburn and Eddie Poole. And now Ella Anderson."

"So we potentially have five victims and several who escaped the same fate. Plus there was the girl who was never found after the moose hunt. Who knows how far back this could reach. We likely have more victims."

"Appears that way."

She took a sip of her coffee. "Listen, I talked to Henry Drood this morning, and he had something interesting to say about Eric Bell." As she told Mason about the word *quarry* he'd used, she twisted the still unfamiliar ring on her hand.

Mason's gaze locked on the ring, but he didn't mention it. "That's worth looking into. In spite of everything we've seen, I haven't wanted to believe we could have a hunting group out there killing hikers and transients. It's too horrific. And to think it could be occurring in my jurisdiction—" He broke off and shook his head. "I'd hate to think any of my neighbors had such a dark side."

"The evidence is mounting."

"At first I thought there might be something connecting the hikers. They wandered onto private property and were chased off by the owners. This is all connected."

"Any news about Glenn? He's been missing nearly a week. Is he even still alive?"

"Nothing new about him. His wife is getting frantic."

In spite of what he'd done, Candace seemed to be sticking with her husband. Annie couldn't fault her sense of loyalty, but it was misplaced with a man like Glenn.

Mason pointed a pencil at her hand. "I see you're sporting an engagement ring today. Looks like congratulations are in order for the two of you. I'm happy for you. When's the big day?"

"The weekend after Dad's," Jon said.

"It's going to be an exciting month with your dad and Martha tying the knot too. Does Bree know?"

"I called her this morning before breakfast and swore her to secrecy. I want to tell Kylie myself."

Mason's gaze slid sideways to Jon. "Cutting it a little close, aren't you? How do you think she'll take the news?"

Annie had tried not to dwell on her daughter's possible reaction. "I'm not sure. She's eight so it's hard to say. I hope to frame it in a positive way that makes her excited and happy." She made a face. "Or at least avoids a tantrum." She rose with her coffee in hand. "We'll let you get back to work. Let me know if there's anything else I can do."

"Will do." Mason was already peering at his computer.

They exited into glowering skies. The downpour had turned to a drizzle, and the temperature had dropped several degrees. Thunder rumbled as they ran for her truck. She threw herself under the steering wheel and slammed her door as lightning ripped from the clouds.

"We have any warnings out?" she asked Jon as he pulled his door shut.

"Gale warning. And six-to-nine-foot waves. The storm will surge again any minute."

She shivered. "I wouldn't want to be out on the water today. I hope Sarah is okay."

The words were out before she realized she'd meant them. Revenge wasn't something she wanted. Sarah had endured enough heartache and pain in her life. Yes, she'd done wrong, but then hadn't they all? Annie was no saint and had no right to judge her sister. Keeping Kylie safe was a top priority, but Annie didn't wish harm on her sister. The two of them were all that was left of their family.

Jon pulled up a page on his phone. "There's something I want to show you. What do you think of this house?"

She took the phone he held out and her breath caught at the house on the screen. "That's the Dalton house." She swiped through the pictures. "Why do you have all these pictures?"

"Dad told me this morning it's going on the market, but they will let us see it first. If we want it, we can save Realtor fees."

"I've always loved that house."

The old Victorian home had been built at the turn of the century by a copper baron. It was on Quincy Hill and overlooked Lake Superior and Rock Harbor. There wasn't a better location in the whole area. She'd loved it even though it had been neglected over the years.

"I know, me too." His steady green eyes held her gaze. "You want to go see it? They're listing it tomorrow."

"I haven't been inside in ages. I'd love to see it."

How could they afford it with the costs of starting up Jon's business? The bank wouldn't give him a loan until his business had been established a few years. She couldn't get her hopes up.

/ / /

Even with the warm dog clutched to her and her windbreaker zipped to her neck, Sarah shivered in the stiff breeze. The wind drove the rain sideways and the force of it stung her skin. The storm howled around her, and the lightning and thunder crashed overhead.

The dog cried and she tried to soothe him, but she was as terrified as he was. "It's okay, boy," she murmured over and over.

All they could do was wait out the storm. If there was a silver lining, it was that the men were unlikely to be out here searching for her. And if the rain had descended soon enough, they might not have noticed the kayak missing.

The kayak!

She hadn't thought about whether its hiding place was safe from the huge waves rolling high up on the sand and rocks. Peering through the curtain of rain, she tried to trace the outlines of the boat, but it was impossible to see. She didn't dare try to feel her way to the boat in case the incoming waves overtook her and carried her out into the lake. No one could last long in those cold waves.

If only she'd sought better shelter for her and the dog. She scooted farther away from the waves, but her back was up against an outcropping of rocks. What if she stacked the rocks and tried to build at least a partial shelter? The thought of letting go of the warm dog didn't appeal to her, but lifting stones would soon warm up her muscles. And if she was able to make a windbreak, it would be worth freezing for a bit.

She pushed the dog off her lap and got onto her hands and knees. Tugging at the rocks, she managed to get one loose, but several more tumbled down the slope toward her. One slammed into her leg, and she cried out.

Maybe this hadn't been such a good idea.

As she moved back toward the dog, her hand touched something slick. She picked it up and gasped. A blue tarp. It might not be a rock shelter, but it would keep the rain and wind off them. Allocating some space for her and Scout to slip into, she weighted down the corners with rocks.

Sarah crawled in first, then lifted the tarp above her head with one hand and coaxed the dog to join her. "Come on, boy. Come here."

His ears flattened, and he crawled on his belly to join her. She put her arms around his wet fur and pulled him close, then let the tarp settle around them. The instant warmth was heaven. Resting her chin on the dog, she closed her eyes. With little sleep last night, she was exhausted from fighting the kayak for so long to get here. Every minute had been a struggle.

When she woke again, she felt deliciously toasty and content. The torrential rains had slowed to a drizzle. She sat up and licked dry lips, and she was ravenous. The thought of bringing food and water hadn't crossed her mind. A person could go without food for days, but water was another story. Was there a source of water on the island? Did she dare drink the lake water if things became desperate?

She was already feeling rising despair about her situation.

After pushing back the tarp, she looked out on her surroundings. Rivulets of water ran from nearly every surface, and puddles formed in mud indentations. If only she had some kind of clean container to catch rainwater. She doubted there would be any fresh spring or good source of drinking water. Superior was supposed to be the cleanest, most pristine water around. Would it be safe to drink?

She might have to find out.

Her body was stiff from sleeping on the rocky ground, and she groaned as she stood and stretched. The highest point on the island was behind her, so she trekked up the rocky slope until she stood where she could see everything. As she suspected, there was no stream. No food. Nothing but trees, rocks, and mud. Wait, where was the kayak?

Panic struck when she studied the area until she glimpsed the bow of the boat peeking out from a bush. At least it was still where she'd hidden it.

Her gaze went back to the water. The rolling breakers and troughs out on the surface terrified her. She was too poor at navigating the kayak to believe she could brave Lake Superior during a gale and survive the journey. The whole space disoriented her too. Which way had she come from and which direction was the mainland? She could no longer tell. There was nothing on the horizon anywhere to orient her.

She tore her gaze from the water to try to decide what to do until she had to make the hard decisions on which way to row. The felled trees might make a better shelter than she had already, and she could cover them with the tarp. The branches would soften the ground. It was a start.

Energized by the thought of at least doing something, she

went toward the grove of trees. Her muscles warmed to the task, and she managed to drag small felled trees into place. She gathered branches and laid them out over the hard ground, then retrieved the tarp. Once it was secured, she crawled inside and sat in her new temporary abode.

It was pretty good, and she wasn't sure how she'd managed to do it by herself. For the first time she thought she might be strong enough to survive this. Maybe.

TWENTY-SIX

THE HOUSE WAS IN WORSE SHAPE THAN JON EXPECTED.
The 1884 structure was sound with a dry basement and a good roof, but the inside was another story. He tried to hide his dismay at the cabinets that were new when Jimmy Carter was president and the way someone had dared to paint the quarter-sawn oak woodwork. The two bathrooms had spongy underlayment from leaky toilets, and every piece of hardwood flooring would have to be refinished.

The place reeked of old, wet wood, yet in spite of the storm raging outside, it felt safe and dry inside.

He finally dared a glance at Annie as they started down the ornate staircase back to the first floor. "Rough, isn't it?"

Her blue eyes shone when she smiled back at him. "I love it, Jon. I've always loved it. The potential for a wonderful family home is here. Five bedrooms for more littles, a huge bedroom for us, and we could take that smallest room next to the bathroom and beside the biggest bedroom and turn it into a master bath so we have an en suite. Nice closets, which is unusual in a house of this era. I'm pretty handy from running the marina all these years, and I can strip the woodwork and paint. We'd need to have it rewired, of course. Maybe new plumbing too. And while we could probably refinish the floors ourselves, I think I'd rather have an expert do them so they are perfect."

His mouth dropped as she rambled on about what she wanted to do with the home. "How'd you see past the dirt and the poor decisions someone made?"

They reached the entry, and she poked him with her elbow. "Hey, I saw through your warts, you know."

He chuckled and draped his arm around her shoulders. "And I'm thankful you did."

Her expression clouded. "Do you know how much they want for it? How can we afford any house right now when you're about to open your own practice?"

"Dad is going to loan me the money. He offered to buy us a house as a wedding gift, but I don't want to do that. I'd want to pay him back."

"Of course." She nodded. "But how kind of him. Your dad is a good man, and you're just like him. So what's our next step?"

He paused before answering. Did he want it even if she did? The amount of work was monumental. "You really want to tackle this monstrosity?"

She walked through the tired entry to the living room and gestured to the large windows. The tumultuous waves of Lake Superior were on full display. "Look at that view. How could we say no? And that fireplace. I know someone painted it, but imagine it in its glory. Think of us on a snowy February day with the flames casting shadows on the wall while we play *Candy Land*. And that hill outside. I can hear Kylie laughing as the two of you go down it on a toboggan."

He could see it all as she laid it out. So vividly he could almost smell the smoke from the blazing fire. "At least the structure is sound. Well, except for the bathroom underlayment. Okay, we'll do it. I'd do just about anything for you, you know."

"I think you're about to prove it." She tipped her head. "How much?"

"Eighty thousand."

"You've got to be kidding! For this beautiful place?"

He dropped a kiss on her nose. "Most people can't see past the seventies cabinets, and it's not like this area has soaring home values."

"But that butler's pantry is to die for! I guess I should mention I want to knock out a wall in the kitchen too." Her blue eyes went soft. "You're going to be Kylie's hero. She's loved this house all her life. The Daltons let us sled on the hill, and Mrs. Dalton would bring us blueberry muffins fresh from the oven. Kylie always said she wished she could live here. It will be a wonderful surprise for her."

The thought of Kylie's excitement added to his determination to make this their home. He took Annie's hand, and they walked out onto the wraparound porch. The rain had stopped again for now. Even though the ceiling and the porch floor needed to be painted, in his mind's eye he saw the swing set he would build and the children romping in the yard. He saw himself with Annie snuggled together on a porch swing. The landscape could be beautiful again. It would take a lot of work, and it didn't have to be done all at once. It would take years, but they'd enjoy doing it together.

He exhaled and hugged her. "I'll let the Daltons' executor know we want it. And I'll tell Dad."

After a few long seconds, she stirred against his chest. "How long before it's ours?"

He pulled away and caught her gaze. "Probably two or three weeks, so I can't carry you across this threshold after the wedding." But he wished he could carry her into a completely redone house.

"That soon? I can't wait! We can work on it while we live in my place."

He couldn't wait to get out of the home she'd shared with Nate though. "Speaking of the wedding, what about a honeymoon?" He held up his hand when she frowned. "I know, I know. You're in the middle of a big investigation. But we should go somewhere just that night and plan something bigger down the road. Do you have a preference?"

She smiled and shook her head. "I'll leave that up to you." She poked him in the ribs. "But don't think you're getting out of carrying me over this entry too. You're a big, strong guy."

"I'll remember that."

"We'd better get going. I'm meeting Anu to sign papers on the cabin she's buying from me."

He went with her toward her truck. What about the lighthouse bed-and-breakfast in Ahmeek? Sand Hills Lighthouse, a little north of Houghton, had been turned into a B and B. It would only be about an hour drive, so they wouldn't be far from home, but it would be far enough to have her all to himself for those few hours.

He'd call this afternoon and book it. Everything was falling into place.

/ / /

When Annie entered Rock Harbor, she parked outside attorney Ursula Sawyer's office. She'd dropped Jon at the Blue Bonnet, and they'd reconnect at dinner. She spied Ursula and Anu already in the office just past the waiting room. Ursula motioned for Annie to join them. Annie touched Anu on the shoulder as she moved to take a seat past the older woman.

Anu seemed her usual imperturbable self with her sleek bob of silver-blonde hair and her impeccable pants and top. Annie could only admire the way she was always put together.

"Exciting day," Annie said.

Anu's blue eyes were serene. "I'm so thankful for you, dear Annie. My contractor will begin the remodel on Monday."

Annie had endured a pang or two of regret over selling the cabin, but Anu's obvious excitement soothed that pain. "I can't wait to see what you do with it."

Signing the papers and the money transfer were quick processes even with Ursula explaining every clause. In her fifties, the attorney had never married, and she and Anu were longtime friends. Anu followed everything she said without question, and Annie did the same even though the legalese was over her head.

When it was done, Annie leaned back in her chair. "How about a banana split to celebrate?"

"I can come along, but I have cut out sugar to help with my cancer fight," Anu said.

"Well, I wouldn't dream of eating one in front of you. Let's opt for coffee instead. Coffee is better than ice cream any day."

Ursula rose and tucked a strand of her straight brown hair behind one ear. "You two go ahead, and I'll join you when I get these papers transmitted."

"We'll save you a seat," Annie promised.

They went out in the wind and walked down to the coffee shop. The rich aroma of coffee and cinnamon rolls vied for first place, but Annie didn't want to make Anu's diet harder on her. She placed their order for coffee only and paid while Anu grabbed them a table by the window.

Anu's expression was pensive when Annie sat down and slid

the coffee across the table to her. "You seem a little sad. Regrets about the cabin? It's not too late to back out."

Anu made an obvious effort to alter her expression, but the shadow lingered in her eyes. "Oh no, no. I am very happy with my purchase. It is Max, you see."

Annie took a sip of perfect, strong coffee. "He didn't want you to buy the cottage?"

"He wishes to marry me," Anu said. "While he has no objection to me having a project like the cottage, he says we would live on the island."

"Not in the winter. It's brutal out there and difficult to get to the mainland. The cottage would make the perfect winter retreat."

"It is not so much where we would live. It is that my hesitancy has shown me I am quite unsure of how I feel about Max." She took the lid off her latte and blew on it, then took a sip. "He is a most wonderful man. Kind, considerate. But I feel as if I perhaps do not know his deepest feelings. On the surface he seems eager to open up, but when I recall our conversations, I realize I am the one who did most of the talking. I know very little about his past and how he feels about the most personal things."

"Have you talked to Max about it? Encouraged him to open up?"

Anu put the lid back on her drink. "Oh yes. He will give me some slight bit of information, but I still know very little. My first husband had many secrets I did not know or even suspect. I never want to be in that situation again."

Annie struggled to remember more about Anu's first husband. He'd been assumed dead for many years but had shown up in town six years ago. She hadn't known Anu that well back then, and Annie didn't know all the secrets.

"I understand." Annie didn't want to offer advice when Anu was so much wiser. The older woman had probably thought it all out before she said a word. "What are you going to do?"

The shadow in Anu's eyes deepened. "I shall make one more attempt to persuade him to lower his guard. If that is unsuccessful, I do not believe I will go forward with the relationship."

"I hope he is willing to let you in. I've always liked Max, and I'd love to see you settled and happy."

The darkness in Anu's expression vanished, and she laughed. "Oh, my dear Annie, I am most happy. A man is not what gives me contentment. Only God can do that. I would have liked companionship and a true commitment like you have with your Jon, but God has sustained me these many years, and he will continue to do so."

Anu's strong faith was one of the many things Annie loved about her. "I know you're right."

They drank their coffee and chatted while they waited for Ursula. "Has Max ever mentioned how that woman he found on his island got along? Sarah mentioned he'd had his staff take her to the hospital, but I never heard if she was released."

Anu frowned. "He never discussed this incident with me, though I was there when the bloody jacket was found. It is yet another example of the way he is so private. I will ask him though."

"That would be great. I wanted to ask her how she came to be injured out there. She might not have been chased like a couple of others, but I wanted to make sure there's no connection. I still don't even know her name."

She spotted Ursula hurrying toward the coffee shop as the rain let loose again. "I'd better get Ursula's coffee now. She's going to need it."

TWENTY-SEVEN

SITTING ON THE BLUE BONNET'S SWING WHILE GULLS
swooped overhead, Jon scrolled through his contacts, and his finger hovered over the entry for Lars Pederson. Like his dad said, Lars would likely be the calmer of the two. Maryanne tended to explode and then need time to cool off.

His dad patted Jon's knee. "Make the call, Jon. If it turns nasty, give me the phone, and I'll handle it."

Jon nodded and touched the Call icon.

Lars answered on the second call. "I've been expecting your call for days." His voice sounded weary.

Nothing like plunging right in without pleasantries. Jon cleared his throat. "Lars, you and Maryanne know me well enough to know I *want* you to be involved in Kylie's life. So does Annie. Has she ever gotten in the way of you seeing your granddaughter?"

"You mean *your* daughter."

Jon winced at the venom in the older man's voice. "If you'd talked to Kylie about this, you would know Nate is her daddy and always will be. I'm going to do my best to be there for her, but Lars, come on. You know how much I loved Nate. You really think I'd try to ruin his memory? Do you honestly believe I would do anything to harm you or Maryanne? Think, man. You know better than that."

The silence on the other side was deafening, but Jon held his peace and waited for Lars to think it through. They had a long history together. Nate had been like a brother to Jon, and both of his parents knew it.

"Why did we have to find out this way? It was a shock."

"How do you think I felt? I had no idea I had a daughter. I missed out on eight years of her life, but you know what? I'm glad Nate had her in his arms. I'm glad Nate died knowing Kylie loved him with all her heart. He never had to know the truth. And you saw Annie and Nate together. You know they loved each other. She was a good wife to him. They had a great marriage."

No one would ever know how much it cost Jon to admit all that aloud, but he owed Nate. Nate had stepped in when Jon left Annie to face the future without him. Nate had picked up the pieces and loved her well. Jon could face that now after Annie's reassurances yesterday. He might not have been able to say all that so easily without that comfort.

"I appreciate you saying that," Lars said in a gruff voice. "I'll see what I can do with Maryanne. She's been on a tear about it all."

Jon didn't doubt it. He'd seen Maryanne in a state before. "I appreciate it, Lars. I mostly called to reassure you that I want you both to be part of Kylie's life. My dad wants that too. Remember, we missed out on her early years.

"You've never seen her excitement when you guys call or when she gets a card or gift from you. She's over-the-moon excited. She adores you guys, and you're also her link to her daddy. I don't want that to change. There's room for all of us. Love is like that. It doesn't matter how many people you love, there is always room for more."

And when he spoke those words, he felt the truth of it in his gut. He might wish Annie had never had another husband in her life, but there was room for Jon in her heart. He knew she loved him. Knew she wanted to be with him. Nate had never taken Jon's place—he'd had his own place in Annie's heart, a place he'd always occupy. And Jon's place was secure. He'd been her first love, the love of her life, and he had come back into that same spot. Their love would only grow from here.

He hoped he could keep that knowledge firmly in mind as they created a life together.

Lars heaved a sigh on the other end of the phone. "It helps you said that. I'll drop the suit. Maryanne will buck me at first, but I'll make her see reason. We don't want to hurt Kylie. Nate's death hurt her enough. Can we have her for a week this summer?"

"I'm sure Annie will be thrilled that you want her. You want her in California or are you coming back up here?"

"In California. There is a lot we'd like to show her. I'll fly up to get her, and one of us will bring her back."

Jon could hear her squeals of excitement in his head. "I don't think she's flown before. That will be an exciting journey for her, but most of her joy will be coming to see the two of you. When do you want her?"

"I'll talk to Maryanne and see when we want to arrange it. When does school start?"

"The last week of August, so we've got time to get it on the schedule."

"Thanks for calling to sort this out, Jon. I don't think anyone wants us to be estranged. And honestly, what would we do with a child to raise? I tried to tell Maryanne, but she was hysterical."

"Do you think she'll go along with this?"

"I'm calling the attorney before I tell her. It's a done deal. She'll be all right. Thanks again."

Jon put down his phone and got up. "I think we both need a cherry Popsicle after that torture, Dad. But he's dropping the suit, and I didn't even have to pull out the big gun of the DNA test."

His dad rose and clapped him on the back. "I think there's a whole box of Popsicles in the freezer. Martha might even let us raid the gluten-free brownies. After our reward, I'll help you draft the offer for the house."

Jon couldn't wait to tell Annie the news. One more thing out of the way.

/ / /

The wind began to die down as the sun sank toward the horizon. Sarah licked her dry lips. She'd give about anything for a sip of water. She glanced at her watch. Just after five.

Exiting the shelter, she studied the waves. They were not as violent as they had been, and the sun had begun to peek through the storm clouds. The air smelled fresh and clean after the violent storm. With the sunshine, she didn't need her jacket, so she peeled it off and left it in the shelter to go closer to the shore.

After a stretch and a yawn, Scout followed her. He went straight to the water and slurped from the waves. Maybe Sarah should do the same, but she wasn't ready to go that far yet. If the breakers continued to die down, she might make it to the mainland in a few more hours. Though the thought of rowing in the dark felt daunting, maybe there would be lights to guide her to Rock Harbor or even a house along the shore.

The dog's ears stiffened, and he turned to stare to Sarah's left. A low growl rumbled in his throat, and his tail pointed straight out. Sarah tensed and turned to see what had upset him. At first she saw nothing, but she thought she heard a motor. Then she saw the bow of a boat slicing through the waves toward her.

She called the dog to her and ran for the sparse trees inland where she'd left the shelter. She quickly took down the tarp and stuffed it under the branches. But where could she hide with the dog?

Her gaze fell on a rocky outcropping. Flat on her belly, she might not be seen. She sprinted for it with the dog and threw herself onto the ground. She looped her arm around Scout's neck and pulled him below the rocks with her. As the sound of the engine grew louder, she remembered the kayak.

She dared a peek above the rocks and saw the boat idling offshore. One of the men from last night had binoculars to his eyes, and she ducked back down. Maybe he wouldn't spot the kayak, but its bright color was hard to miss. Her heart pounded in her ears as she waited to find out her fate.

There was no doubt in her mind they were searching for her.

She dared another glance above the rocks. One of the two men jumped over the side of the boat into the shallow water. Was there anywhere better to hide? If only she had a cave or a big tree to climb.

The dog whined, and she shushed him with a touch. She picked up a rock and hefted it in her hand. It was the only weapon she had, but it wouldn't be effective in a direct confrontation. She'd have to ambush the guy.

Creeping along the rocky landscape, she moved toward where she'd left the kayak. Maybe she could knock him out while he bent over to retrieve it. If he had a gun, she could take it. While she'd never shot a gun, how hard could it be? Point it and pull the trigger.

But when she peeked up again, the man wasn't moving toward the kayak. Instead, he was making a sweep of the island. He was easy to spot in his red plaid shirt. He'd stumble across her hiding place any second. She had to come up with another plan.

Her throat tightened at the thought of being found. She looked around again. There was a tree whose branches might bear her weight. Maybe she could launch a rock at his head from above. Or just hide. The dog would be found, but maybe they'd think she perished in the water.

A vain hope though. The kayak had clearly been pulled ashore. The men would know she had to be here somewhere and wouldn't give up until they found her. Could she get the kayak to the water and escape before they saw? She shook her head. Even if the searcher didn't see her, the other guy still in the boat would notice. He was scanning the area with binoculars.

She scrabbled back on her belly toward the trees. It was only when she reached the trunk that she realized she'd have to stand to climb it. The leaves were four feet from the base, and the men would immediately see her.

She was doomed to be found. Could she get the dog to attack? She put her hand on his head. "Attack!" she said in a hoarse whisper.

Scout looked at her with soulful eyes, and his tail thumped the ground. Not a surprise there, but all hope left her chest. She might as well rise holding her hands up.

But she couldn't bring herself to give up all hope. Maybe they'd get called away or someone else would come. She had to cling to the possibilities.

She crawled back to the rocks and peered up again. Her slight movement had caught the man's eye, and he grinned and came toward her. His red hair glinted in the sun breaking through the clouds.

"There you are. I knew there was nowhere to hide here. Come on out, and I won't hurt you."

She clutched the rock and stood. "What do you want?"

"Just a little game. It will be fun."

She knew better from the glint in his muddy-brown eyes. Before she had a chance to change her mind, she launched the rock at his head. To her amazement, it struck him on the forehead, and he stumbled with a groan.

But he didn't go down. His fists clenched, and he came toward her. "That's going to cost you."

TWENTY-EIGHT

BY DINNERTIME JON HAD A SIGNED PURCHASE AGREE-
ment for the house in hand as well as a lease for the downtown
property. It had been a productive afternoon. He eyed his car as
he got out in the lot at the B and B and locked it. Tonight he'd put
it up for sale online and see what happened.

Though it saddened him to let it go, it was the right thing. The
red Jag wasn't a family car. What would Annie think if he showed
up one of these days with a van? He grinned at the thought as he
jogged up the walk to the house.

Annie met him at the front door, and he swooped her into
his arms. "It's done, love. We can start work on that aging beauty
in a few weeks."

She whooped and kissed him. "I can't believe it! Kylie will be
over the moon. I can't wait until she gets back."

"I called Lars too. He agreed to drop the custody suit."

She kissed him again. "Where's your Superman cape?"

He held her close against his chest. "In my pocket."

Her satellite phone went off, and she stepped back to answer
it. "LEO Pederson. Oh, hey, Max."

When Annie's smiled dropped off, Jon knew something was
wrong, and he stepped closer.

"No, I haven't heard from Sarah." She glanced at Jon. "You haven't heard from her, have you?"

"Nope."

Annie's eyes went wide as she listened. "I'll talk to Mason, and we'll come right away."

"What's happened?" Jon asked when she ended the call.

"There's a missing kayak and Sarah isn't at her cabin. No one has seen her all day. He sent out some of his men to find her, but they haven't had any luck and are on their way back to the island. She has to be there somewhere."

She called up Mason's number. "Mason, have you heard from Sarah?" She bit her lip. "Okay, I'll call out the Coast Guard."

When she ended the call, Jon grabbed their windbreakers from the front hall tree. "Where should we search if she's not on the island?"

"She's not a good kayaker. If she's flipped it, she's probably not still alive." Her voice quavered. "I want to check that little island between the mainland and Tremolo Island. Maybe she washed ashore there. Rather than get my boat, I'll grab one from headquarters. It's bigger and will handle the waves from the storm better."

In minutes they were on the boat and heading out in the choppy waves. The bow cut through the water as Annie, face set and strained, stared at the horizon. Jon used binoculars to study their surroundings, but he saw nothing but white foam and flotsam as they headed out to the little scrap of land on the horizon.

Nothing moved on the little wisp of land, and he didn't think anyone could hide there without him spotting her. Annie cut the engine, and the boat chugged slowly the last few feet. Jon tossed the anchor overboard, and Annie hopped out before he had a second to react. He followed her, and this time she didn't tell him to stay aboard. She'd want all hands on deck to try to find her sister.

Angry or not, she still loved Sarah. It was something that would never change, and one of the many things that drew him. Her devotion and commitment wasn't something easily set aside.

He wasn't on the rocky shore more than two minutes when he caught a glimpse of green and spotted the kayak. "She's here!"

Annie saw it, too, and ran to yank it from the underbrush. She cupped her hands to her mouth and shouted for her sister. "Sarah!"

Only the gulls answered her, and Jon joined her in calling out Sarah's name. "You go that way, and I'll go this way."

They circled the island and ran into each other in fifteen minutes with no sign of her sister. An interesting arrangement of tree branches caught his eye, and he jogged farther inland to have a look. It appeared to be deliberate, and he found a tarp tucked under the leaves. There were scuffle marks and dog prints in the sand too.

"She's been here!" he shouted to Annie.

Annie joined him and they both yelled for Sarah again, but the place felt deserted. The dog didn't bark either.

"She's not here, love."

"I don't think so either. But she's been here, so how did she get off without the kayak?"

Jon studied the landscape and wandered over to search for any prints in the sand. Sarah's small footprints were scuffed with larger prints. "See here. I think someone picked her up. Maybe the men Max sent after her?"

"Let me call him."

While she talked to Max on the sat phone, Jon made another sweep of the area. It made no sense that whoever found her didn't take the kayak back.

Annie's blue eyes were full of confusion. "They didn't find her. Max just talked to the guys."

"What about the Coast Guard? Could they have gotten here first?"

"They would have called me. They knew I was heading here."

"Where do you want to head next? Are there any other islands out here?"

"There's another one on past Tremolo, but it's deserted too. And there would be no reason she landed there. Whoever took her had to have taken her to the mainland. Let's head back and see if a stray fisherman found her. She might be at the marina or the fishing dock in Rock Harbor. If she didn't know we were looking, she might not call me."

Jon heard the regret in her voice and suspected she was ready to make amends with her sister.

/ / /

No one had found Sarah, dead or alive.

Evening had fallen over Lake Superior, and Annie's hope of finding Sarah alive had fallen with it. Hugging herself against the chill of the air, she stood on the porch of the Blue Bonnet Bed-and-Breakfast and stared out at the water reflecting the stars overhead. The Coast Guard reported no trace of her. Annie had spoken to every fisherman and boater she could find at the fishing dock and her marina. Michelle hadn't seen her. Few people even floated past the little spot of land in the big lake, let alone stopped.

Sarah had just . . . vanished.

The door banged behind her, but she didn't turn. She'd known Jon would follow her out here. His palpable concern all afternoon had been her bulwark.

He dropped both arms around her from behind and rested his chin on her head. "I'm sorry, love. I'm praying someone picked her up that we haven't talked to."

She leaned back against his broad, warm chest. "We both know Superior's lethal power. If the waves didn't get her, the cold would."

"But she didn't capsize. The kayak wouldn't have been pulled up from the water like that. She had to have been there."

They'd been over and over the possible scenarios, but nothing hopeful had panned out. She didn't even know what the next best move was. Superior still held the bodies of Nate and her parents. People living along these shores had to come to grips with the reality of the big lake's dominance.

"I have so many regrets."

"You did a lot for her, Annie. Taking her in, giving her a job, even bailing her out. You don't have anything to regret."

"She's my sister. I should have accepted her apology."

"You have a responsibility to Kylie. That transcends everything else."

Annie knew in her heart he was right, but that didn't make this suffocating pain any better. Sarah had died out there without knowing Annie was ready to open her arms to her again. That she was prepared to be a true sister to her, to love her and protect her. She was even going to give her the marina.

Sarah died without any of that.

Jon stirred and dropped a kiss on her hair. "I've had this

crazy idea. I didn't want to entertain it, but I can't go to sleep tonight without mentioning it. Is it possible the hunters found her and took her?"

Annie stiffened and turned to face him. "Th-that's a crazy idea, Jon."

His green eyes were somber in the wash of the porch light. "I know. But nothing makes sense about her disappearance. She should have been on the island. If she'd died in the lake, we wouldn't have found her kayak. The dog was clearly with her too. Something doesn't smell right about all of it."

He was so right. She tried to wrap her head around the possibility. Though outrageous and unlikely, what did she have to lose by assuming it was possible? "I could talk to Candace one more time. If Glenn was involved, she might know where his most important hunts usually took place. If we knew where to search, we might find her in time."

The chances of this working were so slim, she couldn't even name the odds against it happening. But any chance was better than no chance.

He glanced at his phone. "It's only eight. We could go see her now."

"Let's do it. I'm never going to sleep tonight anyway." She put her arms around his neck and kissed him. "Thank you."

He held her for a long moment. "Want me to drive? I just listed the car for sale. I might not have another opportunity. Someone will snatch up that beauty."

Her heart squeezed at how much he was willing to give up for Kylie and her. "Someday maybe you'll have another."

His grin was crooked but heartfelt. "You and Kylie are worth ten Jaguars. I don't need a sports car when I have you."

He pulled out his keys and jangled them from his fingers. "Let's go. We might not have much time."

Her smile faded at the reminder of what her sister might be going through. Were men chasing her through the trees even now? Was she hiding in the woods or a cave somewhere? Had men already killed her?

But no, she couldn't think like that.

She ran with Jon to his car and got buckled in. Staring out at the dark night as he broke the speed limit getting out to Glenn Hussert's house, she prayed for Sarah's safety and for her own acceptance of what the next few days might hold.

The lights blazed out of the Hussert windows when they pulled into the drive. She was out of the car almost before it rolled to a stop. Jon was right behind her as she ran to the porch and jammed her finger against the doorbell.

When Candace didn't answer right away, Annie pounded on the door with her fist. "Candace!"

Finally, footsteps came toward the door. "Hang on, I'm coming."

Candace was dressed in jeans and a jacket as though she'd either just gotten home or was getting ready to go out. She was smiling until recognition flashed across her face. "You're the park ranger."

"We need to talk to you. It's urgent."

"I was just about to go out. You can't stay long." Candace grudgingly stepped aside to let them in.

"My sister is missing," Annie said. "We've been investigating a string of dead and missing tourists, and we believe there is a group operating up here that hunts people. People they think no one will miss. I'm afraid they've taken Sarah. If you know anything, anything at all, Candace, tell me now."

Candace took a step back. "That's monstrous."

"I know. Where is Glenn's favorite place to hunt? That would be a good start."

Candace's gaze darted from left to right, and she finally shrugged. "They usually go out by Fourteen Mile Point."

Annie should have thought of that. Jon had found Eddie Poole out that way. It would take a while to get back into that area in the dark, but they needed to go now.

TWENTY-NINE

AT JUST AFTER TEN, THE LIGHT WAS STARTING TO SOF-
ten over the north woods. Jon switched on a powerful flashlight
before they stepped into the deeper darkness of the forest. It felt
like a wild-goose chase, and he knew Annie held even less hope
than he did. But they had to try. He wanted to lift that heavy pall
of grief and guilt from her blue eyes if he could.

His boots tromping on the ground released the scent of pine
and moss. He held back branches for Annie when he could, but
much of the time, she plowed through quickly as if she knew
where she was going. And maybe she did. This wilderness area
was well-known to her, though the gloom would distort it.

She stopped and examined tracks in the dirt under a large
oak tree. "Several people were here, likely men from the size of
the prints."

Jon didn't answer. They both knew most of the prints would
be left from legitimate hunters. There was no way to figure out
what had been happening in here. If they found something
belonging to Sarah, it would be reason enough to call in more
searchers than the two of them. Annie hadn't wanted to bother
Mason or the SAR dog teams when the chance of success

was so slight. They didn't know for sure Sarah had ever been here.

They trekked deeper into the woods until the only light bouncing along the ground was the beam from his flashlight. The thick foliage blocked any bit of moonlight or starlight. Jon wasn't sure which way was out and which led deeper into the forest.

Annie followed a slight deer trail that veered off to their left. "Let's try this way."

"I'm not sure how we'll get out of here."

"I know the way."

Mosquitoes swarmed his head, and he waved them away. There was repellent in his backpack, but he hadn't bothered with spraying it on, so he paused long enough to remedy that oversight before jogging to catch up with the noise of Annie's passage through thick brush. The sound of waves hitting rocks rose above the buzz of the insects, and he knew they'd gone as far west as they could.

She stopped and sighed. "I guess we turn back when we reach the shoreline." She stood still while he sprayed her down with repellant, then took the can and sprayed some on her hands to wipe on her face.

They stepped out of the forest onto pebbles and sand. A sliver of a moon gilded the landscape with silver, and the sound of the water intensified.

Jon touched Annie's hand. "There's a cabin. Did you know it was out here?"

It was set back in the trees, and the bit of light escaping the edges of the curtains was nearly obscured by the thick bushes that seemed to be trying to reclaim the small structure. It was so dilapidated that it had to be a hunter's cabin that was rarely used.

Someone was inside now though. He heard some noises from beyond the battered door.

"Let's check it," she said. "I've never seen it, though I've kay-aked past here before. It's almost as if it was hidden on purpose."

And maybe it was. It was so well screened by vegetation that a hunter could have used it as a deer blind. He followed her to the door, which was only about two feet by five feet. He'd have to duck to go inside.

Annie rapped her knuckles on it. "LEO Pederson. I'd like to talk to you."

Her strong, assertive voice caused a flurry of thumps from inside. And a weak cry of "Help!"

Annie tried the door, but it wouldn't open. "It's locked."

None of the window openings would be large enough to climb in. "Let me try to force it."

She stood aside, and Jon rammed his shoulder into the door. It cracked but didn't budge until the third try, and as it gave way, he nearly fell into the room. Annie barreled after him with her gun drawn. Jon regained his balance and glanced around the space, dimly lit by one kerosene lamp on an upended crate. There was little furniture, just a bed where a figure lay.

Annie approached the man. "How can I help you?"

Jon kept the distance between them small in case the guy made a move, but as he neared, he recognized Glenn Hussert.

Annie's gasp came at the same time. "Glenn?"

Jon trained the flashlight beam on the man. His head was wrapped in a dirty bandage, and he looked rough with sallow, pasty skin and dark circles under his eyes.

"Help," he whispered again.

His lips were cracked, and Jon searched for a water bottle.

When he found nothing, he fished one out of his backpack and handed it to Annie. She helped Glenn take a few small sips, and he fell back against the cot and closed his eyes.

Annie touched his shoulder. "How did you get here, Glenn?"

His head lolled, and he didn't answer.

"Let me examine him." Jon touched Glenn's carotid artery and found a faint, rapid pulse. Likely very dehydrated. His emaciated state made Jon wonder if he'd eaten much at all since he was spirited out of the hospital, where he'd been fed via an IV.

"He's in rough shape," he told Annie. "I need to get him to a hospital."

Annie yanked out her satellite phone, punched several buttons, and shook her head. "It's dead. I don't think I charged it last night. I'll have to hike out to where I can get a signal and call for help. You stay here with him. You're the doctor."

It made sense, though there was little Jon could do in the wilderness with no equipment. "Be careful. And hurry. I don't like his pasty skin. He needs an IV immediately for one thing. It's hard to know what all is wrong."

"I'll be right back," she promised. "If I go south along the shore, there's a small area with cell coverage. It shouldn't take me more than fifteen minutes to reach it. I'll call for a chopper. There's enough room to land it on the beach."

He watched her rush for the door with a vague sense of unease before he turned back to Glenn.

/ / /

Annie's chest burned and her legs ached from her hectic run along the uneven ground along the water. Darkness had fallen completely, but moonlight lit her path along Lake Superior. Hoping she'd find cell coverage sooner than she expected, she paused several times to check her phone, but it wasn't until she reached a familiar stand of conifer trees that she managed to get one bar on her phone.

She walked toward the trees and sat on a rock to rest while she called for help. Her phone was nearly dead, and she wished she'd thought to recharge it on the drive out here.

She called Mason's number and started talking as soon as it connected. "Mason, I've found Glenn!" She told him how she stumbled onto the missing suspect and his condition. "We need an EMS chopper. He's in a bad way. I left Jon with him, but he has nothing to treat him with, no meds, no IV. I think you can land on the beach."

She gave him the coordinates, and he promised to send out a helicopter followed by law enforcement and forensics. When she ended the call, she pulled out a bottle of water and chugged it, then replaced the empty bottle in her backpack to carry out of the woods.

Out on the water she saw the flickering lights of a passing boat. There'd been no sign of Sarah, and Annie struggled with the rising guilt again. There was so much she should have done and said. Now it was too late. She'd never see Sarah again.

She stood to start the trek back to the cabin so she could be there to wave the chopper down to the right place. A twig snapped behind her and she turned as a figure came barreling out of the forest. Her first instinct was it was a bear, but she quickly placed it as a burly man with a ski mask over his head. Though her hand reached for her gun, the guy crashed into her and bore her onto the sand. His breath smelled of cigarettes and breath mints, and his jacket stank of animal.

The breath went out of her, and her head slammed into a rock. Stars swam across her vision, and her arms went weak as she flailed around to try to escape his grip. The encounter felt weird and off since he said nothing. His hard hands pressed her shoulders back against the ground, then he lifted her and slammed her down again. He did that repeatedly so her head banged onto the rock over and over.

She was barely clinging to consciousness when he flipped her over and bound her wrists together. "Let me go," she whispered.

He still hadn't said a word, and the silence seemed demonic and evil. It heightened her terror. What kind of monster clutched her in its grip? Barely conscious, she didn't have much fight in her to resist his efficient binding of her hands. With her trussed up and helpless, he rolled her onto her back again, then yanked her into a sitting position. In seconds she was hauled up and flung over his shoulder. Instead of heading into the forest, he turned toward the water and Annie closed her eyes to the sound of a motor chugging closer.

When she opened her eyes again, she was in a small room with no windows. Her head pounded, and she forced back nausea with every beat of her heart. There was one small kerosene lamp that left most of the tiny room in shadows. The unpainted concrete floor radiated cold and damp, and when she touched the wall, it felt like concrete too.

Was she buried in a concrete box? She ran to the door, a small steel one, and pounded on it. "Let me out!" She kicked it with a boot, but all that did was make her head pound more.

With a final yank on the doorknob, she went back to the metal cot and sank onto the hard mattress. Who had taken her and why? Was she about to find out what was going on in her beloved Upper

Peninsula by being a victim herself? Her hand went to her holster. Empty.

But she wasn't without resources. If the hunters came after her, they would find out they faced a formidable adversary. She knew these miles of wilderness. It would be the worst fight of their lives. She would not let them win. There was too much to live for—Kylie and Jon. She would use every ounce of strength she possessed to fight.

There wasn't enough space to pace the way she wanted, so she forced herself to conserve her strength, to lay back on the hard, flat pillow, and rest. She closed her eyes, and her headache began to ease. The determination coiling in her chest began to radiate strength to her arms and legs.

Whoever had taken her would not find her an easy target.

THIRTY

SARAH WAS COLD, SO COLD. SHE HADN'T FULLY DRIED from being drenched in the rain. This small concrete cubicle was too damp and chilly to let the moisture evaporate. She'd wrapped the thin blanket around her, but her teeth still chattered.

Fear likely added to that.

The men hadn't spoken to her once they put her in the boat. They'd put a thick pillowcase over her head and had brought her to this dank cell. She had no idea if it was on the island, on another island, or somewhere on the mainland. With the light snuffed out during the ride, she lost all sense of direction and time. They could have traveled an hour or three. It was all the same to Sarah in her terror.

She'd been here for what seemed an eternity. The meal they'd brought her—soup and a peanut butter sandwich—was still untouched on a tray by the door. The faint aroma of chicken noodle soup left a stench in the room, and the thought of eating made bile rise in her throat. All she wanted was out of this dreadful concrete box.

What did they intend to do with her? Whatever it was, it couldn't be good. She'd seen their faces, and while she didn't know their names, she could describe them to law enforcement. That would seal her fate right there. They couldn't let her go.

The lock on the steel door snicked, and she shot to her feet facing it. At least her hands were free now. The door opened, and one of the men stepped inside. In the bit of light from the lantern, she got a good look at him. He was in his late twenties with thick brown hair and a full beard. She had no idea of his name, just that he worked for Max. Max should have vetted his employees better.

His hazel eyes raked her over, and he smiled. "Ready?"

"For what?"

He leaned against the doorjamb. "We're going to turn you loose. If you can find your way to town, you're home free. We won't follow you any longer."

It sounded way too easy, and she could tell from the glint in his eyes he didn't expect her to make it to safety. "Where are we?"

"In the U.P." He snickered and folded his arms over his chest.

"Back on the island? If I can make it to the big house, am I safe?"

"We aren't on the island. Max isn't going to save you."

So they must be somewhere on the mainland. Sarah took encouragement from that fact. There might be a hunter out there with a gun who would help her. Or hikers with an ATV. She might not have to hike out of the wilderness on her own.

She was good at climbing trees too. All she had to do was escape them. There were only two of them, after all.

"I'm ready."

He nudged the food tray with his foot. "I don't think you are. We want to give you the best chance possible. It's not fun when the quarry is too easy. Eat your food. We'll give you water and some granola bars to keep your strength up. It's always better when we can extend the fun two or three days."

Sarah's gut did a slow somersault. It sounded like they'd done this before. Her sister had mentioned missing hikers, and there was that body that had been at the dock when she'd first started working at the marina. One of their victims?

His smile was more of a gloat. "Eat. Rest. We start at daybreak."

Sarah said nothing as he backed out of the room and flipped the lock again. Her only hope was in getting out of here and into the wilderness. She didn't know the area well, but she'd hidden from them before. One skill she possessed was how she noticed things and saw opportunity.

She forced herself to take the tray and carry it back to her cot where she choked down the now-hard peanut butter sandwich and the cold, congealed soup. The food wanted to come back up, but she followed the unappetizing meal with a swig of water, then stretched out on the cot and closed her eyes.

She didn't think she would sleep, but exhaustion turned off her dreams and anxiety, and she slept until the door clicked again. When it opened, the other man stood in the doorway. She saw a bit of moonlight streaming into the area behind him. While she had no concept of time in here, she must have slept several hours, which was good.

"Where's my dog?"

"Around. He's a good boy. I like him."

"Could I have him with me for company?" Why was she even asking? Scout was liable to be a hindrance. She'd worried he might bark or whine and give away her location, but the thought of facing these men by herself terrified her.

The man hesitated, then shrugged. "Let me check with the boss." He backed out and locked the door behind him.

Sarah looked around for anything she might take with her as

a weapon. Nothing. She'd have to find something out in the forest. They hadn't even given her a spoon for the soup. She'd had to pick up the bowl and drink it like water.

The lock clicked again, and he was back. The dog was at his feet, and Sarah couldn't hold back the soft cry of joy. Scout shot from behind the man and ran to lick her hand.

She knelt to bury her face in his musty-smelling fur. "Good boy," she crooned.

"The boss thought it might make the hunt more fun. I hope you know what you're asking though. The dog leaves tracks too."

She hadn't thought of that, but she couldn't be sorry for her request. At least she'd have company, and if they killed her, she'd die with her arms around the dog's neck. It was better than dying alone.

But she didn't want to die. Not without telling Annie how sorry she was. She had to live and get back to town. Making amends was the most important thing to her.

/ / /

Annie had been gone longer than Jon expected. Had she run into a bear? Or maybe she'd fallen and was lying injured out there in the forest somewhere. He monitored Glenn's pulse and breathing every couple of minutes. The man was in a bad way and needed to be back in a hospital as soon as possible.

How long did Jon wait before he set off to find Annie and call for help if it didn't come in a timely manner? The indecision made him pace the small cabin.

Then he heard the *whop-whop* of helicopter rotors. She'd gotten through! Maybe the pilot had landed and picked her up to save her from making the trip back. With a final check on

Glenn, he darted from the cabin and ran for the beach where the landing lights shone on the open space. He waved his hands to let them know they'd arrived at the right spot, then backed away to a safe distance.

It was too dark to clearly see inside the chopper, but there were several figures, and Jon waited for Annie to come bounding out.

The door opened, and two paramedics ducked under the rotors and ran toward him. "Where is he?" the woman asked.

Jon gestured behind him and to the left. "Inside the cabin. Where's Annie?" he called after them as they headed for the building.

The male stopped and turned. "She said she would head back here. I thought she'd be here by now."

The unease he'd felt intensified. Something was wrong. "You can take over with Glenn. I'm going to go find Annie. Maybe she fell and is injured along the way."

The paramedic nodded. "Call if you need us to get her." He hurried to join the other paramedic in the cabin.

Jon first checked with the pilot to make sure she hadn't seen Annie walking along the shoreline as she flew the chopper. The woman had seen nothing. Jon told her he would be unable to call for help so to watch for a flashlight signal as they flew out.

He took off for the edge of the beach and followed it. Clouds blew across the moon and held the hint of rain. He wasn't exactly sure where cell coverage started, so he stopped often to check. He also called Annie's name throughout the trip to where she'd told him she was heading. All along the shoreline, he saw no sign of her. The fifteen minutes along the water seemed to take forever. He rounded a corner and squinted. Hadn't she said something about a stand of conifer trees?

He approached the trees and tried his phone again. It lit with one bar, and he quickly called up her number. As it connected, he heard something ringing. He whirled toward the sound and saw a light flashing by a rock.

Annie's phone and gun lay on the sand, and a wave of fear washed up his chest. "Annie!" He walked back toward the forest calling her name over and over. No answer.

He flipped on his flashlight and scoured the beach area for clues as to what had happened to her. Some indentations in the sand caught his attention, and he studied them.

He was no tracker, but even he could tell a scuffle had taken place here. There were multiple footprints near where he'd found the phone. He resumed his search and found more prints by the water. Someone or *someones* had likely taken her out of here by boat.

And it hadn't been willingly. She wouldn't leave her phone or her gun out here like this. The people who had abducted her would have tossed it aside or forced her to abandon it so they couldn't be tracked.

His heart in his mouth, Jon called Mason, who answered on the second ring. "Mason, have you heard from Annie?"

"Not since she called to let me know she'd found Glenn. What's up?"

Jon told him about the markings on the sand and her abandoned phone and gun. "Could she have been taken out of here by boat?"

"Possible. I'll notify the Coast Guard. It had to have been right after we spoke."

Which meant it had been about an hour as near as Jon could gauge it. Her abductors might have had time to get to their destination. "What if the Coast Guard doesn't find her?"

"I don't know, Jon. There's no way of knowing where to search for her. I'll ask rangers and other law enforcement to be on the lookout for her, but we don't know why she was taken. Or where. Did the paramedics get there? How's Glenn?"

"The paramedics took over, and I left to find Annie. He's not in good shape. I'm not sure he'll make it."

"They're taking him to Houghton."

So the chopper wouldn't come this way. "Could Annie's abduction have anything to do with Glenn? Maybe the perp is whoever spirited Glenn out of the hospital."

"Possible. You found him in his favorite hunting area. Maybe Annie saw something incriminating or they were afraid she might, so they got her out of there."

The strain in Mason's voice caused Jon's worry to spike. The chances of finding her weren't good. "Maybe Candace could give more information. Annie found her husband, and she might be grateful enough to turn over any other info she might have."

"Maybe." Mason didn't sound hopeful. "I already let her know Glenn has been found, and she's on her way to the hospital."

"If I get there first, can I ask her?"

"Yeah, go ahead. She might be sympathetic to you since you're engaged to Annie. I'll be there as soon as I can."

Jon had no better leads to follow than Candace, so he ended the call and tried to figure out where they'd parked. The map he called up on his phone wasn't very detailed. He might not find his way out of the forest.

Just as he'd decided his best course of action was to go back to the cabin and hitch a ride with the chopper, he heard the sound of its rotors fading as it headed toward Houghton. Too late. Jon would have to figure this out without Annie.

THIRTY-ONE

IT WAS AFTER 5:00 A.M. BY THE TIME JON MADE HIS
way out to his car. He'd parked it where the road ran out and the
fire trail began. He'd already wasted so much time, and he didn't
want to drive to Houghton and back again if he wasn't going to
get anything out of Candace Hussert.

His car appeared to be untouched. He checked his phone
and discovered five messages from Mason. He started to call him
back, but his phone rang with another call from the sheriff.

"Hey, where are you?" Mason sounded worried. "I thought
you'd be at the hospital before now."

Jon slung himself behind the wheel and started the car. The
cooling rush of air over his hot cheeks gave welcome relief. "Uh,
I had a little trouble finding my way back to the car."

To his credit Mason didn't laugh. "I already talked to Candace
and told her what was happening out there. She is positive you
are right where Glenn and his buddies always went hunting. It's
one of the most remote tracts left in the U.P. Rather than come
back here, you might search out there. But be careful. If a hunting
group is out there tracking Annie or Sarah, they'll be dangerous."

"What about the dog teams?"

"Too dangerous. Most of them are women with small children. I don't want to put them in the middle of a dangerous hunt with the possibility of bullets flying. I'm calling in the state police for assistance. They understand the danger."

He didn't like it, but the sheriff was right. Though the dogs might have been able to find Annie, Jon didn't want to see Naomi or some of the other ladies in the crosshairs of a scope. He ended the call and rummaged in his backpack for a bottle of water. Even though it was warm, the wetness soothed his irritated throat. He'd been so focused on finding his way out of the forest that he hadn't paused for anything. Every second he wasted was one too many when he knew Annie might be facing the fight of her life.

He finished his water and thought about what to do while he watched dawn touch the shimmering forest leaves with light. He'd be able to see better, but so could the hunters. And if he did find Annie, how did he defend her? He had her gun, but nothing more. He'd give anything for a couple of big-game guns. And if this search went on until night, he'd love to have night-vision goggles. The hunters would have every tech at their disposal.

Were there any cabins nearby? He hadn't noticed any on the way in. He launched the browser on his phone and found a topo map of the area. There weren't any cabins for miles. It would be faster to ask someone to bring him some rifles.

He called his father. "Dad, I have a problem." He launched into explanations but didn't get very far before his dad interrupted him.

"I'll be right there with some rifles, son." His dad sounded alert even though it was barely dawn. "And I bought some night goggles the other day on a whim so Martha and I could watch the wildlife at night from the cabin. I'll bring them too. Give me your coordinates."

Jon rattled them off. "Leave them in my car, and I'll circle back to get them. And Dad. Be careful."

"I'm not in any danger, but you are. Praying for you all. Stay safe."

Jon put his phone away and opened his trunk to see if he could find anything of value he could use in the search. He stuffed a pair of binoculars, a small foldable shovel, rope and string, a warm throw, and bottles of water into his backpack. There was a hunting knife and fishing string in his tackle box, so he took that too. He almost didn't see the can of bear spray in the back, but he grabbed it. He tossed in some jerky and nuts as well, then zipped it up and slid his arms into the loops. After stuffing Annie's gun into the waistband of his jeans, he surveyed the trunk one last time.

His golf clubs caught his eye. The nice heft of a metal driver might come in handy. He pushed as much of it into the backpack as would fit and angled what stuck out along his side and out of his way. He was as ready as he'd ever be. If only he had a real GPS, one that didn't depend on cell service. But he was stuck with what he had.

Where in this huge tract of land did he focus? What would make sense for hunters? He downloaded the topo map before he lost cell service again and studied it. It would need to be the least accessible and least likely to run the risk of having regular hunters wander into their domain. So not near water sources that might pull in game that would be a draw for regular hunters. Nor near fishing spots.

One area stood out to him. The beach along Lake Superior was rocky and not welcoming to boaters. No river or stream running through most of it. And it was about as far away as possible. If he was wrong, he'd hike for hours in the wrong direction, but if he was right, he might land right in the middle of all of it.

And he might need the rifles his father was bringing. If he headed to where his gut was leading him, he couldn't easily circle back and get them. But if he found Annie, they could beat feet here as fast as possible and would have the guns waiting for them.

He couldn't stand here and worry all day. Annie could be in trouble even now, and he needed to find her. All he could do was trust that God was leading him in the right direction. He shut his car door and headed for the hum of mosquitoes and the shadows of deep woods.

Hang on, love. I'm coming.

/ / /

Though Annie wasn't hungry, she choked down the breakfast of a cold omelet left inside her door. She would need every bit of strength and cunning she possessed if what she thought was going to happen this morning transpired.

She'd prayed off and on all night, but she felt alert and refreshed in spite of the broken sleep. The plastic fork would be of no use to her, so she left it on the paper plate. There was no weapon of any kind she could spot in the tiny cell.

But she knew the woods. She'd find something out there, and she would beat these men who took her. When the door opened, her confidence faltered. Joel West stepped into the room. He wore a Hawk tee.

"We meet on my turf this time, chickie." He tossed her a backpack. "Put that on."

Her gaze went to the big rifle dangling from his left arm. A Mauser with a Swarovski scope. A tingle between her shoulder blades made her feel as if he was aiming it at her back even now.

She didn't move. "Where do you want to take me?"

"Out. Snap snap."

She didn't take well to orders like that, so she stared back at him with her chin high. "What does the Hawk tee mean? I saw a picture of Glenn dressed in one."

He smiled. "I'm the hawk. The boss was letting me know I got to take charge of the next hunt. And this time that's you."

His hazel eyes went even colder, and he slipped the rifle off his shoulder and into his hands. "Now get moving unless you want me to shoot you where you sit. No skin off my nose if you want to give up."

Annie wasn't a quitter. Maybe she should make him think she was too frightened to be much of a challenge. She worked up tears and put a quiver in her voice. "Just let me go. I won't tell anyone about you. I have a little girl at home. Her name is Kylie. Her daddy died, and she needs a mother." Talking about her daughter closed her throat, and she couldn't go on with it. It was too close to the truth.

He stared back impassively. "Move."

Tears didn't move him, but maybe her display had made him consider her with more contempt. She forced herself to her feet and shouldered the backpack before going ahead of him out the entry. For an instant she thought about slamming the door shut and locking him in, but he came after her too quickly for the idea to take shape.

Outside her cell another concrete area led to several other metal doors. More cells? Could her sister be in one of them? "Sarah!" she called.

The blow came out of nowhere and knocked her onto her face. She rolled over to see the butt of the rifle descending again, and she rolled out of the way. Her head rang with the impact, but she managed to regain her feet.

"Don't do that again, or next time I'll bash your brains in." He gestured with the rifle. "Outside."

The door he indicated was steel as well but wider and taller than the cell doors. She twisted the knob, and it opened easily. The birds sang and the serene blue sky looked down on her as if there was nothing wrong in the world. But not even the sweet aroma of the wildflowers in the area could mask the reality.

She was staring at a killing field.

She sensed the dark pall over the area in spite of how attractive it appeared on the outside. She swept her gaze over the area, searching for landmarks to orient herself to her location. Even though she had no phone to call for help, if she could figure out where she was, she would know which direction to head.

She stopped in her tracks and turned to face the evil man. "Now what?"

"Now you run. If you can find your way to civilization, we'll let you go. Otherwise." He grinned and made a cutting motion across his throat. "I think you'll make a fine quarry."

Quarry. That word again. These guys were exactly who she'd thought. "How many of you do I have to outrun?"

He lifted an eyebrow as though he'd never been asked that question. "That's for me to know and you to find out."

She started to snap back a sharp comeback, then remembered her strategy and hung her head. "Maybe you're right." Plopping on the ground, she crossed her arms over her chest. "Just shoot me and get it over with."

She took a quick peek at the displeasure on his face and suppressed a grunt of satisfaction. He saw her as a helpless female who wouldn't be much competition.

Let them take her for granted at their own peril.

He nudged her with his foot. "It doesn't play out that way. Get up and start moving."

"Or what? I already said you could shoot me now. What more can you do to me?"

"If you're lucky, you might meet up with someone you know. That'll make it more fun."

She couldn't swallow a gasp. "Sarah? You have Sarah here too?"

Maybe her sister wasn't dead. She scrambled to her feet, all thought of pretense gone. "Where is she?"

"The stakes are higher now, aren't they? It's not just your survival but hers as well. We thought that would make a nice incentive. It's different from anything we've ever done before too."

She shuddered at the confirmation these men played such a heinous and deadly sport. "Do I get a head start?"

"We don't always do that, but you're such a pansy I think we'd better give you one. We don't want the fun over too soon."

"How much time do I have before you start searching for me?"

He glanced at his watch. "You've got one hour."

"You swear or is it a trick?"

"Do I look like the kind of man to joke?"

She shook her head in a placating motion so he didn't see the glint of rage she was sure was radiating from her eyes. "Thank you for the extra time. Is there any area off-limits?"

"What do you think?"

She didn't answer and set off at a run into the deepest part of the woods. Her strategy was forming as she ran. First, find Sarah. Then circle back and enter the building with them out hunting for them. They surely had a working phone in there somewhere.

THIRTY-TWO

SARAH HAD A HEAD START OF AN HOUR, BUT THAT TIME was long past. The men could be sneaking up on her even now. She was hopelessly lost in the thick trees that blocked out the sun and left her clueless on which way was north, east, south, or west.

Branches swatted at her face and tripped her up as she tried to move quickly but quietly through the forest. Birds took flight overhead, a telltale sign to her pursuers of her location. How was she supposed to evade capture out here? There was no good place to hide, just trees and more trees. She'd give anything for a safe cave right now.

Though was anywhere safe?

She paused and bent over to catch her breath. The dog licked her chin, and she let him. Her chest heaved with the effort to draw in enough oxygen. If she could keep up a fast pace, maybe she'd find her way out of here. Her gasps slowed, and she stood to examine the area around her. Was there anything that might help her figure out how to get out of these woods?

She'd tried climbing a tree early on, but the immensity of the north woods appeared to go on and on. Each way she turned was a vast wilderness of trees on three sides with the lake on the fourth side. She'd thought of heading for Superior, but if she followed the shore, they'd almost certainly find her, and she'd have no place to run. The lake would hem her in. Trying to swim out wasn't an option when there was no sight of land out there. The cold would soon take her down.

Her best chance was to beat this wilderness.

A twig snapped, and she froze to listen. It came from her left, near a big pine tree. Sarah whirled to run, but the dog whined and ran toward the sound. "Come back, boy," she whispered.

She should run, but she didn't want to leave him. His tail swished, but the silly dog liked everyone. Though he hadn't liked the men who'd grabbed her off the island, so maybe that was a good sign.

"Good boy," said a familiar voice softly. "Where's Sarah?"

Annie?

Tears filled Sarah's eyes, and she ran toward the voice. "Annie, oh Annie! Is it really you?"

At the sight of her sister's face, Sarah flung herself into Annie's arms. The solid feel of her, and the warmth of her arms made the fear fade for a few minutes at least. Sarah clung to her as her sister held her tight and patted her back. She had to choke back the sobs. The men might hear.

Sarah lifted her head and took a calming breath. "Do you know how to get out of here? How did you find me?"

"You and the dog left tracks anyone could follow." Annie wiped the tears from her cheeks and shook her head. "The men took me, too, Sarah. I haven't figured out where we are yet, but I hoped I'd stumble across you. The man who sent me out told me I might find you. I'm so glad you're still alive. And now there's two of us. We have to outsmart them."

"Wait, what? They're chasing you too?" Her sister was in this pickle with her. That wasn't good. In fact, it was terrible. Sarah would rather lose her life than know Annie might be killed too. Her death would leave Kylie alone.

They couldn't let that happen. "I hope you have a plan."

Annie rubbed the dog's head. "The first thing on my list was to try to find you." She put her hands on her hips and glanced around. "I'm going to climb that tree and see where we are. Maybe I'll recognize something."

Sarah didn't tell her she'd already tried that. Annie was well versed in these woods. She'd surely recognize something and know how to get them out of here. Annie knew everything about survival, and she was in law enforcement. Handling criminals was what she did.

Resting her hand on Scout's head to keep him quiet, she watched Annie climb the big oak tree until her figure disappeared into the leafy curtain of leaves. Sarah wanted to call out questions, but she didn't dare raise her voice. She didn't know how many people were after them or where they were.

The seconds stretched into minutes, then Annie's boots appeared followed by the rest of her as she emerged from the overstory of leaves. Once her sister was on the ground, Sarah leaned in close. "Any houses or civilization?"

Annie shook her head. "Nothing but trees." She rooted in the pocket of her jeans and pulled out a pen. "I'm going to make a compass."

Reaching into the backpack she wore, she extracted a small first-aid kit and broke off a piece of thread, then pulled out a small needle. She knelt by the dog. "I won't hurt you, boy."

Holding the sharp point of the needle toward her, she

rubbed the eye of the needle against the dog's fur. *Rub, rub, rub.* Sarah lost track of how many strokes Annie made with the needle along the dog's fur.

When her sister was satisfied, she put a strand of thread through the eye of the needle and doubled it. Then she fished out an almost-empty plastic water bottle and poked the needle through the cap by pressing it hard against the tree trunk. When she was able to draw it through to the bottom, she tied a knot in the top and let the needle dangle into the bottle.

She screwed the top onto the water bottle. "I need to climb up again and get a feel for north and south." Holding the top of the bottle in her teeth, she climbed the tree again.

Sarah held her breath and prayed this crazy thing would work.

/ / /

Annie hadn't made a compass since she was in Girl Scouts, and she smiled as she shimmied back down the tree with the marked bottle in her hand. Sarah stood with her back to the tree watching the thickest part of the woods. Annie didn't want to break her bubble, but the men were more apt to come from an easier direction. Any hunter knew to find the path of least resistance. For one thing it was quieter, but it was also less tiring.

Annie held up the bottle. "Got it."

She moved away from the trees and held the bottle still until the needle settled and swung in the north to south direction. It was exactly where she'd placed it when up in the tree. This thing worked. Rubbing the needle in the dog's fur had magnetized it.

She pointed to the south, on the same trajectory she'd been on when she ran into Sarah. "This way."

They moved through the forest, skirting the brambles and the thicker brush as best as they could. Annie would have liked to have had the time to ask Sarah questions about what she'd seen and what the men looked like who had taken her. There would be time for that later. They had to get to safety first.

She checked her watch. Ten in the morning. She'd been walking nonstop for four hours. No wonder her muscles ached and she wished she could fall into a soft bed of pine needles for a while. The men would be on them in no time if they did though.

She'd thought to see them before now. Were they deliberately watching them from afar and laughing at their feeble attempts to survive? Annie didn't want to believe it, but she didn't know why they'd been allowed to go this far without a confrontation.

Maybe they were waiting for dark.

She picked up the pace. These woods would be terrifying in the dark. Never knowing when a shot would ring out from the trees or a man with a knife would come rushing toward them. They had to find their way out.

She led the way, pausing often to recheck the compass. From her perch in the tree, she knew it wouldn't be a short walk to get out of here. The terrain seemed to go on forever. She'd seen only rocky terrain this direction, and she hoped when they arrived, they might find a good place to hole up for the night.

She did *not* want to try to rest in the woods, exposed to the murderous stares of the men who hunted them. From the curve of Lake Superior she'd seen, she believed they were in the vast forest south and east of Fourteen Mile Point. Going on that assumption, if they pressed on south and a little west, they should run into some hunting cabins. None would be close, but it was better than heading north toward Houghton.

"Can we rest a minute?" Sarah whispered from behind her.

Annie turned to see her sister's pale face. Sarah bent over and threw up, and Annie grabbed water from her backpack. "Here, take a sip. Easy."

Sarah sipped the water and closed her eyes. "Thanks. I don't feel very good." She looped an arm around the dog's neck and buried her face in his fur.

Annie kept an eye on the trees around them while she let her sister sit. "Are you sick?"

"I don't know. Maybe. I let the soup they brought sit all day. Maybe I have food poisoning." She sent a pleading gaze Annie's way. "If you have to leave me, I understand."

Annie squatted beside her and stared deep into her blue eyes. "Sarah, I will never leave you. Never. Don't even think for a minute I would do that. I came out here to find you, and we are both walking out of these woods together."

Her voice trembled, and she cleared her throat before she stood and gazed around at the possible places where they might rest out of sight of any hunters. Maybe the trees? But could Sarah climb in her condition?

A tall oak tree caught her attention. Was that a deer stand in it? She walked over to inspect it, and sure enough, a sturdy platform was wedged into a crook of the tree. It wasn't that far up either. Maybe she could help Sarah get up there, then use pine branches to brush away their tracks. She could then make new tracks leading away from here before she doubled back to rejoin her sister.

It seemed a doable plan.

She returned to Sarah's side and took her arm. "I have a plan if you think you can get up that tree into the stand." She pointed it out.

"I think I can," Sarah said. "But what about the dog?"

Annie had forgotten the dog. "I'll hide him nearby where he can't make tracks."

"I don't want you to leave me."

"It will only be for a few minutes. Once I get you up there, you can sleep while I throw the hunters off the trail." She explained her plan to her sister, but Sarah appeared greener by the second.

She threw up again. "Sorry."

Annie handed her the water bottle again. "It's not your fault. Let your stomach settle a minute, and we'll see if you can get up there."

She saw a deer trail leading deeper into the woods. It would be a good decoy direction.

"I think I can go now," Sarah said.

Annie helped her up, and they went to the tree. There weren't any low-hanging branches, so Annie laced her fingers together for Sarah to step into. She boosted her up a foot or so, then got under her and let Sarah put her foot on her shoulder to help her scramble up the rest of the way.

She disappeared into the leaves. "I'm on the blind. Hurry back, Annie. I'm scared."

"I'll be right back." Annie called the dog to her and picked up some pine branches as she went. She wasn't about to tell Sarah she was terrified out of her wits too.

THIRTY-THREE

ANNIE'S LEGS AND ARMS ACHED WITH FATIGUE, BUT she pressed on with the task. The tracks they'd left quickly disappeared under the sweep of pine branches.

When she came to a small stream, she decided it was the perfect place to double back. She took off her boots and waded through the water downstream about a hundred years. The cold, wet mud under her feet was slippery, and it took longer than she would have liked. She put her footgear back on and laid a false trail that led away from where her sister was hidden. When she reached a rocky hillside, Annie beelined for the stream, sweeping away her tracks again.

A few yards from the stream, she paused and wiped perspiration from her face with the back of her hand. Her stomach rumbled, and she took out a jerky stick. Sarah was probably hungry too, and Annie hadn't thought to leave her with food. She'd assumed the backpack her sister had contained the same items the men had given her, but she should have checked.

A snap of a twig made her freeze, and she whipped her head in the direction of the sound before diving into nearby underbrush. She held her breath as she heard the mutter of a couple of male voices. It had to be the hunters who were following their tracks. She didn't dare part the leaves to look at them. They were too close and might see her pale face in the leaves.

It sounded like at least two, maybe three.

"They're leaving a trail even a beginner could follow." The voice sounded like Joel's.

"I thought the ranger might make this more of a fun challenge," said another voice.

Annie didn't recognize that guy. Someone coughed, and her breath seized in her chest when a familiar voice spoke.

"Don't assume anything. I know Annie. She's resourceful."

Max Reardon? Annie had to be mistaken. She had to know for sure, so she eased a leaf out of the way and peeked through to see the three men down the way and just across the stream. There was no mistake. The third man was Max, dressed in camouflage gear and leaning against a tree while he rummaged in his backpack.

How could he be part of this? He was a pillar of the community, involved in all kinds of good things. He was wooing Anu too. Even Annie's parents had respected him. Why would a man like that put his reputation and his life on the line for something so horrific? What kind of darkness lurked behind those kind eyes? The reality of it took her breath away.

Joel gave a derisive laugh. "Is that why you didn't want us to grab her in the first place? You're afraid she'll make it out?"

"I don't doubt our ability to find them. Sarah will slow her down. I actually like Annie, but she's tenacious. I knew once she put her whole attention on finding us, we'd have to take her down. And here we are."

"And a fun two-for-one. It gives better odds for each of us to make a kill. I like it," Eric said.

Annie eased the leaf back into place and put her head down as she tried to assimilate this reality. Max was at the heart of all this. Probably the leader. It broke Annie's heart to think how this would hurt Anu. But then, she'd expressed misgivings about how Max had seemed secretive, so she might not be as surprised as Annie thought. Anu's instincts were good, but Annie's had failed her when it came to Max. She breathed in quietly and tried to manage the impulse that made her want to charge out of this hiding place with fists flying.

How dare he do something like this? How could he and those men chase down human beings? It was abominable.

The sounds of them moving away shook her out of her anger. Once they were out of sight, she wiggled out, grabbed her pine branch, and rushed to the stream. After taking off her boots and socks again, she waded down the stream for about a mile, then regained the bank. Once her feet were dry and shod in her foot-gear again, she took a path back to the tree. She made sure no sign of her footprints showed. In some areas, she hopped from rock to rock and in others she swiped the marks away with the branches.

She didn't think they could trace her back to where her sister waited with the dog, but they needed to hide and rest a few hours before they risked it. She prayed Sarah was feeling better. They needed to be ready to run at a moment's notice, and her sister could barely walk when Annie had left.

She reached the tiny clearing where she'd left Sarah. Waiting a few minutes in the shadows, she studied the terrain and searched for any bootprints leading into the area. Once she was satisfied the men hadn't arrived before her, she swept her prints away as she approached the deer stand. Once she was next to the trunk, she peered up and saw Sarah's foot dangling just over the side.

She didn't dare call to her in case the men were nearby. It would be impossible to climb the tree with the pine branch in her hand, so she threw it as far as she could toward a similar tree, then reached up and began the climb. Her fatigue slowed her down, and she was panting by the time she rolled over onto the floor of the stand.

Sarah was out cold. She hadn't even noticed the noise of Annie's climb or the way the stand moved when it took her weight. Annie decided to let her sleep. She took off her backpack and used it as a pillow to try to get some rest herself.

Every muscle in her body ached, and she should have been able to sleep, but every time she closed her eyes, they popped back open. The flutter of wings, the croaks of frogs, every rustle from the wind through the trees had her pulse ratcheting up. It was going to be a long night.

She only prayed they could stay hidden in the tree until daybreak tomorrow.

/ / /

Night descended with a cooling breeze that did little to drive away the mosquitoes that came to feast on her flesh. Sarah pulled a rain slicker out of the backpack the man had given her and huddled into its protective folds. She pulled her knees to her chest and wrapped the ends around her bare legs too. There was no repellant in her pack, probably because the men wanted her to be miserable. They were happy to provide things that could extend their fun, but they didn't want her to be too comfortable.

Bare arms unprotected from the biting insects, Annie slept

beside her. Sarah couldn't search for a cover for her since she was using her backpack as a pillow. Maybe there was something else in Sarah's pack. She rummaged through and found a light throw she draped across her sister.

Annie roused immediately, and she sat up. "Sarah? You okay?" Her voice was a mere whisper.

"I'm feeling much better," Sarah whispered back. "I didn't hear you return. Did everything go okay?"

"I think I was successful at throwing them off our tail." Annie huddled inside the thin blanket. "Thanks for this. The mosquitoes are vicious." She waved the bugs from her face.

"Where's the dog?"

"I didn't see him when I got back. He was either sleeping or wandering somewhere. I'd hoped he'd stay put so he didn't leave tracks. He might circle our tree and lead them here."

Sarah heard the worry in her sister's voice and wished she'd been smart enough to leave the dog behind. If they were found, it would be her fault.

The night was pitch-black in the forest. "What time is it?"

"I don't dare light my watch. I can't see the moon to estimate it without climbing higher. We'd better stay put and try to sleep."

"I'm not sleepy now, but I could try." The whine of the mosquitoes was enough to keep anyone from sleeping.

In the darkness Sarah heard the faint *zing* of a zipper before Annie pressed a throw into her hands. "Thanks."

She pulled it over her head and burrowed into its folds. The instant silence from mosquito wings was a blessed relief. She tried to curl up enough to sleep, but the deer blind was narrow and hard. Neither of them had much room, and she was conscious of how Annie had to hug the side of the blind to keep from falling off. How she'd done it while sleeping was a mystery.

Annie shuffled beside her and came closer. A fold of the blanket lifted, and her sister moved under it with her, spooning against Sarah's back. "I'm going to adjust both blankets so all our skin is under cover. Hold on."

With a few deft movements, Annie moved things around before snuggling in close enough that the warmth of her body radiated to Sarah. A faint memory came of being in a makeshift "tent" in their bedroom bunk beds just like this.

"I think you read me books like this when we were little. You had a flashlight you took from Dad's toolbox. He always knew where to find it."

"You're right," Annie said. "Your favorite was *The Little Engine That Could*."

"I think I can, I think I can," Sarah whispered. She hadn't remembered that book until now.

"We have to cling to that right now. We have to believe God will help us out of this terrible spot we're in. He's already led us to each other, and I'm glad I have you with me."

Tears sprang to Sarah's eyes. She'd never expected Annie to forgive her when she didn't deserve it. "They would have already killed me if you hadn't found me, Annie. I can't believe men would be so cruel."

"I saw the men." Annie's voice vibrated with a tight rage. "I know who the leader is."

"That guy with the beard?" Sarah shuddered at the memory of him.

"It's Max. Max was with them."

"Are you sure? I can't believe he would do this."

"I saw him clearly. I recognized his voice before I saw him."

Sarah struggled to take in the enormity of the news. It had to feel like a huge betrayal to Annie. She'd liked Max.

Annie threw her arm over Sarah. "I'm sorry, Sarah. Sorry I didn't forgive you sooner. I sent you straight into the lion's den when I had Jon take you to Tremolo Island. If not for me, you wouldn't have been caught up in this. He would have gone straight for me when I didn't give up the investigation."

Sarah reveled in her sister's embrace, the first true expression of love she'd had in all these years. Every moment of this terror they'd lived through so far was worth it for these few minutes of knowing Annie loved her.

"It's not your fault," she said. "I'd rather be here with you right now than living life the way things used to be. I won't ever let you down again, Annie."

"We all fail. I'm sure I'll fail you again, even though I don't want to. But when I do, remember I love you and I'll never stop."

The women lay snuggled together, and Sarah had fallen asleep. She wasn't sure what time it was when Annie's grip tightened around her. "Shh," she said in a barely audible whisper.

Sarah strained to listen, but it was hard to hear past the blood pounding in her ears. Then the snapping of twigs penetrated her terror. Someone was out there. Maybe more than one.

Had they been found? She didn't want either of them to see her. Her terror had her huddling under a blanket like a child afraid of the dark. What was out there was worse than any night terror she'd experienced as a little girl.

Now she knew boogey men were real and that they could reach in and change life as she knew it. The men chasing them would slaughter them like deer and laugh while they did it.

THIRTY-FOUR

JON KNEW THE MINUTE THE DOG CAME BOUNDING toward him that Sarah had to be out here somewhere. And if Sarah was in the forest, maybe Annie was too.

He knelt and rubbed the dog's ears. "Good boy!" The golden wiggled all over and licked his face. His whine sounded urgent. "Where are they, boy?"

The dog turned and plunged into the darkness, and Jon struggled to keep up. The beam of his flashlight bobbed along, touching first the path and then the thick brush barring his way. The dog paused occasionally as if to allow him time to catch up. Several times Jon lost sight of the dog, and his euphoria began to fade. How long had he trekked these deer trails? An hour? Two hours?

Finally the dog lay down. His tongue lolled from his panting mouth. He was as hot and tired as Jon. Maybe more so. Jon glanced at his watch. Nearly three in the morning. He retrieved a bottle of water from his backpack and glanced around for something to hold the water for the dog. He pulled out a granola wrapper, and he layered it in his palm to try to hold enough fluid to give the dog. The golden eagerly lapped it up, and Jon gave him more and more until the bottle was gone.

His lids drooped, and Jon would have to sleep for an hour

before hitting it again. His fatigue would make him miss signs he might otherwise see, and he was not a good tracker on his sharpest day. He pulled out a blanket and curled up with the dog.

When he opened his eyes again, dawn's fingers had lightened the forest enough to make out the pine trees around him. He sat up and groaned as his still-healing shoulder protested his position on the hard ground. The dog sprang up with an eager bark. His tail swishing, he stared at Jon with expectant dark eyes, then gave the little grumble Jon had gotten used to hearing from him.

Jon reached into his backpack and got out two meat sticks. He unwrapped one and gave it to the dog, who gobbled it down. "Ready to find them?" He ate his own breakfast while he jogged behind the dog, who seemed to have found new energy.

The dog stopped and whined. His ears went back, and he crouched with his belly to the ground. Jon went on full alert and listened to the way the singing of the birds had stilled. Hunters nearby—or worse? He dove for a nearby bank of bushes and lay still. The dog crawled to join him, and Jon put his arm around the animal to keep it still and quiet. Whoever was out there had terrified the dog.

Twigs snapped, and he caught the smell of a cigarette on the breeze. A deep cough was followed by a curse, then a man said, "You need to give up those cancer sticks."

"Mind your own business," another man snarled.

Jon didn't recognize the voices. He stayed motionless, and as the men passed by, he caught a glimpse of the guys dressed in camouflage and carrying high-powered rifles with scopes. Bigger firepower than they'd need for squirrels or pigeons that were the only game in season now.

"The women outfoxed us," one of the men complained. "That

ranger is a smart one. We never should have let her hook up with her sister."

His mouth went dry as he realized these guys were hunting Annie and Sarah. Jon didn't have a big enough gun to take them on. The most he could hope to do was pick them off one by one. He wasn't the sharpshooter Annie was, but he might be able to wing one in the leg, then dash away and wait for the other one to come after him. He'd just need the right setup.

Noiselessly, he pulled his gun out and edged a leaf out of the way with the barrel. He took aim at the back of the closest guy's knee. His palms began to sweat, and his hands shook with the weight of how important it was to be accurate. He'd only have one chance at making this work.

His finger tightened on the trigger, but before he could squeeze off a shot, the dog burst out of the bushes from beside him and gave a ferocious volley of barks. Jon pulled the barrel of the gun back before the men could spot the metallic gleam of it.

Both men turned to face the dog, and the one with curly red hair sticking out below his hat laughed. "Gonna eat us, dog? Betcha can't get in a good bite before I put you down."

Jon recognized Joel West with the full beard. Was the redhead Eric Bell?

"Leave him alone. He's just scared." He crouched and held out his hand. "Come 'ere, pooch. Want something to eat?" He reached into his pocket and pulled out a half-eaten jerky stick.

Stiff-legged, the dog backed away, but his barking petered off to a low whine. When the man held the food closer, the dog snagged it with gentle teeth and chomped it down.

Joel stood. "See, told you he was just scared. But if he's here, the women have to be close. Where are they, boy? Can you show us?" The dog lay down and stared as the guy cursed and spit on the ground. "Stupid animal. Search for prints. Maybe we can follow the dog prints."

Jon hadn't been careful about tracks. His one thought had been to find Annie, and he'd blundered through the woods like a moose. The guys would find their way right to him with a short search. He turned his head and looked behind him. Thick brush lay that way and would make too much noise. The way to his right was just as bad.

He either had to go to the left or plow right out in front of them before they found him.

/ / /

"The dog was here at some point. I think they covered their tracks as they left." Max's voice held no trace of the fatigue Annie felt even after sleeping a few hours.

Was the man a machine? And the guys with him had tracked them through the night. Annie thought a glimmer of daybreak hovered over the tops of the trees, but she wasn't sure.

She put her hand over her sister's mouth to make sure an involuntary gasp didn't come out as she awakened. Sarah jerked but said nothing. Annie pressed her cheek to Sarah's in reassurance. So far the men didn't know they were up here.

"Looks like the dog slept here," one of the other men said from farther away.

"Any sign of where they went?" Max asked.

The silence below stretched out as their feet crunched in the dirt and rocks. "There's a path here in the vegetation. Maybe they passed us on our way here. Not sure where they were headed."

They were falling for the fake trail Annie had laid. If she hadn't been holding Sarah, she would have attempted a silent fist pump. Her sore muscles were worth it if it fooled them even for a while.

A slight tickle started in her nose. She clamped her nostrils shut and tried to take deep breaths through her mouth. She couldn't sneeze, not now. The sensation grew, and she swallowed several times. Clearing her throat gently and noiselessly didn't help. Her eyes watered with the effort to hold it in. She put her sleeves to her nose and softly blew. The desire to sneeze only grew.

Go, go now!

If only they would leave the area, but they continued to tramp around the tiny clearing. They were right under them. One sound and one of them would fire a volley of shots into the tree.

"We've rested long enough," Max said from right below her. "Let's get going."

Finally. Annie held on with every bit of her strength as the sounds below moved away. When she couldn't hear any more tromping, she held her arm to her face and sneezed as gently as she could. It sounded to her ears like a bomb, but she knew it couldn't be that loud. She sneezed again, and the tickle was gone.

The minutes ticked by, and dawn began to soften the edges of the darkness. How far had the men gone?

"I have to go to the bathroom," Sarah whispered.

And there was nothing to use up here. They'd have to climb down. Sarah had probably held it in like Annie had tried to hold back the sneeze and was probably just as miserable. She could ask her to relieve herself up here and let it trickle down, but they needed to get going anyway. The men might circle back.

Annie released her and threw back the blankets. "I'll go first and help you down."

She stuffed her belongings back into the backpack, then leaned over and let it drop to the ground. Sarah did the same with hers. Annie swung her legs over onto a lower branch and began to climb down. She let go a few feet above the ground and landed on her feet, then reached up to help Sarah.

Light was beginning to pour into the forest, and she could see Sarah's frightened face. "It's okay. I've got you. Hold on to the brace of the deer blind and drop your legs over the edge. I'll stand on the backpack and you'll be able to reach my shoulders with your feet."

"I'll try."

Sarah's face disappeared, and her legs came over the side. Annie stepped onto both backpacks to hoist her height up. Sarah's feet were almost to her shoulders. "Stretch down just a bit. You'll be able to feel my shoulders with your toes."

Sarah's foot grazed Annie's shoulder, then the other one landed too. Annie braced herself against the tree trunk to take her sister's weight. "Grab the tree to steady yourself."

Sarah reached out for the bark and clung to it while Annie steadied her sister's legs and managed to lower her to the ground. They were both breathless when Sarah was safely standing on her own two feet.

Annie pointed to a thickly forested area. "Go over there. I'll scout around and make sure they aren't doubling back."

She waited until her sister nodded and headed toward the seclusion of the forest before she found a pine branch and followed the tracks left by the men. There was a niggling sensation in her back, a warning that something wasn't quite right, but she wasn't sure if it was fear or an internal warning she couldn't place.

The tracks split into two, one going forward and one to the

right. She stood and stared as she pondered what that meant. Did they think their quarries were up ahead and they sought to ambush them, or was it something else? Adrenaline shot through her at the possibility they'd seen something in the small clearing that had given away their location. Maybe the hunters had split up to ambush them in the clearing.

She whipped around to run back and warn Sarah and found a rifle aimed at her head. Max's grim face peered down the length of the scope.

She took a step back. "Max, I never expected you to be in on this. I trusted you. How could you do this?"

His brown eyes flickered with a hint of regret. "I didn't want to, but you wouldn't listen, Annie. Nothing dissuaded you from investigating. You left me with no choice."

"Why, Max? How did a good man like you get sucked into something so heinous? Was it Sean?"

He barked out a laugh. "You think Sean corrupted me? It was the other way around. I was searching for hunting grounds like this when I had him build my house. You'll never understand it." He lowered the rifle. "I find it difficult to shoot you while you're staring at me, and it's too soon to end the game. My men will want in on the final kill."

"I-I can go?"

"For now. The other guys are catnapping. We'll be right behind you when they wake."

As she darted past, he grabbed the branch from her hand. "I suspected you were wiping out your tracks. No more of that."

She didn't answer but ran as fast as she could back to get her sister. He might tell her she couldn't hide their location, but she wasn't about to listen.

THIRTY-FIVE

A SHOUT CAME FROM THE WOODS, AND JOEL WHIRLED just before the butt of his gun was about to move away the foliage in front of Jon's face. Joel trotted toward the sound. "What's got your Speedos in a wad?" He sounded annoyed.

Jon let out the breath he was holding. This was his only chance to wriggle out of here. He scooted toward the only clear path to his left, and the dog followed him. It seemed a hot, miserable eternity before he hauled himself out from under the underbrush and stood. The dog emerged and stood waiting expectantly for Jon to give him direction on where they were going.

Jon checked which way was west on his phone and decided it was the opposite way the men had gone. He glanced over his shoulder and moved as noiselessly as possible along the deer trail meandering in front of him. The way was rocky, and he prayed his footprints wouldn't be as visible with so much rock. It would take a miracle to find Annie undetected. There were more than two men—that much he knew—and they were clearly experienced hunters, while he would be hard-pressed to take down a deer.

He made good time hurrying along the narrow path, and he tried to stay away from the shrubs where he feared he'd leave evidence of his passage in bruised and broken leaves. He guessed he was leaving a trail even an amateur could follow.

The dog gave a small yelp and darted past Jon's feet. He leaped over several shrubs and plowed through a stand of small pines with his tail in a happy plume. Annie and Sarah? Almost afraid to hope, Jon ran after him. He fought his way through pines so thick he couldn't breathe until he stood under a tall oak tree whose shadow had smothered out most of the vegetation under it.

His eyes widened at the sight of his Annie. Her blonde hair was bedraggled and full of twigs and leaves, and her blue eyes stood out in sharp contrast to her muddy face. She knelt beside Sarah, who was on her knees with her arms around the dog's neck. Jon had never seen a sight more wonderful than Annie alive and breathing. He'd been so afraid.

"Annie," he croaked.

She jerked, and her eyes went wide. She leaped to her feet and hurtled toward him to hit against his chest in a satisfying weight. He hugged her and fought tears of relief. "I thought I'd lost you," he murmured against her hair.

Her arms about squeezed the life out of him, and he could feel her terror in their grip. He hung on to her and tried to give her as much encouragement with his embrace as he could. Though they were far from safe out here with those men stalking them, at least they were together.

She pulled away and peered up at him, her blue eyes pools of anguish. "Jon, *Max* is behind this! I thought he was a good guy, a friend. Someone I'd hoped to be almost part of the family when he married Anu. If for no other reason, I have to get out of here and let Anu know what kind of man he really is."

He gripped her shoulders. "Listen, I've got rifles back at the car by now. My dad was dropping some off. If we can circle back, we can at least be armed."

Though he planned to shove them all in the car and hightail it out of here.

He pressed a kiss against her forehead and stepped back. There would be time for more once they were safe. Every second counted right now. "Do you have any idea where we are? Anything seem familiar?"

She shook her head. "I'm all turned around. I lost my make-shift compass and most of the time I can't tell where the sun is, so I've been wandering around lost."

He thrust his phone into her hand. "I have a compass. I downloaded a topo map of the area before I came in here with no signal. It might help."

"Oh, it should!"

He told her his password and she punched it in, then studied the compass before she opened the map. Her finger traced a fire road. "We might be near this, but I can't tell for sure. If we could get to the fire road, we'd have an easier time of finding our way out of here."

"But Max and his men will also have an easier time finding us," Sarah said. "I think we need to start laying traps for them. Just making a beeline out of here is going to get us shot. You know it will, Annie. Those men have done this often. It's a sport to them."

Annie gave a reluctant nod. "She's right, Jon. Those guns are enticing, but if we forget who we're facing, we'll be dead in no time. They have a lot of firepower. And they're expert marksmen, well versed in tracking. There are three of them—Max, Joel West, and Eric Bell."

"So we do something unexpected, whatever that might be."

"I'd thought about going back to the cells where they held us. There was a building I thought they might be using as an armory. Getting into it might be a problem, but I think they will suspect we'll try to hike out of the woods. They won't be expecting us to go deeper in."

"Let alone going to their stronghold," Jon said. "How far away is it?"

"Probably a four-hour hike, so the trick will be staying alive long enough to get there." Annie turned to her sister. "Your idea of traps is great, Sarah. If we could find some string, I could set snares. I've got ideas for other booby traps too. Just not many resources."

Jon reached for his pack. "I just might have something useful."

/ / /

Annie set Jon to making punji sticks as they walked along. With his knife he sharpened six sticks to a point. They moved as fast as they could, but Annie kept making direction adjustments and leading them through carpets of pine needles that she could brush out with a branch.

Jon showed her the sticks. "I had no idea the woman I loved was such a warrior. I hope you don't ever use these skills on me."

She wanted to smile, but with her focus on survival, all she could do was make a grimace she hoped he'd take for genuine. "This kind of thing is mostly illegal. If I had any choice, I wouldn't be using them. If none of the hunters fall into this, we'll have to come back later and take it out. I'd hate an innocent person to be injured by the traps."

She surveyed the surroundings, then pointed out two trees about five feet apart. "Sarah, tie a trip wire between those trees. Make it about three inches off the ground. Close enough to the ground it's hard to see but high enough to trip the ankle. Jon, you use that that little shovel and dig a trench three feet past the trip wire. Dig down about a foot. I want them to trip on the wire and fall onto the punji sticks. If we can mess up a knee, they'll have trouble following us. Their companions will have to carry them out."

"You think they will or maybe just leave them until they take care of us?" Sarah asked.

"They're friends, so I hope they have enough concern for each other so we can rattle them as they rescue their buddy. But with such heartless men, it's hard to say. I'll gather leaves and pine needles to cover the trench."

They all set to their various tasks. Once Annie had a pile of debris collected, she grabbed a pine branch and retraced their steps. She wanted to leave a clear trail to this spot, so once she backtracked and erased her steps behind her, she planted her feet carefully the way she wanted them to go and led them right to the trench.

Did they have enough time? There was no way of knowing how closely the men were behind them. She'd tried to cover their tracks the best she could, but there were three of them and a dog, and it was slow going, even though they'd traveled single file to make it easier. The only comfort she had was that the hunters would also be traveling slowly to try to read the signs in the forest. These men took hunting seriously. They didn't go charging carelessly when they wanted to make a big sport of it.

That would take away the "fun" for them.

She found it hard to believe anyone could be so twisted and cruel. *Evil* was the real word. There was evil in the world, and the three of them faced it right now.

When she reached Jon and Sarah again, the booby trap was nearly ready. She helped Jon secure the stakes in the ground, and then she hid them with leaves and pine needles. Jon and Sarah both watched her quietly, and she could sense the fear from her sister. She wished there was time to reassure her that everything would be all right. Annie wasn't sure she could say the words with any kind of sincerity.

The odds were against them.

After testing the strength of the fish wire strung between the trees, she nodded. "I think we're ready. You two go ahead, and I'll leave tracks in the opposite direction of where we're headed. You're going to come to a fork in the trail about a mile up. Keep to the right side. It's the trail back to their headquarters. I'll lay a false trail the other way and join you at the cells."

Jon frowned. "I don't like it, love. We should stay together."

"It has to be this way, Jon." She took her gun from him. "We'll leave a trail like an elephant if we all stay together, and I need them to think we're trying to escape, not head back to where we started. I won't be long. Hurry as fast as you can. When you get there, see if there's a way to break in to that building and get weapons. Sarah, you check out the cells where they had us locked up. See if there's anything we can use for weapons in there. I'll hurry as fast as I can."

Both Jon and Sarah didn't budge, and she gave her sister a small shove. "Go. Right now. We don't have much time."

With reluctance Sarah turned and trudged up the narrow game trail with Scout trailing behind, and Annie pushed Jon after her. "I'm fine. Hurry." She wasn't sure at first if he'd comply, but he finally chewed on his lip and followed after Sarah.

Annie wasted no time in brushing away any marks they'd left before she circled back toward the fire road she'd seen on Jon's map. She didn't want to make it too obvious, so she hopped on rocks, carefully displacing a needle here and a leaf there. She lingered to pull some leaves half off a thick thimbleberry bush before doing it all over again.

She reached the fire road and stared longingly down its length until it disappeared into the green depths of the forest. If only she dared to run for all she was worth for help. But it would be suicide, and she'd promised Jon she'd be right back. He'd be worried. Even if she made it—and she held out no real hope she would—she'd be gone for hours.

Max and his men would kill her and turn back to find the others. No one would escape their net with her gone. She trudged a few yards along the fire trail and found a few rocks leading off into the woods. The perfect spot to slip off and circle back.

THIRTY-SIX

WOULD THIS NIGHTMARE NEVER END? MUSCLES ACH-ing, Sarah trudged through the bugs, the humidity, and the stench of rotting vegetation in the final trek to the place where she and Annie had been held. The sight of the metal roof on the block building of cells squeezed her chest.

She trusted her sister, but it seemed insane to her to walk right into the lion's lair. Sooner or later the hunters would come back here—either with Annie's dead body or another victim. Sarah didn't want to be around for either of those scenarios.

Jon made less noise than she did, but his passage along the path was far from silent. The two of them made enough racket to stop the birds from chirping, and anyone nearby would stop and check it out. But Annie had seemed confident of her plan.

Sarah stopped before she stepped out from under the shelter of the trees. "What time is it?" she whispered to Jon.

He glanced at the phone. "Three. Annie's been gone for two hours. I don't like it."

"I don't either." She also didn't like the thought of moving out into clear view of anyone who happened to still be here. But maybe the place was deserted.

She eyed the three buildings spaced around the clearing. All were block style with metal roofs painted green to blend into the surrounding trees. The cinder blocks were the same color. A chopper or plane flying over this area likely wouldn't notice the structures. The largest one held the prison cells. Another appeared to be a utility shed, and it didn't have a lock on it like the other two. The third one had two locks and no windows, which was why Annie had thought it might be an armory. Sarah had her doubts. She suspected the men kept their guns with them.

But it might stockpile ammo.

Jon stepped past her as if he was tired of waiting for her to make a move. "I'm going to see if there's anything in the utility shed to help us gain entry to the other buildings. There might be keys or tools we can use."

He dashed toward the farthest building and slid open the barn-type door. Sarah waited for a gunshot or a shout to ring out, but only birds chirped in the trees. After a moment, she followed him, but she expected a bullet in her back at any moment.

She stepped into the shed's cooler interior and glanced around. Sun streamed through the fly-speckled windows and shone on the rough plank shelves holding cans of paint, insecticide, and various cans of other utility items. Several boards with nails pounded into them had been attached to the block walls. Tools hung from the nails. A chain saw leaned on the wall in one corner along with a push mower. Lengths of galvanized and plastic pipe leaned against another corner wall as well as a sump pump. Just about anything she could imagine in a utility shed was in here. It might be a treasure trove for her inventive sister.

Jon took a quick look around, then turned and peered above the door. "A set of keys!"

"I'm surprised. I really thought we'd have to figure out a way to break in."

Jon reached up and retrieved the key ring. "There are four. Hopefully they open all of the buildings. Let's check out the building Annie thinks might be an armory."

He ducked out of the shed and went to the building across the clearing. By now, Sarah had quit expecting to be shot at any minute, but she wished Annie would get back. Every minute without her sister made her anxiety tick up a notch. Sarah followed Jon and watched as he inserted one key after another until there was a satisfying *click* as the first lock opened. He did the same with the second lock on the door and laid both padlocks on the ground.

"We're in." He put his shoulder into the sliding door and opened it as wide as possible. "Bingo. Annie was right."

Sarah blinked at the array of guns and boxes of ammo around the interior. She wasn't a gun expert, but even she could recognize assault weapons and high-powered rifles. It appeared like enough firepower for a small army. Maybe this was the hunters' fallback position if they were holding off the authorities.

She followed Jon inside. "Do you know what we should do with all this stuff?"

"I can figure out our best weapons. And when Annie gets back, she might have some ideas on putting alarms and booby traps around to warn us when the men are approaching." He glanced at the time again. "I wish she'd get back."

Sarah nodded, but she had a sinking feeling in her gut that her sister was in trouble. Neither she nor Jon knew a thing about tracking, so taking weapons and trying to find Annie would be a useless endeavor. Knowing Jon though, she was sure he'd charge hell with a water pistol to find her sister. And Sarah wouldn't be far behind.

They wouldn't go down without a fight, and these guns might equalize the battle a bit. She'd never shot one, but she'd try her best. Jon picked up one of the biggest, deadliest-looking rifles.

He searched through the boxes of ammo and loaded it, then handed it to her. "It's ready to shoot. Just point and pull this trigger right here."

She nodded, but the thing felt like an anchor in her hands. It was so heavy she'd have trouble holding it up. "I think I'll need to prop it on something."

"We'll construct a wall for defense or shoot out of the shed's windows if we're attacked."

His lips were pressed in a grim line as he loaded gun after gun and carried them to the shed. They were preparing for war.

/ / /

Every minute that passed without Annie was excruciating to Jon. For now, he would do as she asked and get them armed and ready. When she got here, they might take the guns and hike out, but he'd let her make the call on what to do.

The weapons were loaded and ready against both walls by the windows of the shed. "Grab a gun and let's check out the cell block. What did you see when you were in there?"

"Just cells with steel doors. Like a prison, which is what I'm sure they used it for."

Jon stuck a SIG Sauer gun in his waistband, then grabbed an automatic rifle before heading to the cell block. He fiddled with the lock and found the key that opened it. The door opened with a rush of stale air that held the stench of human waste. He stepped inside and looked around the concrete interior.

The steel doors of the cells lined the hall, and he went through the building opening every door to make sure no other prisoners were trapped inside. Each cell held a small cot, a bucket for a toilet, and nothing else. And each one stank of despair and fear. He hated the thought that his Annie had endured this. Sarah too. No human being should be locked in here, waiting to be hunted down like an animal.

The last door opened into a bunk room, which was probably where the hunters rested. It contained a toilet and supplies. There was a closet stocked with dried soup packets, granola, and jerky, and he stuffed handfuls of granola and jerky into his pockets. They might come in handy.

He checked the time again. Five. Annie had been gone four hours, much too long. He'd been sure she'd be back by now. At least he hadn't heard any shots fired. Should they search for her? She'd been very specific in her directions. He backed out of the last cell and checked for a phone anywhere. Nothing. Cell phones didn't work back here either, but the men probably used satellite phones. If only he'd had one to bring in here with him.

"Find a phone?"

He turned at Sarah's timid question from the open doorway and shook his head. "Nothing in here. I wish Annie would get back."

"You're thinking of going after her?"

"I'm not sure what to do. I'm not sure where she ended up, and I'm liable to wander in the wrong direction. What if she gets here needing our help, and we're gone? I keep telling myself to trust her the way she'd asked. She hates it when I get worried and think she needs my help. But what if she does need us this time?"

Sarah pushed her stringy hair out of her face. There were circles of fatigue under her blue eyes, and her face was dirty. Angry scratches marred her legs below her shorts, and bug bites covered her arms. She looked spent and exhausted, which was exactly how he felt as well. And he was sure Annie wasn't in any better shape. She'd been trekking out in the woods, covering tracks, and laying down new ones for hours now.

He pushed his worry aside again and stared around the space. "There aren't any windows in here, so I still think the shed is our best refuge to fight from. We can leave the door shut and fight from the windows."

"But what if we fought from the door instead?"

"I think we'd get in each other's way, especially when Annie is here, too, and three of us are fighting."

Sarah clutched her hands together. "You think we aren't going to get out of here, don't you? That we're going to have to disable or kill the men to escape?"

"Probably. Yeah, we could take as many guns and as much ammo as we could carry with us, but they could pick us off one by one from the trees. They probably have tree stands set up all over these woods. They may think we made it out or they might find our trail back. If we are patient, they'll come back here. And we have to be ready and waiting for them. There is a lot more firepower here than they could carry with them, so we have the advantage. Once they are out of ammo, they'll be forced to retreat since we have control of the rest of their stash."

"They could send one person or more."

He shrugged. "One person couldn't carry enough for all the hunters. The main problem is we don't know how many there are. If there are six or more, they could send several guys while we hold them off. But my gut says that would be too many to keep their activities secret out here for all this time. I suspect they have no more than four. Maybe just the three we know about."

She nodded and backed out of the cell block. "I hate this place. I didn't want to shoot from here anyway."

"I think we should move more guns out of the armory. We don't know if they have grenades or anything they could launch to destroy the weapons and ammo. Let's take as much as we can to the shed and into here in case we have to divide up."

And it would help occupy his time so he wasn't so worried about Annie. He prayed for her safety as he began to carry rifles and crates of ammo into the shed. When it was standing room only in there, he transferred more to the cell block. When they were done, the armory was bare bones except for a few empty crates.

He replaced the padlocks and made sure it appeared like the building hadn't been disturbed. The men would be in for a big surprise if they got back here.

THIRTY-SEVEN —————————

IF ONLY SHE COULD SLEEP A FEW HOURS. ANNIE rubbed gritty eyes and surveyed her work. She'd carefully covered her tracks when she went off the fire road, then had waded a distance in a stream before emerging on the side of the water closest to the hunters' compound.

Her stomach rumbled as she shrugged off her backpack, then dried her feet on dry grass and sat down to pull on her shoes and socks. She'd eaten the last of her jerky a while ago, and there wouldn't be more food until she got back with Jon and Sarah. They might have eaten all their supplies as well, but she suspected there would be a stash of edibles at the compound somewhere.

She spied a carpet of wild strawberries and moved over to pick them and stuff them in her mouth, stems and all, so there would be no sign of them. They were fully ripe and delicious, but there weren't enough of them. She glanced around again and found another patch. And another. In a few minutes her belly was full, and she felt recharged to continue the battle instead of wanting to find a cave and sleep for days.

Had Jon and Sarah made it back to the compound? She'd prayed constantly for them to stay safe and to find help at the hunters' headquarters. Maybe they'd found a sat phone or some way to call for help and were even now rescued and waiting for her, but the chances were slim.

She had no idea what time it was, but judging by how hungry she'd been, she thought it was near dinnertime. Jon and Sarah would be frantic, and she prayed they stayed put and didn't come out here looking for her. They'd leave a trail a mile wide for the hunters.

She donned her pack again and picked up the tree branch. She had a vague idea of where she was, and she started off toward another deer trail. She'd lay down another fake trail before heading to the hunters' compound. One false path might not be enough with the wily hunters. She left a footprint here and a broken twig there again until she came to a Y in the path. She thought the left side would take her toward the camp, so she made a few more obvious signs that direction before retracing her way and heading toward Jon and Sarah.

She'd traveled about a mile when she heard voices. There was a large, climbable tree to her left, and she quickly tossed her branch into the bushes and climbed it. She perched on the largest limb with the biggest part of the trunk hiding her from the direction of the sounds. Her pulse roared in her ears, and she barely dared to breathe in the woodsy scent of the bark.

"That ranger is seriously ticking me off," Eric said.

Annie clung more tightly to the tree. Was Eric talking to Max, Joel, or both?

"You complaining about the sport of it all?" Max asked. "Challenging is good. It tests your skills. We could all take a leaf from her book on woods lore. She knows how to hide her tracks, and she has elevated this hunt above all others."

"What if she gets away?" Eric whined. "We've been out here for hours. I thought we'd have them both by noon."

"Quit complaining. You sound like a two-year-old. She's going to make every hunt after this one seem way too easy. We might have to change our possible prey to someone more challenging like Annie."

Just the two of them. Where was Joel? Having him out there somewhere was worrisome.

The voices were closer now. Annie hadn't had a chance to cover her tracks, and the grass below was thick and lush. It would show her tracks way too easily. If they searched at all, they'd find her up here. Maybe they'd see the tracks she laid for them and go that way before they discovered her perch.

"When we find her, I want to make her pay for leading us around like donkeys," Eric said.

"I might give you first shot, but you have to cyclops it," Max said.

Cyclops it? She struggled to remember the reference on the back of a photo they'd found at Hussert's. *Shoot straight.* So the words on the back referred to both who was taking the lead and directions on taking out their prey.

Max's voice grew closer. "One shot is all you get. We don't torture our prey. That's going too far."

Did he think running for her life didn't amount to torture? Had he seen the bleeding blisters on one of his victim's feet? This had been a horrible experience, and it wasn't over yet. She didn't know how it would end, and it might get worse.

There came the sound of a zipper and the ripple of a package being torn open. "Want a jerky?" Eric asked.

"I have some if I want one. I don't want to spend another night out here. We need to find them and end this."

"Maybe Joel has had more luck."

If only she had a way of letting Mason know what was happening out here. She had no doubt he had called in the state police and a search was being conducted, but this area was vast. It would take sheer luck to find them.

"Hey, Max," Eric called. "Crushed leaves here. I think she went this way."

Annie held her breath as their footfalls faded into the sounds of chirping birds and the running stream. But it was a while before she found the courage to drop back to the ground.

/ / /

Seven o'clock. It took all the prayer and strength Jon could muster not to go charging into the forest with a gun to search for Annie. One word kept reverberating in his head: *trust*. Trust Annie, yes. But even more, he needed to trust God for this situation. It was the hardest thing he'd ever done. Somehow, they needed to get out of here to their daughter, but the outlook was so bleak that it was hard to hang on to faith.

But minute by minute, he managed to stay at the ready with his gun.

Sarah returned from a quick trip to the toilet in the bunk room. She appeared about ready to drop. Jon had tried to get her to take a nap, but she'd refused, so he tried again.

He gestured to the bunkhouse. "I'll call you if they come, Sarah. You won't be much help if you don't get some rest. We could take turns standing watch. You sleep for an hour, and I'll wake you so I can sleep a bit too."

She took her spot by the window. "I know you. You're not going to sleep until Annie is back here."

"It's hard to wait," he admitted. "I thought about going just a little ways into the woods and seeing if there's anyone out there."

"All that will do is lay tracks for those guys to see that someone is back here."

It was the same reminder she'd given him for hours, and it was all too true. But how long did he wait? Until the men came busting in here with their guns blazing and he had no idea whether they had Annie with them or she was dead somewhere?

The not knowing was killing him.

A movement caught his attention, and he motioned for Sarah to be quiet as he peered around the windowsill with his rifle ready. The line of vegetation around the perimeter of the clearing shivered as if some unseen hand was moving it. Then a figure moved. The gleam of the sun revealed Annie's blonde hair first, and she stepped into view. Jon didn't think—he just reacted and raced out the door toward her.

Her eyes widened when she saw him, and her mouth trembled as if she was trying not to cry. It seemed he ran in slow motion across the clearing, and it felt like an eternity before he had her in his arms.

He buried his face in her hair. "I was so worried."

"So was I," she murmured against his chest. "I laid several false trails and got lost a couple of times, though I hate to admit it." She lifted her head and looked out at the compound. "Where is Sarah?"

"In the shed. She's standing guard. Let's get inside before those guys show up." He led her toward the building. "We transferred all the weapons and ammo into here in case the hunters tried to take out the armory. I found a box of grenades, but I'm not sure what to do with them."

They reached the utility shed, and she stepped inside. Sarah let out a strangled cry and stumbled toward her sister. Annie embraced her and patted her back as she heaved huge sobs against Annie's chest.

"I thought I'd lost you forever," Sarah said in a choked voice. "We were so scared. We didn't know what to do."

"You did exactly what you should have and waited for me." Annie let go of her and swept her hand around the space. "And look at this. We're ready for a war, and it's a good thing because I think we're going to have one. I'm sorry to say I doubt my ruse will delay them for long."

"You think they know we're here?" Jon asked.

Annie shook her head. "It's hard to say, but I erased every track I saw. I hope they come waltzing in here with no idea we're going to take them down. I left a trail toward the booby trap you made in hopes one of them would step into it, and they'd need to come back here to give him aid."

She stepped over to examine the boxes and guns. "Lots of ammo."

"What can we do to help?" Sarah asked.

Before she could answer, they heard a man screaming obscenities out in the woods. He sounded like he was in pain.

"I think someone just made contact with your punji sticks, Annie."

She grabbed a gun. "Everyone, take your stance. Aim for the chest so you're more likely to hit them."

Jon kicked the door shut before the first men arrived, and he rested his gun on the windowsill. These guys were going down.

THIRTY-EIGHT

THE BELLOWING GREW LOUDER, AND ANNIE'S PALMS began to sweat as she squinted down the barrel of the gun. This thing was high-powered, and it had been a long time since she'd fired an assault weapon. The yelling was half angry and half pained, and she knew if the injured man had his way, he'd make her pay for what had happened to him.

"Steady," she whispered to Jon and Sarah. "Don't fire until they're close enough that we won't miss."

The rifle felt unwieldy in her hands, and she made the instant decision that she wouldn't need something this powerful to take down one healthy guy. The injured man wouldn't be much of an adversary.

Two figures burst from the trees. Eric Bell assisted Joel West. Blood poured from Joel's left knee, and he could barely stagger into camp.

Eric led him toward the cell block and left him sitting on the ground and rushed toward the door. "Sit here while I get supplies."

"I need pain meds!" Joel yelled after him. "Bandages and antibiotic cream too."

"You guys focus on Joel, the injured guy, while I handle Eric,"

Annie whispered. "Don't let Joel go for his gun." Her finger tightened on the trigger, and she gently squeezed off a shot.

A shout almost instantly followed the sharp report from her gun, and Eric stumbled and went down clutching at his knee. He spewed obscenities and curses as he rocked back and forth.

Annie kept her gun trained on him. "Throw down your weapons, Eric! It's over."

"Annie?" His voice held disbelief. "It's not supposed to happen this way."

She could have said so many things—like sometimes the underdog fights back. That good always wins in the end, even if they are overcome in this world by evil. That sooner or later your sins will find you out. But she held all that in and shouted again for him to throw down his weapons.

"You want me to shoot the other knee, Eric?" she called. "I'm not alone. The next bullet will be through your head and your friend's head. We're done playing your games. You're never going to stalk any kind of prey again from inside a jail cell."

She saw his decision to reach for his gun before he could make a move, and she put another bullet right by his other knee. He yelped and scrabbled back toward the door, but he had nowhere to go. They'd made sure the door to the cell block was locked and inaccessible. These guys had no cover and were sitting ducks.

"Throw your rifle as far as you can." She knew Jon and Sarah were watching Joel West and had to trust he'd had the sense to stay still.

"All right, all right!" Eric shrugged off his rifle and held it by the barrel, then tossed it out into the yard where it hit five feet away from him.

"Now your knife. And your pistol," she yelled.

His scowl deepened, but he yanked up his pants to reveal an ankle holster. He tossed the handgun and knife beside the rifle. She would have to go out there and make sure he was disarmed.

She grabbed a coil of rope and a knife. "Watch him."

"You can't go out there," Jon protested. "Max and other hunters could show up anytime."

"Sarah, you keep an eye on the perimeter and on the other wounded guy. We can't cower here inside when I need to make sure he doesn't have any other weapons on him. I need to tend to their wounds and truss them up. I'll be fine."

She didn't wait for an answer but opened the door and stepped out into the late-afternoon sunshine. This standoff was far from over. But she couldn't make the mistake of assuming these defanged snakes out here were harmless. When she least expected it, one of them could turn and bite.

Eric's dark eyes were full of hate. "Max will make you pay for this. You think you've won, but you don't know who you're up against."

"It's true I misjudged Max, but he doesn't know who he's up against either. I'm not a victim. Not ever." She wanted to kick him in the injured knee, but she restrained her base impulse. "Put your hands behind your back, Eric." She cut a piece of rope.

He sneered but did as she ordered, and she bound him, then unlocked the cell block. She gestured for Jon to help her, and they dragged him howling and writhing with pain into a cell inside. She slammed the steel door shut as Jon went to get West. As they exited the block building after locking up Bell, she heard a shot zing out and saw dirt and grass kick up by the other hunter. He must have been making a move for a weapon.

Her scalp prickled and she stared carefully around the perimeter. He'd given them no trouble, so what if he was trying to provide cover for Max or another of the hunters? She spotted a glint of metal in the trees and made a dash for the utility shed.

"They're coming!" She dove inside and Jon slammed the door behind him. A bullet zinged against the outside of the metal door.

The battle was about to get real. She glanced at Jon, then froze. "Where's Sarah?"

Jon's green eyes widened, and his gaze swept the room. "She was right here when I left to help you haul the men to the cell."

The door had been open. Had Sarah sneaked out for some reason? Annie couldn't imagine what could drive her sister to leave the protection of this building. Now she would have to go out there and find her.

/ / /

The instant Sarah saw the woman's outline, she knew it was Michelle. And Max had her. There'd been no question about telling Jon because he would have stopped what she knew she had to do. Sarah and Michelle had been through too much together for her to abandon her to Max's plans.

Leaving the big gun behind, she stuck a knife into her waistband and gripped a fully loaded pistol in her hand. Maybe it was stupid, but Max wouldn't be expecting her to come running. He would be looking toward Annie, who was the professional. By the time Sarah had slipped out the door and into the tree line behind the building, she'd realized it was probably foolhardy. She'd never even shot a gun before. Did she think she was G.I. Jane or something when she had no skills like her sister?

But too late to back out now, even if she wanted to. Maybe God would see her desire to do good and help her. She couldn't count on it though, not after what she'd done.

She crept through the underbrush and made her way through gaps in the shrubs toward where she'd spotted Max leading Michelle. When had he gone after her and how had he gotten her? Annie had thought she would be safe out at the marina in that little cabin surrounded by people. Maybe Anu had mentioned it without thinking.

Every snap of a twig or rustle of leaves made Sarah wince. When she reached a path of pine needles, she was thankful for the silence as she moved. Any hunter would know she was coming, but she didn't know how to be noiseless like Annie. The more the scales fell from her eyes about her false memories of her childhood, the more she realized what a remarkable sister she had. But Annie couldn't do it all. Sarah had to at least try.

She found a rocky path through the trees and went that way. Was that a voice she heard or a bird? Creeping closer, she strained to hear and recognized Michelle's voice.

"What are you going to do with me?" Michelle was crying.

"What has always been planned." Max's steely tone held no hope of changing his mind from whatever he'd concocted.

Sarah crouched behind the large trunk of an oak tree and peeked out into the small clearing where Max had Michelle. Michelle was in yoga pants and a tee, and her dark hair was up in a ponytail as if she'd been exercising. Max's gun was slung over his shoulder, but Sarah had no doubt it could be in his hands in seconds.

Her fingers tightened on the revolver, and her hand shook as she brought it up to aim at the man she'd liked and trusted. He'd taken her in when Bree was out of town, but he'd had such an evil motive behind his kind gesture. The betrayal stung in such deep places in her heart, but despite the evil she knew existed inside of him, she found it hard to think about putting a bullet in his head. But she had to do it. She couldn't give him the opportunity to get to his gun. Hitting him in the leg or arm wouldn't put him out of commission. He was too dangerous.

Steady, steady.

Her arm strengthened at her internal order, and her finger tightened on the trigger. Just as she was about to squeeze off a shot, Michelle moved into her way. Sarah bit her lip and took several deep breaths as she waited. She silently urged her friend to step out of the way.

A squirrel scolded her from a branch near her face, and Max's gaze swung that way. In an instant he had Michelle in a lock hold with a huge knife at her throat. "Sarah, how nice to see you here. Come on out or I'll slice this pretty lady's throat. Oh, and toss that cute little peashooter onto the ground."

His cold brown eyes made her shiver, and she knew he would do what he said if she didn't obey. She lowered the gun and tossed it into the grass a few feet away. Maybe she could make a dive for it at the right time.

"Come out and join the party. I never dreamed you'd be foolish enough to leave Annie's protection. You'll be a much stronger bargaining tool than Michelle, though I think she might have been enough to gain me access to my camp. I wasn't sure she'd answer my text and come, but women are so easy to fool."

His voice went even more steely as he said "my camp." Their occupation of his property had bothered him more than they'd realized. Well, at least more than Sarah had thought it would. Annie was the strategist, and she probably had expected Max's anger.

The knife at Michelle's throat moved, and a trickle of blood ran down to her chest. "I said come out," Max barked.

Sarah moved from behind the tree trunk and approached. She kept her eye on the gun in her peripheral vision. There surely had to be a chance for her to grab it and get a shot off. "Why, Max? Why would you do this?"

He shrugged. "I'm not going to debate it with you—it just is. My friends and I find it good sport to eliminate frivolous people who don't contribute to society. Look at you, Sarah. What have you ever done to better the world around you? Am I any worse because I take people like that out?"

Sarah couldn't argue that she deserved better treatment. "But what about Michelle? And Jon and Annie? Michelle's helping women and working on the environment. Jon is a doctor! And Annie helps people every single day, yet you plan to kill her."

"Jon and Annie were unfortunate enough to get caught up in the fallout. Michelle, too, for that matter. I wish I had a choice there, but I don't. So let's get this over with. Annie will surrender willingly when she sees I have her beloved sister. Move."

He released Michelle with a shove and had his rifle in his hands in moments. Sarah had no choice but to go before him with Michelle.

THIRTY-NINE

JON BARRED THE DOOR AS ANNIE MOVED TOWARD IT.
"You're not going out there, Annie. If anyone goes, it needs to be me. Kylie is expecting to see you tomorrow. You have to think about our daughter."

Despite her mutinous expression, he held out his hand. "Think, Annie. As long as you are free and in charge of these weapons, we have a chance. If Max takes you, what am I going to do with them? I don't have your skills or training. Sarah needs you here, and so do I."

The fight went out of her eyes, and they filled with tears. "I don't know what to do. I thought I was trained in every type of situation, but there's no tactical guide for what to do when your sister is being held by a maniac. I'm sure Max has her by now. Why would she have gone out there by herself? I don't get it."

Jon didn't either, but they didn't have time to argue about the unknown. He moved past her and began to tuck grenades behind his back at his waistband and into his pants pockets. "I think these might be handier than guns or knives. I'll take the usual weapons as well just so I have something to throw down when he disarms me. How do I use them?"

"These are V40 mini grenades, which will make it easier to stow them out of sight. But don't be fooled by their size. They are still very dangerous." Annie showed him how to pull the pin. "Get it away from you as quickly as possible. You've got just seconds before it explodes. Do you have a plan?"

"I thought I'd go out with my hands up and tell him you're out scouting, so he will have to make do with me."

"Those grenades won't help you if he's got Sarah right beside him." A frown crouched between her eyes as the wheels turned in her head. "I'm going to yell to Sarah to run. When you hear that, grab a grenade and throw it to the side of where Max is standing. Even if Sarah is near, his body will help block the shrapnel. She might be injured but I think she will survive. If it lands right."

The worry in her eyes told him she wasn't sure about this plan. He kissed her quickly with fervor. "I know it's not perfect, but we're running out of options."

As he moved toward the door, he spotted three figures moving at the tree line and squinted to make out their identities. "Max has Sarah and Michelle."

Annie whirled but stayed back where she couldn't be seen. "Michelle? I'll bet Sarah saw her out there and that's why she ran off. She probably thought she could help her, but Max is a hard adversary. Don't trust anything he says, Jon."

"I won't." He moved to the open door and stepped out with his hands in the air. The pistol he'd been using protruded from his front right pocket, and he hoped Max would focus on it and nothing else.

"Let the women go," he shouted. "You can take me instead."

The women were in front of Max, and he gestured with his

gun. "I'll take all of you. Send Annie out too. She's led me on quite a chase, and I want to thank her for making it so challenging."

"She's not here. She went out the window just before you came. She's probably circling around behind you even now."

"Don't trust him!" one of the men yelled from inside the block house.

"I told you she went out the window," Jon said.

Max smiled. "Nice try. I'm not giving you the chance to yank out that peashooter in your pocket. Toss it away. And there's something else in your pocket. I want it out too."

Jon pulled out his gun and threw it down, then tossed out the grenade in his pocket. He had more he didn't think Max could see from where he stood.

"Ah, I see you made your way into my armory." His voice went cold. "You're going to pay for that." He gestured with the gun. "Come here. I want to make sure you don't have any other weapons before the fun starts."

At least he seemed to have bought Jon's lie about Annie's whereabouts. He glanced at the women with a plea in his eyes and short jerk of his head away from Max. At the same time Annie screamed, "Run this way!" from Jon's right.

He dropped to one knee and grabbed the grenade from his waistband. The women leaped into motion at the sound of Annie's voice, and he yanked the pin from the grenade and tossed it to his left by Max's right foot.

Max saw it and started to run, but it went off almost immediately.

The women dove behind some pine trees as the explosion shook the ground. The tremor it created threw Jon onto his back, and he scrambled to regain his feet.

He scooped up his gun and held it ready, but Max lay motionless on the ground. Had the women survived? And where was Annie? Moving that direction, his gaze darted between Max's prone body and the pines where he hoped to see Sarah and Michelle still standing.

"Annie!" He watched for any movement to his right. "Sarah, Michelle, are you okay?"

Everything in him wanted to see the women, but Annie had warned him not to trust Max, and he didn't dare move away until the man was either dead or completely incapacitated. He went to Max, who was on his belly. Blood poured from the side of his face, and his eyes were closed. Jon grabbed a length of rope sticking out of Max's back pocket and trussed up his hands with them before he checked his pulse. It was thready but still beating.

Now to find the women.

/ / /

The ground's shudder from the grenade threw Annie to the ground. Praying, she had picked herself up and ran to find her sister and Michelle.

"Sarah!" Where was she?

Annie had her gun out and ready. Deep down, she suspected Max might be a demon incarnate and would survive the blast. But she hoped she was wrong and he was at least unconscious.

A moan came from the stand of pines to her left, and she went that way. She found Sarah on the ground and knelt beside her. The coppery scent told Annie she was injured before she saw the blood matting her sister's blonde hair. More blood coated her cheek. Her lids fluttered, but her eyes didn't open.

Annie touched her neck to check her pulse. She had trouble finding it at first, then sighed when she detected it. Faint, but there. Her right pupil was dilated, and Annie thought she'd suffered a concussion. She needed to get help.

A moan came from behind her, and she found Michelle behind another tree. There was a gash on her arm, but it wasn't bleeding much. There was a goose egg on her forehead that was concerning though. Annie checked her pupils, too, and found them of equal size, so she should be okay. She'd likely hit the tree during the explosion and suffered the contusion.

She didn't want to leave the women, but she had to see if Max had survived the blast. If she was sure it wouldn't put Jon in jeopardy, she would have been shouting his name, but if Max was still out there, he'd likely hear too. She pushed back pine branches and hurried through the underbrush to where she'd last seen the men.

A flash of red caught her eye, and she saw Max lying bound on the ground. He wasn't conscious. Relief made her knees weak. "Jon?" she called.

There was no answer, so she called for him again, and this time he came charging out of the trees behind her. She went into his embrace with a cry of relief. "I was so afraid," she whispered.

He held her close for a long minute, and his kiss was like coming home. She sank against him with no strength left. These past few days had taken everything from her, but they'd survived. They'd managed to defeat Max and his men.

He pulled away and ran his hands over her arms. "Nothing damaged?"

"I'm fine." She took his hand and pulled him toward where she'd left the women. "I need you to check Sarah and Michelle though. I think Sarah has a concussion, and Michelle will need stitches."

He went to Sarah first. "I don't like her color. She's pasty." He checked her pulse and pupils. "Yeah, she has a concussion. We need to watch her. Head wounds bleed a lot, and she's lost a lot of blood. We need to get her to a hospital. I'll hike out to my car and call for help."

"I'll go. I'm not sure you can find your way out of here."

"There's a compass in the armory. I saw it."

"But you're the doctor. You're needed here. I can move quickly." Annie could tell Jon didn't like it, but she knew she was right.

"Let's get the women inside out of the elements. Let me check Sarah's spine and neck." Jon ran his hands over her limbs and neck, then nodded. "I think it's safe to move her."

He picked up Sarah and carried her into the clearing. Annie rushed ahead and started to open a cell door but shuddered and changed her mind. Sarah would hate to wake up there, so she hauled out a mattress and had it ready in the armory building as Jon came in with her sister in his arms. He laid her down while Annie grabbed another mattress for Michelle.

Sarah was beginning to stir by the time he got her settled on a mattress. Her blue eyes, so like Annie's, finally opened, but she kept blinking like she couldn't really see. "Annie?" she whispered.

Annie knelt by her. "I'm right here. You're going to be okay. The danger is over. We have to go get Michelle, but we'll be right back." She gave her sister a few sips from a water bottle Jon handed her. "Get some rest."

Sarah closed her eyes again, and Jon stood. "I'll go get Michelle."

"I'll come too."

They went back to the pine grove, but Annie stopped. "She's gone. I know this is where we left her."

Jon pointed. "There's blood spatter."

They pushed through a thicket of blackberries, and Annie spotted a figure stumbling through the pines. Michelle.

The woman staggered, and Jon rushed to catch her and ease her to the ground. "Here, get some water in you. Just small sips."

She took the bottle he handed her and took a couple of small drinks.

He reached into his pocket and handed Annie his phone. "I put a pin in my car's location before I set off. Once you have service, it will lead you right to the car. And here's the key." He pressed both items into her hand. "And hurry. Both the women need to be in a hospital."

"I'll be quick."

He took her shoulders in his hands and pulled her in for a kiss before she left. Her lips were soft and pliable under his, and she kissed him back with enthusiasm. He pulled away reluctantly. "I always knew you were amazing, but even I had no idea just how amazing. Hurry back."

She nodded and set off into the trees.

It would take at least a couple of hours to hike out to his car, and that's *if* she was lucky enough to find paths through the heavy vegetation. She eyed the glowering sky. And if the weather cooperated.

FORTY

MAX WAS CONSCIOUS BY THE TIME JON STEERED HIM into a cell, but the older man met every question Jon asked with contemptuous silence. Mason would have his hands full with the man, and Jon couldn't wait to see Max squirm. He hated to think of how this would affect Anu though.

He left the prisoners with water and jerky, then kept the women hydrated as best as he could. Michelle complained of a headache, and he gave her ibuprofen that lessened the pain enough to allow her to fall asleep. He let Sarah sleep but woke her every hour to check her pupils and see how she was feeling. Her right pupil looked more dilated, and at one point, he thought she might have had a mild seizure. He had few resources to help her while he waited to hear from Annie.

It was dark by the time he heard the *whop-whop* of a helicopter rotor. He dashed from the armory and flicked his flashlight on and off to signal the pilot. Once the chopper's landing lights came on, he got out of the way of the blades and wind. His biggest relief was that Annie hadn't run into trouble on the way out. He'd be able to relax once he saw her beautiful face in the light of the chopper.

The chopper blades settled on the grass, and the rotors began to slow. The door opened, and Jon charged from the armory's doorway when he spotted Annie. He ducked down and grabbed her hand to draw her away from the helicopter and out of the way of the paramedics hopping out behind her.

He swept her into his arms. "You made it!"

She kissed him before she answered, a lingering embrace full of relief and promise. "It was slow going, which is why we're so late. A quick stop to get me, and we found the clearing after a few trials and errors. I couldn't drop a pin here since I didn't have service, so I had to use the compass and my memory." She turned to follow the paramedics into the armory. "How's Sarah?"

"I think she's a little worse. She may need surgery to relieve a brain bleed, but we need to run some tests and see what's happening in her brain. We should go to Houghton. She'll need a good neurologist."

Annie nodded and peered over to the man tending to her sister. Sarah was out, and she wasn't rousing as the paramedics took her vitals and inserted an IV. Annie tensed as she watched the scene unfold. Jon wished he could have had Sarah awake and smiling, but he was growing more worried by the minute.

Michelle was going to have a black eye to go with the goose egg on her forehead, but her color had improved all through the afternoon. Jon thought she'd be fine with some rest. He dropped his arm around Annie and pulled her out of the way as the men finished with Sarah and loaded her on the litter. Michelle got aboard on her own power.

"Mason will be here soon to take custody of the men. Where is Max? I'd like to talk to him."

"In a cell." He paused to tell a paramedic there were injured men in the cell block too. "Their conditions are stable, and I don't think the sheriff will want you taking them out of here without guards. They're dangerous."

The paramedic glanced up briefly. "We'll be with these women for a bit. I'll check the men when I can."

Jon took Annie's hand to walk with her to the cell block. "Max and the other hunters are in individual cells. Good luck. He hasn't been exactly talkative."

"I'd like to know how this started—and how we might find the remains of the people he's killed. I'm sure their families would like closure."

He doubted Max would tell her anything. He'd keep his mouth shut and demand an attorney. But Annie had a way with people, so maybe she'd make more headway than Jon had.

They entered the dim coolness of the block building, and Jon blinked as his eyes adjusted to the darkness. The two closest hunters sat up on their cots and started demanding to be let out. Jon blocked out their voices and pointed. "He's in the cell across from the hunters' bunk space." He led her down the hall and stopped at Max's cell.

Max looked worse than when Jon had brought him in. His skin was pasty, and blood still leaked from the wound on his head. Bruises had sprouted on his arms and face, but his brown eyes stared impassively out of his swollen eyes.

"So you won, Annie. I underestimated you. I should have killed you as soon as we took you."

Annie laced her fingers into the steel cell grate. "Where are the bodies, Max? Give the families closure and tell me where to find them."

He smiled, and the expression was hideous with his swollen

features and bloody lips. "I don't know what you're talking about, Ranger Pederson. I have no bodies. In fact, the only charge you can bring against me is abduction."

"Oh, I'm sure the sheriff can come up with a few more. Attempted murder for one. We all heard what you planned for us. The sheriff will layer on enough to make sure you never see the outside of a cell again."

Max's eyes sparked with malice. "I have the best attorney money can buy."

"Your money won't save you, Max. Neither will your attorney. And what about Anu? Don't you care how this will hurt her?"

He shrugged. "She already told me our relationship is over. I am too closed off for her liking. I don't think she would have appreciated getting to know me better." His chuckle held no real mirth.

Jon took Annie's hand. "I hear ATVs. I think Mason and the state police are here. Let them handle this scum."

/ / /

Annie's beloved U.P. was safe from the human predators who had stalked this pristine wilderness. The breakfast aromas in the Suomi Café were soothing and familiar. She picked at the omelet Molly had brought her and looked out onto the dim sunrise over Rock Harbor. She couldn't quite wrap her head around everything that had happened.

Jon reached across the booth table to take her hand. "You look tired."

"I didn't sleep much last night." They'd gotten to her cottage at three. It had taken hours to tell law enforcement everything and to ride an ATV back to Jon's car to drive out of the forest. It was only five now, and though she'd laid down and closed her eyes briefly, her thoughts wouldn't turn off. "I texted Anu and asked her to meet me here. She had heard I was missing but didn't ask any questions. Mason may not have had a chance to tell her what's happened yet. I suspect he may still be out at Max's compound."

Jon's strong hold on her hand brought comfort. He'd been a rock through all of this, and she'd been uncertain any of them would survive.

Jon gave a final squeeze of her fingers and picked up his fork. "I'm famished. Oh, and I checked on Sarah and Michelle this morning. Michelle was released a few minutes ago, but Sarah was admitted for observation. Her concussion has improved, though, so I suspect you may be able to spring her later in the day. Once that right pupil shrinks back to normal, they'll let her go home to recover."

"Thank the Lord," Annie said. "She didn't look good when they loaded her in the chopper. I'm going to take her to my cottage. I've been aloof from her for too long. She proved herself all through our ordeal."

Jon's gaze went over her shoulder. "Here comes Anu."

Annie turned and waved to the older woman, who nodded. Anu was smiling, so Annie suspected Mason hadn't dropped the bombshell about Max yet. It was going to be up to her to deliver the blow as gently as possible. If only Bree had returned, but she wasn't due back until right after lunch.

Anu's smile faded when her gaze swept over Annie's face as Annie rose to hug her. The older woman didn't release Annie's shoulders after the hug. "My, Annie, you are exhausted. You should have gone to bed instead of meeting me this morning. Though I will say, I was most happy to hear of your rescue. And I have good news about my cancer—there was no spread. So it is over. No more treatment will be necessary."

Annie embraced her again. "That's wonderful news!" Her pulse blipped at the trust on Anu's face. She slipped back into her seat and moved over to make room for Anu. "Have you talked to Mason?" She was sure of the answer before she asked.

Anu shook her head. "Just a brief text. He said there was much to tell me about what has been going on in the forests, but that you were safe. That was my main concern. I prayed constantly for all of you."

"Those prayers were so needed. We barely survived all of it." Annie wet her lips and swiveled on the bench seat to hold Anu's gaze. "There has been a hunting group operating in our area, Anu. They targeted people they thought could disappear up here without too much media attention. My investigation got too close to the ringleaders, and they decided they had to take me out. They planned to use Sarah to lure me in and eliminate the threat. But they have all been taken down. Mason has them in custody."

"There is something you are not telling me, my dear Annie. Who was involved?"

There was no gentle way to drop this bomb. "Max Reardon was the head of the group, Anu."

Anu reeled back as though she'd been slapped. The color washed from her cheeks, and her blue eyes went wide. "I-I cannot quite believe it, but I can see from your expression this is true. You are quite sure?"

"He hunted me and Sarah across miles of forest for two days, Anu. He and his friends were relentless. They called it a sport.

They have killed others, but Max refused to tell me where to find the bodies. I think he might have had genuine regret that you would be hurt by this."

Anu shook her head. "Do not try to spare my feelings. A man who would do something so horrendous has no tender feelings in his heart for anyone." Her eyes filled, and she looked down at her hands in her lap.

Annie had never seen Anu cry. She'd always been so strong through adversity, so reliant on her faith. This had rocked her world, and Annie wished she could have spared her. "You might be able to help, Anu. Maybe Max would tell you where we could find the bodies. I'd like to provide closure for the families who have no idea what happened to their loved ones."

"I do not wish to speak to him. I do not wish to ever see his face again," Anu said.

"I know, and I wouldn't ask if it wasn't of such great importance. I don't know that Max will tell you, but it's our only hope to bring those young men and women home to their families. No threat of punishment will break him."

Anu buried her face in her hands. "I had thought I might come to love him at one point. How well he hid his true nature."

"I trusted him. He'd always been so kind to me, and I never dreamed he could hide such darkness."

Anu lifted her head to reveal wet cheeks. "I will try. That is all I can promise. A man like Max is unlikely to respond to any plea. Is he at the jail yet?"

"I think he's at the hospital. He suffered injuries from a grenade during the final battle."

Anu gasped. "A-a grenade?"

"He had a virtual armory out there, Anu. Assault rifles,

grenades, timers, all kinds of ammunition. We don't yet know how long this has been going on either. At least as long as he's rented our island, but it could have started before that. He used to come for hunting trips before he decided to make Tremolo Island his home. This liaison with the other hunters could have been going on a long time. He confirmed Sean Johnson was part of it, and those women he killed were part of a hunt. We may never know the truth of that unless one of the hunters talks."

Anu's mouth flattened. "I shall do what I can to find out."

Annie wouldn't want to be Max when Anu faced him.

FORTY-ONE

THE VISE AROUND SARAH'S HEAD HAD LESSENED, BUT that had allowed the pain in the rest of her body to complain. She moved like an old woman as she got into clean clothes. She'd been told Annie had brought them, but she didn't dare hope things would remain good between them. Life would likely go back to normal, and she'd be on the periphery of Annie's life. She told herself that would be okay and was what she deserved.

It felt great to be free of the IV and other monitors, and Sarah wanted nothing more than to step outside and feel the sun on her face. To feel the breeze off the water and to hear the birds sing would be heaven after what she'd been through. She was alive, and so was Annie. That meant everything.

She turned at a knock on her hospital room door. Annie poked her head through the opening. "I hear you're ready to get out of here. Scout is waiting for you too."

"I get to keep him?"

"I talked to Ella's family, and they agreed to let you keep him. He's waiting at the house."

That was all Sarah needed to hear. "I'm ready." She slid her feet into flip-flops. "I can't wait to get out of here and away from machines and antiseptic."

Annie smiled and nodded. "I get it. Let's go outside. There's something I need to talk to you about."

Here it comes. Sarah swallowed down her fear and hurt and followed Annie down to the first floor and out into the sunshine. She drank in the view of Lake Superior from the park area at the side of the building. "This view never gets old."

"No, it doesn't." Annie held out her left hand, palm down. "Did you notice my engagement ring or were there too many bullets flying around to notice?"

"I noticed. I'm happy for you and Jon. You deserve to be happy, and I know Jon loves you."

"We're so blessed to have gotten a second chance." Annie sat on the bench by the bank of flowers and patted the space beside her. She waited until Sarah settled. "We're going to get married next weekend. Neither of us wants to wait, so that means making plans quickly. I have to tell Kylie yet when she gets back. Bree and the gang stopped for a late lunch but should be here within the hour. So I thought I'd better get those plans going. I need a maid of honor."

Sarah gave an inane bob of her head. Nothing like twisting the screw to bring her here and tell her she was going to ask Bree to be her maid of honor. But it was okay. She'd cheer on her sister from the back of the church and try not to make any ripples.

Annie handed her a small box. "I'd like you to wear this when you stand up with me."

What did she mean? Sarah's head hurt too much to fully track what Annie meant, so she opened the box and stared at a beautiful yellow necklace flanked by blue. "Is that a goldfinch?"

"It is." Annie leaned in closer and touched the stones. "The bird is made from sea glass from our beach, and the blue stones are sapphires that match the ones in my ring. Henry made me three of them while I was missing. One for me and one for Kylie. And one for my maid of honor."

One. Two. Three. Sarah's mouth dropped open. "Wait, are you asking *me* to be your maid of honor?"

"Of course I am. You're my sister. Kylie will be flower girl and wear one, and I'll wear one too. So we can always remember God's faithfulness. He sent a goldfinch to comfort Kylie when she was trapped and alone, so we know he is with us. The necklace is a reminder of that."

Sarah's eyes burned. *Don't you dare cry.* But the tears spilled down her cheeks anyway. "I—I thought you'd ask Bree."

"I would have if you hadn't come home. I love you, Sarah. I've always loved you. We're going to move past everything as a family." Annie's voice wobbled, and her eyes filled with tears too. "I never want to be without you again."

Sarah flung herself into her sister's embrace and let the tears fall against Annie's blue tee. "I'm so sorry for everything, Annie. So sorry. I was a little crazy or something. I believed so many things that I see now were wrong."

Annie held her tight. "I forgave you already. It's in the past, Sarah. Let's make wedding plans and forget about it. I'm going to sign the marina over to you. It's more than I can handle, and you'll do a great job with it. I'll teach you everything I know, but you've always loved the cottage. The loons don't even give you the creeps the way they do me."

Sarah pulled back and wiped the moisture from her face. "But where will you live? You and Jon and Kylie?"

A smile lifted Annie's tired face. "We're buying a house! It's one Kylie and I have always loved. It's going to take a lot of work to bring it up-to-date, but I don't mind. I'll take any help you want to offer. We have wallpaper to strip and floors to refinish. And painting. Lots of painting."

"I can do that!" Was this all true or some kind of wonderful dream? Sarah couldn't believe Annie would welcome her into her life so completely. A series of beautiful impressions spooled out in her mind: Christmases with the family, jumping off the dock with Kylie, painting with Annie, and taking charge of the marina. Her own business.

Her jubilee faded. "What about the kidnapping charges?"

Annie smiled. "Daniel is working with the attorney, and Mason thinks the charges will be dropped. Your help in bringing the hunting group to justice will help. It will take a little time, but we think it will all work out."

Annie had told her God was good, but Sarah knew she had so much to learn yet about that goodness. And she was ready to learn.

/ / /

Annie sat with Jon behind the mirror looking into the interrogation room. The tiny viewing room smelled of Mason's burnt coffee and mints. It was dark except for a glow from the computer screen and a clock. Annie scooted her chair closer to the window and studied the occupant in the other room.

Max looked rough with bruises and contusions on his arms and face. His wounds had been mostly superficial, and the hospital hadn't held on to him long. They didn't want to deal with all the security if he didn't need the nurses' care.

Max was unshackled and sat in a relaxed posture on a chair,

with his hands folded in front of him on the table. He wore an orange jumpsuit, and his salt-and-pepper hair was unruly. He surely knew Annie was watching him as he stared defiantly right back at her through the two-way mirror.

Annie wasn't sure she'd ever be able to close her eyes and not see his face as he was ready to shoot her dead. The man she'd liked and trusted was a monster behind his handsome exterior. He'd probably already lawyered up, but at least Anu would try to penetrate his guard.

The door opened and Anu entered. She paused and waited a moment. "Max," she said in a soft voice.

When Max saw her, the indifference fell off his face, and his posture changed to tense and expectant. Clearly he hadn't been expecting Anu to show up. Did he think she'd come to bail him out or help in some way? He had to know better.

"Anu, you need to leave. Now," he said.

The plea in his voice was hard to miss. And who could blame him? No one would want to face a pure soul like Anu when his sins had been found out in such a public way.

Anu went around to the other side and pulled out a chair. "I asked Mason to let me speak to you alone. I did not think he would allow it, but he made a special concession for his mother-in-law." Her long gaze swept Max's head and down his arms. "You were injured by a grenade?"

Max's head bobbed. Annie had never seen him so discomfited and uncomfortable. He was usually the master of any social situation and worked to put other people at ease. His wealth had always given him a stature, but that had left him now, and he seemed shriveled and defeated in this drab room.

Anu folded her hands and leaned forward. "Why, Max? The

man I thought cared about me should have been incapable of something like this."

He shrugged, but he couldn't meet Anu's gaze. "I can't answer that because I can't remember exactly how it started, Anu. I am sorry you're hurt though. I'm not sure why you're here. You already told me we didn't have a future. I doubt you've changed your mind now that I'm in here."

"I still care about you and what happens to you. I just knew I could not build a future with a man who kept so many secrets. Now I know why you held yourself back. You feared I would discover this, did you not?"

He inclined his head and shrugged again. "I've never met anyone like you, Anu. So kind, so caring about other people. So good. *Good* is a word I don't use lightly. Few people have that goodness you seem to radiate."

"That is not me, Max. That is God. And even now, he loves you."

He waved his hand. "Don't talk to me about your religion, Anu. You came here for a reason, so you might as well get it off your chest."

"I wish to know where to find the bodies of your victims."

His answering smile held no real mirth. "Annie put you up to it, didn't she?" He stared toward the two-way mirror and waved. "Nice going, Annie. Hit me where it hurts."

Annie reached for Jon's hand and clutched it. "Whatever works, Max," she whispered.

Jon moved his chair closer to hers and slipped his arm around her. "Steady, Annie. Maybe he'll spill it."

"I don't think he will. He's so hard." Her eyes filled at the thought of the families without answers.

Jon brushed his lips across her cheek, and she leaned her head against his and prayed for Max to do the right thing. Just this one time.

"Please, Max. Where can we find them? Their families need to know."

He sighed. "The lake keeps its dead. I didn't handle any of the cleanup."

"The names?" she coaxed. "That would help at least."

The door opened and Mason entered. Anu frowned, but he put his hand on her shoulder. "There's no need for you to have to beg this man for anything, Anu. Eric Bell told us everything. He gave us a list of the victims. Seventeen in all. There were three hunters: Max, Bell, and West."

Annie gasped at the number. Seventeen people had perished in these twisted hunts. It seemed impossible.

In the interrogation room Anu stood and moved toward the door. "I will pray for you, Max." Her voice was choked as she was let out and the door closed behind her.

Mason crossed his arms over his chest. "The list Eric gave me of the hunters included Glenn Hussert. What role did he play?"

"Ask Eric."

"I did. I wanted to see if you'd tell me the same thing he did."

Max shrugged. "Then you already know he saw us one night and insisted on joining the group. He was a weak link though, and I was sure he would blab once he was able to talk. I hoped he'd pass on his own in the cabin, and I wouldn't have to deal with him."

He sounded morose, and Annie shuddered at the regret in his face. It wasn't regret for what he'd done but sorrow that his hunting spree had come to an end.

She brushed her lips across Jon's neck. "Let's get out of here.

I need to shed the slime of all this off me. I can't listen to any more."

"Want to go see our new house?" He pulled keys from his pocket and jangled them in front of her.

She gasped. "How'd you get the keys?"

"Dad's got the title company working extra hard on it, and he promised the Daltons a five-thousand-dollar bonus if we can close in two weeks."

She glanced at the clock. "It's two. Bree should be back with Kylie. Let's take them all over to have a look. I'll tell Kylie about the wedding."

His smile went even more tender. "I love to see you smile like that. It's been a long, hard road but we've made it, Annie."

She stood and drew him into a tight embrace. "You're never getting away again, mister."

"I wouldn't think of it," he said before he kissed her.

FORTY-TWO ————————

THE SOUND OF KYLIE'S LAUGHTER MADE JON SMILE. HE stood back by the blackberry patch inhaling the aroma of leaves and fruit. From his spot on the bench he could see the whitecaps out on Superior rolling to shore. Two gulls landed nearby and stared at him with black eyes as if they were willing him to produce some bread crumbs. "Sorry, no food."

Annie pushed Kylie in a swing. Their daughter's blonde hair flowed out behind her as she leaned back and pumped her legs to go higher. The reunion had been sweet. She'd even spared a hug for him after she squealed and about squeezed her mother's neck off. They'd never been apart like this before, but Kylie seemed to have weathered the separation well. And at least she'd been gone during those tortuous days when Annie was missing.

Sarah, Bree, Kade, and their kids had loved the house, and the Matthews family had left to head home and unpack. Sarah was weeding the rose garden on the other side of the house, so this was a good time to talk about the wedding.

Jon rose and went to join his girls. Annie and Kylie, two peas in a pod. He imagined Annie had looked exactly like Kylie at age eight. He watched his daughter's legs rise high above the grass and swing back the other way. He stepped in front and pushed her while Annie pushed from the back. She was like her mother—fearless. The height and speed of the swing didn't dim those blue eyes one bit.

"How about ice cream pretty soon?" he called.

"Yes!" Kylie put down the toe of her sandal to begin to slow the swing. "Can Sarah come with us?"

"She sure can," Annie said. "Scout and Milo can come too."

Jon slowed the swing and stopped it. "Your mom and I have something we want to talk to you about first though."

"Okay. Can I feed the gulls while we talk?"

Annie looked in her purse. "I have some granola." She handed a packet to Kylie, who tore into it and broke it into pieces.

"There are going to be changes in our life, honey," Annie began.

Kylie nodded expectantly. "Like moving here."

"Yes, that's a big one. But what happens first is important too."

"You're going to marry him, aren't you? I mean, he can't live with us otherwise."

Annie shot a bewildered glance toward Jon. "That's very true. And you're right. We will get married first. I want you to be our flower girl. What do you think about that?"

Kylie thought about it for a minute. "Can I pick out the dress?"

"Yep. I thought we'd go shopping tomorrow. I need to find a dress, too, and I'd like you to help me pick it out. You and Sarah."

"Is Sarah going to come with us to this house?"

Annie shook her head. "She's going to live in the cottage at the marina. But she'll come visit anytime she wants. And we'll go see her. We have a lot we need to teach her. She'll be my maid of honor."

"That will make her happy."

Annie knelt in front of Kylie and put her hands on her

shoulders. "I want you to remember that even though things are changing, one thing will never change: I love you very much and so does Jon. We might have some rough patches adjusting to everything, but as long as we remember how much we love each other, it will be all right."

Kylie shot a quick glance at Jon. "Do I have to call you Daddy?"

Jon hid his disappointment at the "have to" comment. "Not until you want to. Your mom and I always want you to remember your daddy Nate who loved you. You could call me something else. Dad or Pop or Papa or Father would work. Or Jon for now. But I hope you can learn to love me, too, one of these days."

"I already kind of do. I mean, you saved me. And you saved Mommy. It's hard not to love someone who does that. But you're not my daddy. I'll think about what to call you. Maybe *Isa*. Anu has been teaching me more Finnish words. I'm part Finnish, you know."

Jon blinked at the Finnish word for *father*. "That would be okay too. Whatever you want to do is fine with me."

"Okay. Can we get ice cream now?"

"One more thing." Annie pulled out a velvet box. "This is for you to wear at the wedding."

Kylie opened it and stared at it for a long moment. "It's my goldfinch! The one God sent me."

"It is. And this will be yours forever. Whenever you see it, I want you to remember God is there for you even when we can't be. And he's brought Jon to us. We're going to be a family."

"Can I have a brother or sister?"

Jon couldn't help but laugh since he and Annie both wanted more children as soon as possible too. "I think you'll be an awesome big sister. Do you promise to help change diapers?"

She wrinkled her nose. "Ew, I guess. That's a lot to ask."

"Big sisters have a lot of responsibility, but I think you can do it. We'll see what we can do about that request." Annie stood and held out her hand. "Let's go get some ice cream."

They walked around the end of the house to get Sarah, and Kylie ran to show her the necklace. Sarah showed hers off to Kylie, too, and the four of them walked down the hill toward town. At the bottom of the hillside, Jon turned to stare back at the house as a shaft of sunlight shone on the welcoming front door.

He couldn't wait to carry Annie over that threshold. Just nine more days and she would be his. He slid his gaze to his daughter. He'd had no idea how loving his own child would change his life in wonderful ways. He'd even had an offer on his car, a good offer. Enough to pay for the lease on his new office for several months.

Life couldn't get much better.

///

Annie stared at herself in the mirror. She'd resisted a white dress since she'd been married once before, but Bree and Kylie had talked her into one. The handkerchief hem just brushed her knees, and the bodice skimmed the tops of her arms with the lace sleeves trailing down.

Kylie twirled in her frilly blue dress. "You are so pretty, Mommy."

"And look at my big girl! All grown up in your lace dress." Annie touched the flowers in Kylie's updo, but they seemed secure. "You and Aunt Sarah look like sisters now."

Kylie gave a nod of approval to her aunt. "Don't be so scared,

Aunt Sarah. Everyone will be watching Mommy anyway. That's what Anu told me when I told her I was scared."

Sarah's blonde locks gleamed in the new chin-length cut. She seemed older and more serious now, but then Annie thought she probably did, too, after all they'd gone through this summer.

The wedding music wafted in the open window of the living room at their new home. Jon awaited her out on the lawn of the Dalton house. But it was the Dunstan house now. They'd managed to sign the papers just yesterday, a whole week early. Her new dad had managed to move heaven and earth to get it done.

"You're up, Kylie," Annie said.

Her daughter straightened her shoulders and picked up her basket of rose petals gathered from the garden outside. "I'll see you in a few minutes, Mommy." She took Sarah's hand and the two of them went to the front door.

Annie followed and hung back as Kylie sprinkled petals across the porch and down the steps to the tulle arbor where Jon waited with his dad and Martha. The newly married couple looked as happy as Annie felt. She drank in the sight of Jon while his gaze was fixed on their daughter as she performed her duties with grace.

Then a brown-and-black streak came tearing across the yard and jumped on Kylie. The puppy knocked her down and the rose petals spilled onto the grass. "Bad Milo!" Kylie began to cry.

Jon rushed to help Kylie to her feet, and he scooped up the petals and deposited them in her basket. "It's okay, Bug. You're nearly there."

He picked up the squirming puppy and handed him to Bree. She dropped him beside Samson, who quelled the pup with a growl. Milo cowered by his sire's feet and settled. Kylie wiped her face and finished the petal dropping, then went to sit by Bree and Kade's daughter, Hannah. Annie smiled as she watched her daughter's face turn expectantly toward the door to watch Sarah come down to stand on the other side of the minister. She seemed more nervous than Kylie had, but she got through it without stumbling.

Kade appeared by the doorway and held out his arm. Annie took it, and she smiled her thanks. There was a little hole in her heart that her dad wasn't here to lead her down the aisle to her new life, but Kade had been quick to step in and offer. Good friends were the same as family. Sometimes even better.

Her gaze locked with Jon's as she crushed the rose petals underfoot on the way to her new life. His green eyes were alight with love and strength. Nothing had driven him from her this time—not danger or fear or lies. He'd stayed by her side, and she knew nothing but death would ever separate them again. She barely registered when Kade stepped away to let her take Jon's arm.

They repeated the same vows she'd heard all her life. Nothing new and modern for them—they wanted the same vows their parents had taken. Ones that lasted and bound them together. But those vows barely registered even though she meant them with all her heart. All she could hear was the sound of her blood pounding in her veins and the expression on Jon's face.

"You may kiss your bride, Jon," their minister said.

When Jon's lips came down to meet hers, their friends and family whooped and cheered. Annie clung to Jon and tried to hold back the tears. A wedding wasn't the place for them, but she couldn't stop them from flowing. She was grateful, so grateful.

The break of day was here—and it promised an amazing new life for all of them.

A NOTE FROM THE AUTHOR

Dear Reader,

As I write this letter to you, I'm in a mess of emotion. My mother died ten days ago after a heartbreaking battle with diseased arteries and Alzheimer's. I'm thrilled she's with my brother Randy. She never really got over his death, and she's hugging his neck right now. She's getting caught up with my grandparents, whom I loved with all my heart. She's telling my little cousin Tiffany all about how well Tyce, Tiff's son, is doing. He's thirteen now and such a good kid. So while there is grief, there's joy that she's out of that diseased body and mind and is enjoying such good things from God's hand. But there is still her empty chair and my dad's sadness to deal with.

Writing can be so therapeutic. It's a warm, safe place to wrap myself in when there is pain in real life. And writing *Break of Day* proved to be that solace when I needed it. I so loved wrapping up this story and giving Annie and Jon their happily-ever-after. I think Annie might be my favorite character yet, though it's hard to pick. To a writer, our characters are like our children—you don't really have a favorite. But Annie was strong when I was

A NOTE FROM THE AUTHOR

weak. She powered through so many things, and her spirit helped me power through.

I hope she encourages you like she encouraged me!

I love to hear from readers, so connect with me on Facebook, sign up on my website for my newsletter, or drop me an email.

Love to you all,
Colleen

www.colleencoble.com
colleen@colleencoble.com
www.facebook.com/colleencoblebooks

316

ACKNOWLEDGMENTS

AFTER MORE THAN TWO YEARS OF MISSING THEM DEARLY, I got to visit with my HarperCollins Christian Publishing family right after I finished *Break of Day*. What a joyous time celebrating twenty years with my wonderful publishing family! We laughed, cried happy tears, exchanged many hugs, and recounted wonderful memories. Thank you, team—you are the best and I'm so honored to have you by my side. It's been a challenging time for all of you during the past few years—dealing with COVID-19 and navigating the new publishing landscape—but you've done it, all while making sure your authors know you love and appreciate them.

I work closely with my dear Amanda Bostic, fiction publisher. She's more than my editor; she's my friend through thick and thin. I've always told her she gave me my suspense wings and seeing her name pop up in my email or on my phone always makes me happy. Love you, Amanda!

Kerri Potts is my marketing director, and she's always quick to answer me—even when she shouldn't be working. But more than that, she's a dear friend whose smile always brightens my day. Thank you, Kerri! You're the best!

ACKNOWLEDGMENTS

Julee Schwarzburg is my freelance editor, and we've made a great team. She really understands romantic suspense and has guided me through the balance of suspense and romance. Thank you, Julee! I never want to be without you.

My agent, Karen Solem, and I have been together for twenty-two years now. She has helped shape my career in many ways, and that includes kicking an idea to the curb when necessary.

My critique partner and dear friend of more than twenty-four years, Denise Hunter, is the best sounding board ever. Together we've created so many works of fiction. She reads every line of my work, and I read every one of hers. It's truly been a blessed partnership.

I'm so grateful for my husband, Dave, who carts me around from city to city, washes towels, and chases down dinner without complaint. My family is everything to me, and my three grand-children make life wonderful. We try to split our time between Indiana and Arizona to be with them, but I'm constantly missing someone. ☹

Most important, I give my thanks to God, who has opened such amazing doors for me and makes the journey a golden one.

DISCUSSION QUESTIONS

1. Nate's parents reacted poorly when they heard the news about Kylie. What do you think drove their reaction?

2. Jon had to decide whether to tell the police about his suspicions over the death of one of his patients. What would you have done and why?

3. Annie wasn't sure about trusting her sister again. How do you reconcile forgiveness with trust after being hurt?

4. Memories came back to Sarah when she went to the cabin where she'd spent time as a child. What do you find the most evocative of the five senses when it comes to memory?

5. Daniel was thrilled to welcome Kylie as his granddaughter. How easy do you think it would be to begin a relationship with an older grandchild?

6. Jon struggled with what to do about his career. Do you think he made the right decision to start his own practice?

7. Daniel decided to marry Martha after a short courtship. Have you known older people who married like that? Is it a good idea or not so great?

8. Have you ever badly misjudged a person? How do you come to grips with the evil people do when they seem so good?

FAMILY SECRETS CAN BE THE MOST DANGEROUS OF ALL.

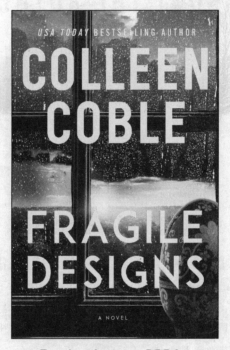

Coming January 2024

Available in print, e-book, and audio

ABOUT THE AUTHOR

Photo by Amber Zimmerman

COLLEEN COBLE IS A *USA TODAY* BESTSELLING AUTHOR best known for her coastal romantic suspense novels, including *The Inn at Ocean's Edge, Twilight at Blueberry Barrens*, and the Lavender Tides, Sunset Cove, Hope Beach, and Rock Harbor series.

/ / /

Connect with Colleen online at colleencoble.com
Instagram: @colleencoble
Facebook: colleencoblebooks
Twitter: @colleencoble